NEEDLENECK

NEEDLENECK

A Noir Novel

E.M. SCHORB

HILL HOUSE   **NEW YORK**

ISBN: 978-0-692-14998-0

for Patricia

In a dark time, the eye begins to see . . .
—Theodore Roethke

*The "Divine Pageant" of the Paradiso belongs to the
world of what I call the* high *dream, and the modern
world seems capable only of the* low *dream.*
—T.S. Eliot

Thou shalt not bear false witness.
The Ninth Commandment

Aspice, viator.
Inscription on Roman Tombstones

PART ONE

IN A DARK TIME

Chapter 1

THE SAINTS AND SINNERS CLUB

Long ago, in a dark time, a young man, apparently uncertain and possibly afraid, stepped into an unfamiliar bar. He felt that he was losing himself, was out in search of that self, desperate to save it. Seated, he looked beyond the window of the dismal barroom, into the bleak, wintry street, as if hoping to find there the answer to a puzzling question, but saw only an old newspaper flash by the steam-frosted window, like a mad, flapping wraith.

Feeling suddenly constricted, he got down from his stool, drew it back from the sticky, initial-carved mahogany bar, and bumped into a young woman who was passing behind him. She laughed, doing a quick sidestep, avoiding a full collision.

"Excuse me," he said, as his stool tipped over. He caught a rising chrome leg in his right hand while smiling an extended apology back over his left shoulder. She was side-stepping perilously over his big, black heels. He righted the stool, then stood dusting his smooth, rust-stained hands. The young woman waited patiently, a good-humored smile on her face.

"Really," he apologized again, his voice cracking slightly with embarrassment, "I am very sorry."

"Apology accepted," said the young woman, with a shrug and a soft laugh.

"No harm done. But I'm glad I'm wearing boots and not nylons." She grinned, winked, and passed down the bar, toward the rear, his haunted, dark eyes following her, and took a seat at the return by the window.

The place was empty but for himself, the young woman, and the bartender, a humorously wicked-looking, wall-eyed old man, who, after drawing the young man's beer, had shuffled off to his post by the cash register, where he stood dozing. The young man pushed back his left sleeve and studied his calendar wrist watch, much aware of the girl's presence at the front-end of the bar. It was just three in the afternoon. The watch was a month old, a Christmas gift from Father Ryan, under whom the young man served as curate at St. Saviour's, a small lower-middle-class parish in the Chelsea neighborhood of Manhattan. Enclosed with the watch was a note, written in Father Ryan's spidery script, that read: *My dear Father Din, I have noticed that of late you do not seem ever to know what time it is. Perhaps this will help. Yours with love in Christ, Father Liam Ryan.* The watch was a fine, sophisticated instrument, but it could supply no answers for the questions that vexed him. Father Din brushed the cuff of his charcoal-grey-tweed jacket back over its complicated face, took a sip of stale flat beer, and tried to think of other, more pleasant things. He wondered about the young woman. He could not remember having seen her come in. He thought that she must have been here, but in the back, when he entered. Surreptitiously, he glanced down the bar at her, caught her eye, and looked away.

He judged her to be about his own age, twenty five, perhaps younger. She was wearing a snug-fitting, burnt-orange turtle-neck sweater, a wide black belt, a long skirt of muted-green-tweed, and black boots, the block-heels of which added about three inches to what Father Din guessed to be a natural height

4

of five-seven. She was perhaps too heavy-breasted to be a fashion model, but she had the general figure and looks of one. Her hair was light-caramel-colored, worn long, and flowing from beneath a Hunter-green, tasseled tam. Suddenly she crooned down the bar, in a rich, soft voice: "Pardon me . . . I was wondering if you'd shoot a game of pool with me? There's a table in the back." Only now did Father Din quite realize that his eyes had drifted back to her. He had been staring at her. He started to speak, but before he could find his words, she had added, sweetly imploring: "Oh, please do! I'd enjoy it so much."

"Well . . . sure. Why not?" Turning to rise, he knocked over his beer glass. He watched as beer ran wildly over the bartop. "Oh, this is awful," he said. He forced a laugh, adding: "You must think I've had too much."

"Now don't go getting paranoid, buddy," the bartender croaked. "After twenty years almost in this business I ought to be an expert on who's had too much and who ain't, and I say you ain't. Now, don't you worry about it; I'll have it cleaned up in a sec. You want a refill?" He had mopped up the bar while speaking.

"Beer isn't the right thing for pool, anyhow," said the young woman, coming up the bar. "It makes you too dopey. If you want to shoot good pool you've got to drink something that'll wake you up. Do you mind if I order for you?"

"Well—"

"Oh, please: let me," she insisted. "Give the gent a Scotch Rocker, Tiger . . . on me."

"Really, I don't think—"

"Now, not a word!"

"You want a fresh one, Toddy?"

"Yeah, Tiger, one for me too." She turned to Father Din. "I hope you don't mind my ordering for you. Sorry, if I'm being presumptuous. Tell yourself that I'm a lonely girl who's gone and let herself get a bit too high." She smiled, her eyes warm and gleaming. "My name's Toddy Muir," she went on, rather breathlessly. "Oh, and this is Tiger—Tiger Hartzmann." The bartender nodded, and placed their drinks before them. "He got that name—Tiger—when he was a wrestler. Right, Tige?"

"Yeah, I used to wrastle," said the bartender, a gleam of suppressed pride in his old-time celebrity surfacing for an instant on his watery wall-eye. "I was on TV nearly four hundred times. But that was a long time ago. Listen to Toddy, she'll have you thinking I still had the diamond belt."

"You *are* still champ," Toddy asserted.

"Listen to the kid!" He gave Father Din a wild, wall-eyed wink. "No, I'm just a tired-out old man. But I held the champeenship gold belt fourteen times. Lost it the last time to the Great Destroyer. Then I had to give up wrastling; it was too hard on my kidneys. I've got what they call a floating kidney. Have you heard of that?"

"Yes, I have," Father Din affirmed. "But I thought wrestling was . . . well, safe, like show business."

"Hell, show business ain't safe," said Tiger. "It wasn't wrastling that started my kidney floating around; it was show

6

business. The first time it bothered me was right after I did a long fall through a skylight at Universal, when I was a stuntman. That was twenty years before I became a wrastler." He shook his great head at Father Din's ignorance. "You kids don't know nothing," he said. "It's the generation gap all over again, only this time it's the Xers versus the baboos."

"Baboos?"

"Babyboomers."

"You tell him, Tiger," said Toddy, nudging Father Din in the ribs with her elbow.

"Well, go ahead," said Tiger, mildly aggrieved, "take your drinks and go shoot pool, before my little girl here has a conniption." He limped back to the cash register, shaking his head, and instantly fell into a doze.

Father Din took the glasses from the bar and handed Toddy Muir her drink. "I'm sorry—" he began; but Toddy cut his sentence short by putting a long, transparent fingernail to her puckered lips. Then she took a sip of her drink, and smiled over the rim of her glass, saying: "You mustn't be so sorry all the time. Repeated apologies can be a sign of emotional insecurity." She studied his face, frowning beautifully. "You have a good face," she went on. "A square jaw—that's strength. And your nose isn't too small. A prominent nose is another indication of strength, and also of leadership. Take de Gaulle, for instance. Your eyes aren't large. But that could mean that you have depth. You know, it's odd; your face is small for such a big man. I'd like to feel your bumps."

"My bumps?"

7

"Yes. You know: phrenology."

"Oh. You mean read my character by interpreting the bumps on my head?"

"That's right. I used to be into all that sort of thing—Tarot cards, palmistry, pyramid-power, astrology, haruspicating. You know—New Age stuff."

"Do you believe in that sort of thing?"

"Oh, I don't know. Not really, I suppose. Of course, I was just joking about the bumps—it doesn't seem believable that doctors once took phrenology seriously. But it makes a more pleasant subject than the daily news, don't you think?"

"Well, I guess you've got a point there. As a matter of fact," said Father Din, inspired, "I do tend to believe in semeiotics—signs, you know. Signs and wonders. I came in here because of the name—The Saints and Sinners Club. Sometimes I feel that God sends us messages . . ."

"Any old how," Toddy broke in, not caring for the direction of the conversation, "I think that you have a good face. That's why I don't like to hear you say you're sorry so often. What have you got to be so sorry about?"

"No," said Father Din, "I only meant to say that I should have introduced myself . . ."

Toddy waited, expectant, but Father Din could think of no name to give but his own. Toddy raised her eyebrows—two long, fine golden feathers—and smiled, blinking. "Have you forgotten it?" She laughed.

8

"Hop, Hopkins," he blurted. "Sam. Sam Hopkins."

"Pleased ta meetcha, Sam," she said, grinning, and using the name in a way that had an element of teasing in it. She grabbed his hand and pumped it. "Shall we play now?"

The backroom was long, narrow and dark; it ended in a twin-doored wall, from which the only illumination, a pair of lighted glass signs reading, left, LADIES, right, GENTS, dimly shown. But Toddy, floating rapidly in the vague light—rather like an ascending angel, thought Father Din—with the certainty of familiarity, found the fine chain—Father Din could hear it clicking against the bulb—and in a moment they stood in a wide, bright circle of light.

"I hadn't realized it was getting so late," she said.

Father Din checked his watch again. "It's after four."

"It gets dark so early in winter," Toddy said, wistfully. "I hate winter. I like to see the sun shining."

"Oh, I don't know," said Father Din. "I rather like winter. It's . . . private."

"I think winter is a downer," Toddy insisted, collecting the balls that were scattered on the table. "It's so depressing. Sometimes I feel that I've lived in winter all my life."

They chose cuesticks and racked up the balls for rotation, which Toddy said was her favorite because it was simple. Toddy shot first, breaking the triangle and scattering the bright balls about the table. The yellow threeball sank. She sank three more lowballs and scratched, sinking the white cueball.

Father Din could handle a cuestick. He often shot pool at St. Saviour's Boys' Club. He was no Minnesota Fats, but here, with Toddy Muir's warm, soft eyes fixed upon him, he bungled even simple shots. But that was of no importance. What was important was that he felt as if he were being caught up in something; as if he had lost control of the situation. Fortunately, there was still time to turn back, from what, he wasn't quite sure. He decided to leave as soon as the game was over.

"You're not from around here, are you?" Toddy asked.

"I'm looking for an apartment," he lied. "What neck of the woods are we in, anyway?"

"Funny you should say that! The locals call it Needleneck, because of the junkies. They've invaded the neighborhood."

"That doesn't sound good."

"No, but it is gentrifying around here, too. In spots. A lot of artists and gallery owners are moving here—where the rents were rock-bottom—but that's beginning to push the prices up a bit. This is still a pretty dangerous area, though. I don't mean to discourage you, but there's a lot of junkies down here, lots of muggings and robberies. A lot of the new galleries are run by women, and the hypes go after them. A couple have been raped.

"You see," she went on, taking aim, "I grew up here. When I was a little girl, there were still flower children and hippies everywhere. But, like they say, the more things change, the more they remain the same."

As Father Din watched Toddy Muir moving about the table, shooting easily and expertly, his thoughts began to shift, to focus with his dark eyes on her long, lithe arms, bending and reaching, capably and rhythmically, over the dazzling green of the felt. There came upon him a pervading sense of unreality, heightened by an undercurrent of nervous excitement. Perhaps it was the drink that had done it. His limit was an occasional glass of Irish whiskey, to keep Father Ryan company. Whatever it was, he had a sense of being out of time, island-isolated. Toddy was lighting a cigarette, long, sandy lashes delicately flicking smoke away. She placed her cigarette on an ash tray, aimed down a cuestick: shot.

Chapter 2

LIVING A LIE

How had Father Din come to this place, to the back room of a bohemian bar, wearing a civilian suit of grey tweed, the very color symbolic of his weakening ties to the Church, the pale and paling ghost of priestly black?

Father Michael Din was born to parents who were born in the middle of the Great Depression. Michael never knew his grandfather, the original "Din" which was an Ellis-Island-rendering of something with a long tail on it. All Michael knew of his grandfather was that he was a socialist and an atheist. He was rarely spoken of during Michael's childhood. Young Michael's own father was a flag-waving patriot, hard-headed and hard-hatted, proud to serve in Korea and, perhaps in reaction to his own father's lack of it, deeply religious. He joined the Jersey City police department after Korea and worked his way up to his Detective's shield. He died of heart failure while young Michael was still in seminary. Din's mother, Elizabeth, believed in staying home and taking care of her man. Her aspirations had matured in the decade that fell between the Second World War, when women manned war-time industry, and the Sixties, when women turned in droves to achieve that which was material and that which was individual. She had been satisfied.

The great and simple secret of Michael Din's life was that he worshiped his father and since childhood had wanted nothing more than to please him and to be as much like him as possible. He had become an altar boy in his local parish because, as his father had put it, "Nothing would make me happier." This presented no problem to young Michael. It pleased his father and he did not see how it could interfere with him becoming a cop, like his father. But it did, for the politically powerful Bishop of his diocese selected him for the priesthood. Detective Din was told and heartily approved. Young Michael died inside, and yet he lived. He would not utter a word against the plan—not spoil what seemed to be the fulfillment of his father's dreams. At fifteen he entered Seton Hall, the prep school of priests, two years later a New Jersey seminary, and six years later a parish in the Chelsea section of Manhattan. During these years, he felt like a sleepwalker, a sleepwalker who was dreaming of another life. Women played a large part in his dreams, their mystery and beauty, and the secular life of the policeman played a part as well; for, in truth, he suspected himself of being his unbelieving grandfather's boy. As a poet knows from his earliest days that he is a poet, Michael knew from his earliest days that he was not a true believer. No, that wasn't exactly it. To be exact, he believed in God, but doubted the relevancy of the priesthood. For as long as he could remember, he felt that he had been living a lie.

Chapter 3

ODD MAN OUT

A hundred and twenty-five subway-roaring blocks uptown from the Saints and Sinners Club, in Harlem, a group of Black Muslim jazzmen had just finished a complex and protracted riff for a temple congregation that showed its approval with slight smiles and nods that seemed no more than a pigeon's involuntary head-thrust. The jazzmen, indeed, most of the congregation, wore what seemed a uniform of white shirts and dark ties and suits. The one jazzman who was out of uniform seemed to be in a sour mood as he shoved his saxophone into its case. He was clearly an outsider, and looked like one who intended to remain an outsider in any given situation—a man who did his own thing. As did the other jazzmen, he took a seat in the congregation, a sullen expression on his face.

Behind the podium was a huge blackboard, at one end of which was a chalk drawing of an American flag with a Christian cross superimposed on it, and at the other end was the half-crescent symbol of Islam. Under the American flag and the Christian cross was written: "Slavery, Suffering, and Death." Under the Islamic half-crescent was written: "Freedom, Justice, and Equality." "Which one will survive the war of Armageddon?" was at bottom-center. With this set behind him, the speaker took the podium, energetically crying, "Welcome to this special teaching!" He was tall, athletic, dynamic. "You are here to get some good news," he cried.

"MAKE IT PLAIN," chorused the congregation.

"Good news for us is bad news for them," he cried, waving at the outward world.

"PRAISE ALLAH!" the congregation shouted.

"What's good for the sheep is bad for the wolf!"

"MAKE IT PLAIN!"

"Freedom for the black sheep is destruction for the white wolf!"

"ALL PRAISE DUE TO ALLAH!"

"When I tell you that the white man is the wolf," cried the speaker, "I tell you the simple truth of history."

"MAKE IT PLAIN!"

"The white wolves are an endangered species. And we must see to it that their conservationists do not put them back in the woods—do not replace the dying breed!"

"SAY IT OUT!"

"Death to the white wolf!"

"DEATH TO THE WHITE WOLF!"

All around the outsider, the sullen-faced jazzman, dark-suited men leaped to their feet to shout approval. He sunk, sprawling in his chair.

"Our God is a live God!"

"YES!"

"Our God is a black God!"

"YES!"

The speaker looked directly down at the sprawling, sullen jazzman. "You are deaf, dumb, and blind," he shouted."You are lost in the North American woods. You are alone with the wolf! The new day is delayed because of you!"

"MAKE IT PLAIN!"

"Man, you must cleanse yourself, physically and morally. You are a swilling body of hogmeat! A floating broth of toxins!"

"MAKE IT PLAIN!"

"The hog is a filthy animal—and you eat it! And when you eat it, you become it—a grunting hog! Hogmeat makes addicts, thieves, and prostitutes! The white devil has fed you on hogmeat until you have become hogmeat! He has fed us his own immorality, until our people have been turned into prostitutes, thieves, and addicts.

"His Christianity has taught us to deal in dope, and you and I know this is true because when we were Christians we dealt in dope and prostitution. Yes, we were liars and con-men and cheating bad women."

"We lied!"

"YES!"

16

"We stole!"

"YES!"

"But now we protect our women and children from the white, Christian wolf!"

"YES!"

"And from the Zionists!"

"YES!"

"All praise to Allah."

"YES, YES, YES!"

Again, the speaker looked directly at the sprawling jazz-man. "Is there one here who would give up the hog?" he asked, with which the sprawling jazzman gathered himself up, rose with a new dignity, and walked up the aisle and out to the street, where he lighted a cigarette and scanned the neighborhood, as if seeking a shock of recognition. "But nothing really changes," he muttered.

Chapter 4

FEAR AT FIVE

Toddy sank her last ball; now the eight ball; now she went around the table knocking the remaining balls (those Father Din had been unable to sink) into a corner pocket. "Well," she said, replacing her cuestick in the rack, "Will you have another drink with me?"

"I'm sorry, but I can't," said Father Din. I have to go now–"

"What? That would be cheating a poor girl out of her just rewards, don't you think?"

Father Din looked blank.

"Well, I won. That means that you have to buy me a drink. You men make the rules, and that's one of them, isn't it?"

"Well, I do owe you a drink," he conceded. "But I can only stay for one."

They sat down at the bar.

Toddy grinned at Tiger. "Two more Rockers, Tiger, if you please. I won, so Hopkins here has to pay."

"I should've warned you," said Tiger, smiling approval on Toddy but with his small, wet, wall-eye focussed on Father Din. "She never loses a game. At least not at that table. She's been shooting back there since she was a kid. I

18

taught her myself, but she can beat me now." He set up two drinks.

"Don't tell him that, Tige," Toddy objected, but full of triumph. "You'll scare him off. And just think: if he keeps on shooting, and I keep on winning, and he keeps on buying, you'll get rich, and I'll get drunk. And that's what we're here for, right?"

"Wrong!" Tiger shook his head. "I like to see you get high, just enough to feel good, Toddy, but not drunk," he said, ambling away.

"Don't worry about me being frightened off," said Father Din, "but, really, I can't play another game. I have to go to work."

"I thought you were down here apartment hunting."

"Well, I was, but I'm also a salesman."

"And you sell at night? It's almost dark."

"Oh—I have to meet a client at his home."

"I've been drinking and shooting pool all day, since this morning. Nobody to keep me company but Tiger, and he's been asleep most of the time. Some Chinaman came in about an hour before you and had three double shots in about thirty seconds and left. He didn't even speak English. He had to point to the bottle. Early this morning old Martha—she's a local character—she came in and sang "Those Were the Days" about a hundred times and had almost as many eyeopeners, but she was still too drunk from last night to make much sense. So you might say that I've been alone all day—

19

until you. When you're alone you don't realize how much you've had." She grew pensive, dreaming into her drink. Tiger lounged against the cash register, softly snoring. "What time is it?" she asked.

"Nearly five."

Toddy took another sip from her drink and said, "You'd better go." Father Din felt as if the lights had gone out. He moved his glass in a circular motion, swirling the cubes in his drink, and then took a sip from it. He looked at Toddy. She was pale, soft. He wanted to touch her cheek. He fought back an impulse to do so. A pang of loneliness overcame him. "Is there anything wrong?" he asked.

She looked up and smiled. "I'm all right." Then, after a thoughtful pause: "You're a nice sort of guy . . . an attractive guy . . . but not very sure of yourself, are you?"

"I guess I'm a bit clumsy. I had a fit of nerves."

"No, that isn't what I mean."

"It must be that I'm not used to the work yet. I'm new at it." He looked at her. "Do you mind if I ask you a question? You don't have to answer, of course."

"What is it?"

"Why is a young, beautiful girl like you sitting alone all day in a place like this?"

Toddy laughed. "What's a girl like you doing in a place like this? Isn't that what men always ask girls in cat-houses?"

"I only wondered if there was anything wrong."

"Wrong? Why do you say that?"

"Well, you looked so—so sad, just then. Or afraid. Are you afraid of something?"

"Nothing I can't handle," she said. She emptied her glass and called Tiger, ordering another round. "You better go now. I didn't realize how late it was getting."

Minutes ago, in an exuberant mood, she had wanted him to stay. Now she wished he would leave. It was perverse of her, to behave so: to make a man feel wanted, needed, when it was his desire to leave, and then to make him feel superfluous when he desired to stay. He was contemplating her motives, when a bull of a man, bald, bullet-headed, well-dressed, came in the door, and she sat up, alert as a doe that has just caught wind of a hunter.

Chapter 5

THE HIGH PRIEST OF THE CHURCH OF MORAL FREAKS

"'Lo, Priestess. Well, no greeting? Still in a snit, eh? Why didn't you leave then? You knew I was coming." Tiger placed a tumbler filled with Scotch and ice in front of the man and stepped back, his wall-eye glaring. The man drained the tumbler, returned it to the bar. "Again!" Now he turned his pale eyes on Father Din. "Who's this?"

"A friend," Toddy said.

"So, she can speak," said the man, turning back to Toddy. "Well, if we're speaking again," he went on casually, "why not answer my question? Why did you stay here if you knew I was coming? You said on the phone you were going to leave. Could it be that you love me after all?" He laughed softly; then he downed his second tumblerful of Scotch and replaced the empty tumbler on the bar. "Again!" he repeated. Tiger snatched the tumbler and went up the bar. "Well?" asked the man. "Could that be it?"

"I despise you," Toddy said, staring into her drink.

The man laughed. "Another aspect of love," he said, lightly. Once more he turned his cold, pale gaze on Father Din. "Could your friend here be the glue that kept you stuck to that barstool? No offense to you, sir," the man added quickly, smiling. "Since Toddy won't introduce us, I'll have to introduce myself." He paused to drain his third tumbler of Scotch, waved a beringed finger at Tiger, indicating that he wanted still another, and turned, leaning against the bar, to fully face Father Din. "I'm called Monk," he said placing a cigarette in a holder and lighting it. A veil of smoke rose back over his endless forehead like a thin peruke of fine grey hair. "Do you find that an odd name?" he asked, the veil rising above his pale eyes, his dark, closing brows.

"No, not so odd," said Father Din.

"Perhaps," said the man, "I should explain. I had a little friend once who insisted upon associating me in his mind with a small, brachinating primate. I suppose it was the short-ened form of the latter that produced the name Monk; but I prefer to think that the name has religious connotations. I am a kind of neighborhood priest, you see. I tell you these things because yours is a new face hereabouts. You aren't from around here, are you?"

"No."

"No, I didn't think you were. You see, I know almost every-one in this area—or know of them—who they are, what they do—it's my business." He drank half the Scotch from his tumbler, mouthed his cigarette-holder, puffed, drew it away quickly. "Yes—as I was saying—I'm a sort of neighborhood priest. When I make a new convert, he always asks me, 'Who are you? Who should I ask for?' and I say, 'Now that you are a member of my flock, just ask for Monk.' I tell them that if they have any trouble finding me all they have to do is ask a cop."

"I don't follow you. Why should they ask a cop?"

Monk ignored him. "So you see, the name has a sort of reli-gious value, don't you think?" He aimed his cigarette at

23

Father Din's forehead and took a long, slow drag. "I see you don't care too much for my humor," he said, smiling. "Yes, I am the high-priest of the Church of Moral Freaks," he added, chuckling softly. "And I guess that would make our taciturn friend here the high-priestess. That's my little joke. You noticed that I greeted her by calling her priestess?" He looked at Toddy. "He isn't a cop, is he, Priestess?" He looked back at Father Din. "You aren't a narc, are you, my friend? I can spot the traces of fuzz in a newborn baby. No, you're a dude. A runaway husband, perhaps? What's your name?"

Father Din decided that it was time to leave. He finished his drink. "Sam Hopkins," he said, putting money on the counter.

"Are you leaving, Mr. Hopkins?" Monk asked.

"I think I'd better."

"Oh. Did you find my description of the young lady offensive?"

"I think you've made several offensive remarks, Mr.— Monk."

Monk laughed. "Well, what would you expect? I'm a priest of evil. Malice is my middle name."

"That sounds more juvenile than amusing," said Father Din. "Otherwise, you sound halfway intelligent."

"I *am* an intelligent man. It's apparent that you are, too." He paused. Father Din was looking past Monk at Toddy. She sat crumpled over an empty glass as if trying to read

24

something in its bottom. Again he changed his mind, deciding to stay a while longer. He called for Tiger to bring him another drink. Purposefully, he did not order one for Toddy. She ignored what she might have taken for a slight, and ordered herself another. She looked foggy, bedraggled, and fearful.

"Juvenile? Not at all," said Monk. "Think about it. Think about war, and of race-hatred; think about your own inner-most secret desires," he went on, in a bland, considering voice, "and you'll see that—like those religious sects where every member of the sect is a minister—we are all priests of evil. All men convert to the Church of Moral Freaks at some point in their lives. I only claim my exalted title as the High Priest of Moral Freakishness by virtue of the life-long effort I've made to rid myself of hypocrisy. Others pretend—even succeed in convincing themselves—that they desire goodness and virtue. I make no such pretense. I like to think of myself as representing the raw malice of mankind, its deep, permanent, bestial nature."

"Not very admirable," said Father Din.

"Naturally not," said Monk. "But that's because men can't face themselves; they can't accept what they are—beasts in a jungle. If they could accept the fact that they were only beasts, they might learn to admire the beast's fang and how and for what purpose he uses it."

Father Din eyed the man. Monk clearly meant what he was saying.

"But things are getting better."

"How do you mean?"

"Psychiatry," said Monk carelessly, "is helping us to see that we are all weak and cruel or cruelly weak in our strength. Vicious, in other words. It's teaching us to be unashamedly what we are. Ultimately, man will lose all of his ideals. He will excuse himself until he goes back down on all-fours to snarl and bite with pride." He laughed, finished his drink, and called Tiger to bring him another. He put a new cigarette in his holder and lighted it. "There's an odd contradiction, however," he resumed, "psychiatry is telling man, in effect, without realizing it, that it's every beast for himself, and individually we like that; but each of us fears the unbridled beast in the other guy, you see, so we support all sorts of laws that prevent—or at least dissuade—us from freely biting others."

"You prefer anarchy?" asked Father Din.

"I prefer law—when I'm the only one breaking it," said Monk. "It keeps the other beasts at bay." He drank the first half of his fourth drink; replaced the tumbler on the bar, snuffed out his cigarette, and put the holder in his breast pocket. "It's been interesting talking to you, Mister—what was it?—Hopkins. I don't often get the chance to talk with an intelligent person. My business, you see. I deal with scum. It's always been that way with me. All my life I've dealt with scum in scummy businesses. Started out as a boxer; then I was a soldier; then I was a thief, and later a private eye. I'm writing an autobiography. You must read it when it's published. That won't be for a long time though—not until after I'm dead. I haven't finished it yet. I've lived a violent life. I like violence; it's in my blood. It turns me on. I'll die violently, I know. By the sword. But that's what I want." He laughed. "I frighten you, Mr. Hopkins?"

"You disturb me . . ."

"Well, that's just as well. Because it's time for you to be on your way. I want to be alone for a few minutes with my high priestess. Yes, I'm afraid the sun goes down, Mr. Hopkins. The sun goes down."

"It's been a cloudy day," said Father Din. "I won't miss it. I've decided to stay."

"Look, my friend. You're a stranger around here. I'm trying to do you a favor. I've enjoyed talking to you, but it's time for you to leave. Go! Now! Don't make a nuisance of yourself. Don't encourage me to hurt you. Because if I should be forced to do that—"

"No!" cried Toddy. She slammed her glass down on the bar. "Leave him alone! He has a right to be here. I want him to stay. It's you! You leave! Leave me alone!"

"Are you drunk?" said Monk, startled.

"Yes, I'm drunk. What does it matter? I'm still sober enough to know where you've been today and that you've got twenty years worth of junk on you."

"Keep your mouth shut," Monk fairly hissed.

"Why should I?" Toddy challenged, her eyes melting with drink and emotion. "I've had enough—enough," she said, bursting into tears.

Monk slipped off his stool, slapped her quickly across the mouth, and then tried to stifle her scream by cupping a hand over her mouth. She bit the hand and pulled free, mouth open, but she did not scream. Her eyes were wide. Monk cursed, holding his bitten hand.

"Get out of here," Toddy said, thickly. Then, in a higher pitch: "I tell you, I can't take much more." She pushed her hair back from her face, using both hands, and turned back to her empty glass. "I want another drink, Tiger." Tiger picked up her glass; looked at Monk: "You can't hit her and get away with it," he said, wall-eye fiery with impotent rage. "I'll take a baseball bat to you."

"I don't see anyone interfering," said Monk, looking from Tiger to Father Din. "How about you, Mr. Hopkins; anything aside from a gloomy look?"

"I'm glad I stayed," said Father Din. He got to his feet. "I think we've all had enough of you."

"Remember," said Tiger, raising a finger in warning, "Lieutenant Figlia's after you. You ain't gonna walk in and out of that station like it was a hotel no more. That's a tough flatfoot, and he don't take bribes."

Monk stuck his cigarette-holder between his teeth. He spoke around it, lighting a smoke. "Mind your manners, you cock-eyed old fool. This place could burn down—like that"—he snapped his fingers. He took the holder from his mouth and exhaled smoke. "O.K.," he said. "None of this is im-portant. Toddy, you stay if you want to, and I'll go. I'm go-ing to be up at your place at ten tonight. If you're sober I'll talk to you then. I'm going to make allowances for you be-cause you're drunk. But if you keep this up, I'm afraid your husband is going to be in for a bad time—a whole lot worse than usual. As for you, Hopkins, you'd better find a hole and

28

crawl into it. And make it deep." He turned and stamped out into the evening dark.

Chapter 6

A RUMOR OF CAVALRY

"I'm sorry I dragged you into this, Sam," Toddy said. "I should have left an hour ago. I don't know why I didn't. I've been thinking about having it out with him for weeks, but I didn't have the nerve to do it when I was sober. I had to get drunk to do it. I guess I'm a coward."

"You're no coward, honey," said Tiger. "There ain't many guys around here who would talk to him the way you did. Jeeze, why did you ever get mixed up with that bastard?"

"You know why," Toddy said, her eyes going hard and cold. "Get me another drink."

Tiger regarded her doubtfully. "Don't tell me I've had too much already, Tiger. I know better than anybody how much I've had, and it isn't anywhere near enough. Now get me another drink, if we're friends."

"You too, Sam?"

"You know, Tiger," said Father Din, "I'm not a drinking man, but somehow tonight I don't feel as if I've had enough either."

"Right on!" cried Toddy. She gave him a poke in the ribs.

"So I was right after all," said Father Din, after Tiger placed fresh drinks in front of them and went up the bar to serve a couple of customers who had just entered, "you are in some kind of trouble. Do you want to tell me about it?"

"Are you sure you want to hear a drunken broad tell her long sad tale of woe?"

"Who is Monk?"

"He's . . . let's say an old acquaintance." She fidgeted with a cigarette and match. "I smoke too much. But nobody I know is trying to quit—anything!" She lighted the cigarette and sighed out the smoke. Then she said, shrugging her shoulders: "Oh, what's the use! He's a mistake I can't undo." She looked hard at Father Din. "You know, there's something about you . . . you make me want to talk."

"Do I? I'm glad if I do."

"Well, Sam," she said, her mood lightening, "you really are something else. Here I thought you were interested in my legs and it turns out that it's the real me you're after."

"I only want to help, if possible."

"That's too bad. I was hoping for something more." She looked quickly away, took a sip from her drink, and looked up again, saying: "I admired you, the way you handled yourself with Monk. Most of the guys I know are terrified of him."

"You'd be wrong if you thought he didn't unsettle me. I find it hard to believe, though, that anybody could mean some of the things he said."

"Oh, he means what he says—somewhere, deep down. He likes to put people on, though. Like that priest of evil

31

business. That's supposed to be a joke, but he means it, too. That's exactly what he is."

"He didn't mean that, about burning this place down, did he?"

"He's had other places fire-bombed. I know that for a fact."

"Then why isn't he behind bars?"

"Nobody'll testify against him. Hell, nobody knows just how many crooks are free because some witness was murdered. It happens all the time."

Tiger wiped the bar. "I see you got a lot to learn, son; Monk shmears the cops. He's like a little king around here. It ain't no secret that he peddles dope and pimps and is into a half a dozen other rackets—gambling, protection, pornography— you name it. That's why I don't mind telling you—every- body knows it. But try to get him on anything and see what happens. I'd have the fire inspectors in here closing me up; and two days later the place would burn down anyway."

"But Figlia's different," said Toddy. "Monk can't buy him off."

"Who's Figlia?" asked Father Din. The name sounded familiar to him. Then he remembered. It was the same name of a young girl whose funeral he had helped to direct.

"A nark. Narcotics. He's on special assignment in this precinct—he used to be in Harlem; and before that over in Chelsea. He had a daughter who O.D.'d on smack."

"That's motivation," Toddy put in. "That's why he can't be bought. And there can't be any question about it: he's here to get Monk."

"He's working in tandem with the local precinct," said Tiger; "the reason bein' that most of the robberies around here are committed by junkies."

"Hey, Tiger!" came a call, and Tiger, cursing under his breath, ambled, more like a shaggy old bear than a tiger, back up the bar.

Chapter 7

ODD MAN IN

The man who called Tiger was a very tall, skinny black man. He wore his hair in a plaster of waves and ringlets that dipped down the right side of his forehead, almost covering and no doubt at times stabbing into his right eye, in the manner of certain black jazz musicians of an earlier era. There was a somewhat feline handsomeness about him, but this was offset to a degree by the shabbiness of his clothes—he wore, following the custom of old-time jazzmen, a satin-collared tuxedo, worn shiny, and a sullen scowl. A battered black saxophone case dangled from one long thin hand; the other hand was waving about and stabbing the air with a long delicate index finger. "You and me, bro, are born pork-chop-sandwich and hot-sauce Baptists. You can change, but you're asking too much of me when you ask me to give up my heritage."

"What'll it be, Tory?"

"Double gin on some cubes."

"And you?"

The man with Tory was about the same age and bore a striking resemblance to him. He looked like Tory might have looked with a close-cropped haircut and a natty funeral director's dark suit—a clean-cut version of Tory.

"He'll have a plain tomato juice, Tiger. Or an Orange Crush. Or moo juice. Ask me how do I know?"

34

"How do you know, Tory?" asked Tiger, one eye eerily focused on Tory and one on the natty dresser.

"Cuz Mister Spit-shine here—he be my righteous Big Bubba. He only eat, drink and do pure things. Sometimes he so goody-two-shoes, he make me sick."

"It's all that gin and hog in you that makes you sick," said Tory's brother. "Gin, hog, and only Allah knows what-all. You are destroying your holy black self with white man's toxins." He looked at Tiger. "Do you have tomato juice? If so, please bring me one, with a twist of lemon." He looked at Tory. "I don't want to be seen standing at a bar. Let's take a table. I'm going to sit over there. Bring the refreshments." He went over and sat at a table in a dark corner, a tall neat figure, crisp and clean in the shadows.

Tory moved up beside Toddy. "Hey, baby, what's happenin?"

"Hi, Tory," she said.

"Do you know what is an evil thing, Toddy? It is, that everyone in this world is out recruiting somebody. Ain't nobody can be what they be without recruiting somebody to be just like they be. Only time anybody is happy is when everybody is just like them. Am I meeting a new recruit, or ain't ya gonna introduce me?"

"Sam Hopkins," said Toddy, "meet Torrance Amsterdam."

"Tory will do fine." He reached out across Toddy and pumped Father Din's hand. "You see that white shirt on Mister Slick over there—Mister Stiff-as-Starch—that's my

35

brother, Morris Amsterdam, A.K.A. Mahmoud Zero—or is it X?—or some such, and he is after recruiting me into the Muslims. But I tell him what a man called Monk tells me: I have already been recruited into the Congregation of Moral Freaks." He began to spit laughter, then went into an aw, aw, aw, aw, aw, and only got ahold of himself when Tiger put a tray of drinks in front of him. "Later," he said to Toddy, flipping Tiger a bill and, without waiting for change, took the tray over to the corner to join his brother.

Torrence and Morris Amsterdam were born outside of Elkin, North Carolina. Their mother and father had picked cotton for wages. Their grandmother and grandfather had picked cotton to hold on to a shanty and a quarter-acre of land. Their great-grandparents had picked cotton for the Amsterdam family, as slaves. *Their* grandparents had been rich in Africa, owning cattle. And so it goes, back into the obscure antiquity of history, the twilight before it, and the darkness before that. Morrie and Tory were jazzmen. Morrie's elegant fingers could make magic on the piano. Tory could blow his soul through the balloons of his cheeks and the brass rigama-role of his saxophone and never run out of it. But Morrie wanted more than a piano player's cigarette; he wanted Justice; and so he became Mahmoud Zero, one of Allah's avengers. Tory, on the other hand, doubted if there was justice in all the universe, ever was, ever would be. But complaints abounded, plaints and complaints, to be screamed, hummed, eased, and jammed out of the big brass mouth of his sax.

Tory and Mahmoud were at the Saints and Sinners Club to meet a couple of Mahmoud's associates. Tory had suggested the spot as a good place for Mahmoud to meet his friends because he liked the place, liked Tiger, and because he was behind in his drinking, at least three gins back. He was al-

36

ways behind in his drinking. Today, he was behind because he had given his brother a hand at the mosque in Harlem, where a sideman had been arrested and a replacement was desperately needed. The Black Muslims have no liturgy. They do not sing in the temple; but they usually start their services with a protracted, sort of progressive jazz riff. Tory suspected that the combo could have gotten along without him. He suspected that Mahmoud had used the excuse of a missing member to bring Tory to the Muslim service, a chance to convert him. After the jazz riff, Tory and Mahmoud had seated themselves among the congregation and heard what Tory suspected Mahmoud thought would be his conversion sermon. At the end of the sermon converts were invited up front. Several former Baptists and Methodists, struck with guilt for having held to the white satan's religion, made their way up to pledge conversion. Tory was not among them. Mahmoud had been hectoring him all the way downtown. He was ashamed, disgraced in front of his brothers and sisters, that his blood brother could not see the Light.

Chapter 8

THE HORSEMAN OF THE APOCALYPSE

"How did you get involved with a man like Monk?" Father Din asked Toddy, realizing that every question was getting him more deeply involved with this strange and beautiful young woman and with the troubles that went with her.

She shrugged. "My husband, Jack, got me mixed up with Monk. Jack and I don't live together anymore. He lives in a loft across the street from my apartment. But we don't see much of each other these days: only sometimes when he comes over to pick up his stuff from Monk. He's a junkie, one of the members of Monk's congregation. He used to be an artist, a painter: he only used the loft for a studio in those days. And the last thing he painted was a portrait of a junkie. He knew this little seventeen-year-old Puerto Rican boy who had been using heroin for years. He got the boy to sit for him, and he worked on the painting for a few months, but it never satisfied him. He felt that he couldn't psyche the boy out. Then he told me that he was going to shoot up with the stuff so he could see what the boy got out of it. Now that really scared me; but he told me not to worry, that one or two shots of the stuff couldn't hook anybody. Well, I still didn't like it, but I didn't like to argue with him in those days. I respected him, you see, and I trusted him. And as far as the painting went, he was right, I guess; because it turned out to be a really wonderful portrait, the best Jack ever did. Not realistic, of course. The face smeared and blended with the background—a kind of dream image, or nightmare. He was offered two-thousand dollars for it at a show he gave a month or so after he finished it, and that was a great price. It was painted over all of these broken, bad-luck mirror pieces stuck on the canvass. It made for a really interesting effect. Sometimes you could see bits of yourself looking back at you from the portrait. Jack said it reflected the society that made junkies, and then he said it showed that becoming a junkie could happen to anyone."

"There but for the grace of God," said Father Din.

"Yeah, that was it."

"What happened to the painting?"

"Jack wouldn't sell it. He still has it up there in the loft with him. He won't part with it. He hasn't had another show, either. That show was even reviewed by some newspapers. One reviewer said that the painting—Jack called it Horseman of the Apocalypse—"horse" is slang for heroin in case you didn't know—'was the biggest step forward in American painting since Jackson Pollock.' By then Jack was shooting the stuff three and four and even five times a day, and always complaining that the stuff wasn't any good and that he needed another shot to get the same high that one less gave him a week before." She looked up at Father Din.

"Monk was Jack's connection. Dedi Pavon, the model, introduced Jack to Monk, and pretty soon Jack was letting Monk use our apartment for his headquarters in the neighborhood.

"Jack's family has money. I guess they think of Jack as something of a black sheep. But they send him a check every month anyway. Which is their way of keeping a hold on him. But junk is very expensive. It was running Jack a hundred dollars a day the last I heard, and it may be several times that by now. I don't ask because I don't want to know." She paused. "But the thing is, Monk offered Jack a cut-rate for the use of the apartment, and Jack took him up on it. I tried to tell Jack that it wasn't the apartment Monk was after, it was power over *us*; but Jack wouldn't listen: he was beyond reason. That was then. But later, when Jack finally saw that what I had told him about Monk was true, he tried to face Monk down. But Monk only laughed in his face. And when Jack lost his temper and took a poke at Monk, Monk threw him out of the apartment. I tried to go with him, but Monk wouldn't let me. I thought then, though, that Jack was saved. I thought he'd go and get the police and have Monk arrested, no matter what it cost him to do it. But within fifteen minutes Jack was back outside the door, begging Monk for a fix. Man, that did something to me. I didn't see how Jack could let Monk throw him out of our apartment and then come back begging for more . . . it was shameless . . . and . . . disgusting. I couldn't help myself, I hated him for it. Well, . . . I hated what he had become. It's awful to find yourself hating someone that you've loved. I wanted to hurt him, to shock him into sanity . . . I don't know what. Anyway, when I heard him crying outside the door like that, all I could feel for him was contempt. Something snapped, and it was all over. I didn't say a word to Monk on Jack's behalf. I just went into the bedroom and got in bed."

She snuffed out her cigarette viciously: looked up. Her eyes glittered and were opened wide as if to hold back tears. The muscles in her jaws were knotted; her mouth twisted. "Maybe it was all those months of watching Monk get more and more power over Jack, and watching Jack let him do it. You wouldn't believe it." She lowered her voice. "It was disgusting. Monk came into the bedroom that night stark naked—carrying his belt from his trousers. He handed me the belt, threw himself across the bed, and stuck his huge, powerful-looking butt into the air. He told me to whip him. I couldn't. Then he told me he'd break my arm, if I didn't. I couldn't. Then he said he'd kill Jack, if I didn't. Then finally I could. I whipped his ass till I raised welts and he loved it. I never had sex with him. Only that. He can't have sex in a normal way. I've been half out of my mind."

"A casebook sado-masochist," said Father Din.

"The weaker Jack got, the more he just seemed to fade away. Monk was in charge of everything. He just took over our lives. It was as if Jack was dying, or dead. And that meant that our marriage was dead, too. I mean, doesn't a marriage die with the death of one of the partners?"

"I don't think so," Father Din ventured in a quiet voice. He felt almost schizophrenic—one minute libidinous and aggressive—one minute counseling like a parish priest.

"Oh, but I do," Toddy shot back. The shock of her own attack upon Monk had temporarily sobered her, but now the drinks seemed to be catching up with her again. She burst into tears, and began fishing in her pocketbook for a handkerchief. She found it, and held it over her face while continuing to sob. All the pent-up emotions of months were released. Finally she stopped shaking and wiped her eyes and face, blew her nose, and smiled sheepishly at Father Din, who had sat like a statue, one big hand on her long, shivering back, while she cried.

Tiger, seeing Toddy crying, had come down the bar to her and now stood, gnarled hands whitely gripping the bartop, in mute empathy. He was visibly relieved when Toddy looked up to smile at Father Din. "There now," he said. "Do you feel better, honey. Are you O.K.?"

"Oooh, Tiger," Toddy sniffed, "you old dope. I'm fine. Women like to cry once in a while; don't you know anything?" She looked at herself in her compact mirror and grimaced. "Oh, I'm a fright! Excuse me," she said to Father Din, "I better go to the ladies room and put myself together again."

"Is she all right?" asked Tiger when she was gone.

"For now," said Father Din. "But she's not all right."

Chapter 9

AT CROSS PURPOSES

Ansar Rashid was in America to serve Allah, or so Mahmoud had been given to understand by Ansar's Atlantic Avenue connections. In truth, these connections had mistakenly thought that they were introducing a member-in-good-standing of Viper-8, whose major effort in the great Jihad was to write letters and make phonecalls claiming credit for the deeds of others, to his American counterpart in the Black Muslims. In fact, Viper-8 had evaporated with the arrest of three of the eight of its total, forlorn membership; and, though Mahmoud was a member in good standing of the Black Muslims, he was no terrorist. Brooklyn's Muslim Atlantic Avenue grapevine, an exchange of tall tales and fantastical gossip, much of it disinformation planted by F.B.I. operatives, had both ends of the story wrong, one end because Ansar was a great self-aggrandizer and the other end because they completely misunderstood the current mission of the American Black Muslims. Mahmoud assumed that he was to show Ansar the American ropes, how the Black American suffered at the hands of the Great Satan. He further assumed that Ansar would take his new-found understanding of the plight of the American Black back to the Middle East and spread the word. Ansar assumed that Mahmoud's purpose was to help him establish an American Jihad against the Great Satan. They had not known each other long enough to know that they were at cross purposes.

Ansar did not like meeting in a place that served alcohol. He was annoyed. "Why have you dragged me to this den of iniquity?" he asked of Mahmoud, throwing his Loden coat across the back of his chair. His every gesture reeked of agitated self-importance. Out of his coat, a cold-weather gift from his Brooklyn friends, Ansar proved to be pot-bellied, soft as a pillow.

"We were in Harlem," Tory answered for his brother, "you were in Brooklyn. This is half-way between."

"Please, Tory," said Mahmoud, "try to be quiet. Listen and learn. Please forgive my brother's intrusive behavior, Ansar. His wits have escaped with the vapor of alcohol. Still, this did seem a convenient place to meet. That is, geographically. My brother lied to me. He told me this was an eatery. I don't like it any more than you do. But—would you like something to drink? I mean fruit juice of some kind, or Co-Cola?" Ansar waved the suggestion aside. "And what about you, Miss Azziz?" Mahmoud asked of Ansar's companion. "A glass of white wine?" Camilla Azziz was a teenager. From Palestine, her family had gone to Kuwait, and then on to Chicago, where Camilla was born, an all-American girl. The face that went with her prime pulchritude did not suit it. It was worried in its frame of wild waves of curly black hair.

"Miss Azziz will have orange juice," said Ansar. He spoke a good, accent-lilted brand of English; but there was something irritating about it, as if there were either a demand, an order, or some kind of sarcasm, in every sentence.

"Let's make an itinerary," said Mahmoud.

"If we do, it may have to be adjusted," said Ansar. "I am here on serious business and could be interrupted at any time."

44

"Woah, woah," said Tory, standing up. "Serious has just hurt my sensitive ears. I'll go get us some drinks." He took the tray and went up to the bar. When he returned, the tray laden with four gin and tonics, Ansar was saying, "Are you sure this is a safe place? That bartender looks like an Israeli agent." Tory was putting the drinks on the table. "You mean Tiger?" he said.

"Tiger," quoted Ansar. "Could that be a code name?"

"Tiger's just a broken down old man," said Tory. "He used to be a wrestler. Years ago."

"I don't trust this place," said Ansar. "And I do not trust this man," he said, pointing at Tory. He looked at Mahmoud with gleaming eyes. "Why has he led us here, to meet in such a place? Could it not be a plot? Camilla, get your coat! We are leaving now. I will not stay in the stench of alcohol," he said, eyeing the four gin and tonics.

"Good," shot Tory, pulling the tray toward him.

"Are you coming?" Ansar asked of Mahmoud.

"Give me a moment," said Mahmoud. "I must speak with my brother."

"We will wait outside." Ansar fairly dragged Camilla to the door.

Tory sprawled at the table, gin in hand. "I think you been put in charge of a coo-coo bird, Mister Slick."

"I can't explain it to you now, my brother, but Ansar may have reasons to take extreme care."

45

"You mean even paranoids have real enemies—eh?"

"I don't like to leave you in this drunken condition, my brother, but at the moment I am called to higher service, in the name of Allah. But it is my ardent hope that you will rethink your life style. You have embarrassed me several times today, but I am your brother and I love you. Please go somewhere and get some sleep. I do not like to think of you wandering the streets in your present condition." Mahmoud leaned down and kissed his brother on the cheek. As Mahmoud pulled open the door to leave, Dedi Pavon brushed passed him, entering.

Chapter 10

TAPERING OFF

When Toddy returned from the ladies' room, she said, "I washed my face in cold water and fixed it up, and I feel positively sober again. I'm so sorry I burdened you with my long tale of woe, Sam. Whatever got into me, I just had to get it out."

"Remember what you told me about apologies: a sign of emotional insecurity, you said."

Toddy laughed. "Who said I was emotionally secure? Anyhow, that only went for repeated apologies, which I don't intend to make. What you must think of me, though. Now, at this moment, I can't imagine myself telling you all those things . . . I don't know what came over me. It's just that I haven't had anyone to talk to. It's been so long since I've really talked . . . And there's something about you . . . you make me feel like talking . . ." She covered Father Din's hand, which was resting on the bar, with her own. "I feel that I know you even though I don't. It's strange . . . you're such a good listener . . . so quiet and patient. Not like a salesman at all."

Gently, Father Din removed his hand, and Toddy moved hers to the pack of cigarettes that lay on the bar, removed one, and brought her other hand to meet it with a flaming lighter. "Smoking is like hoping," she said. "I keep meaning to quit."

Chapter 11

THE LIVING IMAGE

Dedi Pavon paused just inside the door, high-fiving Tory at a distance. Doing a little warming jig, he surveyed the room, his face showing the tell-tale lesions of Kaposi's sarcoma. Father Din had seen many such faces in the last few years, the faces of AIDS victims. The boy was shivering, hunching his narrow shoulders, rocking from foot to foot, rubbing his hands together: understandably, for he wore no overcoat, hat or gloves, only a thin mustard-hued suit, a luminous pink cha-cha shirt, and a pair of blue plastic shoes. Father Din thought the boy was a candidate for pneumonia, and, as if in keeping with this casual prophecy, the boy hacked, hacked again, and fell into an uncontrollable fit of coughing. He tugged a sticky-looking handkerchief from his breast pocket and covered his mouth with it until the fit subsided. He blew his dripping nose, stuffed the handkerchief back in his pocket, threw back his shoulders and, with a brand new grin that displayed a prominent black void of missing teeth, exclaimed, "Ave Maria!" He stepped up to Father Din. "If you spit out there it will freeze and break on the sidewalk like a ten-cent diamond. Amigo, you got to have cold blood to live in this town, you know that?" He laughed ingratiatingly. Then, seeing Toddy, apparently for the first time, he slapped his scarred cheek in surprise. "Ay! I didn't know it was you, with your nose buried in the glass. Is this your friend I have spoke to?"

Toddy looked him over. "Where's your coat, Dedi? Are you crazy?" Then to Father Din: "Sam, this is the boy I told you about, the model for Jack's painting—Dedi Pavon. Dedi, this is Sam Hopkins."

Father Din encompassed Dedi's frail, proffered hand and shook it as if he were rocking a small bird to sleep. "Hello," he said.

"Pleased to dig, mon." Father Din let the hand fly free. "I didn't see it was you, Toddy. I was going to put the con on your friend here, see if he wouldn't like to buy a nice watch, cheap. Hey," he exclaimed, new hope shining his eyes, "maybe you would like that anyhow, eh? I could give you some good bargain . . ."

"Sam doesn't want any hot watches."

"How you know what the mon wants?" Dedi challenged, with the look of an insulted salesman. "You shouldn't bust in when people's doing business. That ain't polite." Then, pathetically: "Besides, you know I'm a sick boy. How'm I gonna buy medicine with you telling people I'm selling hot merchandise?"

"I've already got a watch," Father Din intervened. "Got it just recently." He extended his left wrist. "See?"

"That's a beauty!" cried Dedi, raising his eyebrows. "Damn! Everybody got a watch! What a life! Oof!" He pinched his nostrils against the stink of the world. "I should go back to Puerto Rico. I need the sun to shine on me. I'm a sick boy." He fell silent for a moment, a doleful expression on his face: then, surprisingly, he assumed a bodybuilder's pose, flexing his biceps, and said with vehemence: "I could be Mr. Puerto Rico in six months." Toddy and Father Din laughed. "But who wants to be muscle-bound?" Dedi said, shrugging his shoulders. "I-yi-yi-yi," he cried, rolling his head despairingly, "I don't know what to do . . ."

"Where's your overcoat?" asked Toddy.

"What do I need an overcoat for? I know how to make me warm." He winked. "But I got to get El Dinero, big green daddy, to get what I need. You know Monk. He don't take no watches, hot or cold. *!Ay, ese hombre no me gusta!* But he the mon. He got the smack, so—" He was suddenly overtaken with another coughing fit. When it was over, he went on: "See? I'm a sick boy. Ask my sister, she will tell you. I need medicine. *Caramba*, how'm I'm gonna get the bread?" He took his thin homely face in his hands and swayed it from side to side. There was such a look of despair on that hand-held face that Father Din was tempted to buy himself an extra watch, but the almost certain knowledge that what he paid for the watch would be spent on heroin, combined with the probability that the watch was stolen, militated against the gesture.

Suddenly Tiger came up and took Dedi by the arm, saying: "Not in here, Dedi. I've told ya before, I don't want ya to peddle none of your hot merchandise in my bar. I got enough troubles without that." He pulled the boy toward the door.

"O.K., O.K., mon," Dedi protested, "I only come in this dump to see if my sister was here. Hey, Toddy," he called back, "you seen Pilar?"

"You can see she ain't here," Tiger said. "Come on, now, I got customers to serve."

"I gotta come in to see, don't I?" He called back to Father Din: "You sure you don't need no watch, mon?" Then he was propelled out the door. Tiger stood waiting to see that he was gone. He then turned to clean the table where Tory sat, nursing the last of his gin.

"What's the matter?" said Tiger, wiping the table, "You look worried. Got troubles?"

"I'm worried about my bro. He's too innocent to live."

"Hey, one of your friends must have dropped this," said Tiger, flopping a paperback on the table. "It was on the chair."

"Must have slithered out somebody's pocket," said Tory, thickly, reading its title: *Official Document In-House Circulation Only, Central Intelligence Agency #918593K, Ingredients and Preparation of Home-Made Bombs.*

"Oh, wow!" cried Tory, shaking his head.

Chapter 12

WARNINGS, WARNINGS, WARNINGS!

Tiger went up the outside of the bar and came back down behind it to Toddy and Father Din. "I feel sorry for Dedi," he said, picking up their empty glasses, "but what can I do? I can't afford to buy him no fixes. He spends more on dope in a week than I make, working my ass off." He shook his head. "Poor kid. Remember when I used to let him come in to shine shoes, Toddy? The money he made, he used to go to the five-and-dime and buy things for his sister. He used to come in and show me what he bought her. Fancy can-openers that you screwed on the wall, and sets of steak knives with bone handles: he liked to have a nice home, he said." He gave a sympathetic little laugh. "Hell, he was only about eleven or twelve. You remember, Toddy? You wasn't so much older yourself. But then, you was always in back, shooting pool. We never had much business during the day, and she'd be out of sight back there."

"I was already sixteen or seventeen when Dedi first started coming in," Toddy said. "That was a couple of years after I lost my parents. My dad spent a lot of time here in the last year of his life. Tiger was his friend. At the end, I guess Tiger was the only friend he had; so I used to come in to talk to Tiger about my dad. I was only a little girl then, but in this neighborhood a girl's little girl stage goes fast."

"Your father was a fine man," Tiger said earnestly. "But Dedi and his sister, Pilar—uh, they only had a little room to live in, and no parents neither, none that I ever heard of. Pilar was older—let's see, she'd be, oh, twenty-five now, maybe. She was a pretty kid. Took good care of her little brother, too, for a long time. But she was uh, you know, in the life, a prostitute. I don't judge her for that. How else could a little girl raise a boy all by herself? She could have just given him away, you know. Some of these desperate people do that. They just give their kids to somebody and go off on their own. But not her. And I respect her for that. I don't know how she managed to dodge the authorities all those years. They probably never even knew she was there. But, too bad, somewhere along the line she got on junk. And then later Dedi got on it. "So," Tiger waved his palms, "that seemed to . . . end their lives." He turned away wearing a hopeless face and went up the bar to refill their glasses.

"He's a good guy," Toddy said. "But he's old. There isn't much he can do. I guess there isn't much any of us can do," she added, after a pause. "What time is it?"

"Seven-thirty. Do you have to be somewhere?"

"Monk will expect me to be at the apartment at ten. If I'm not there he'll make it tough on Jack. I don't want to be responsible for what he might do to Jack."

Tiger brought their drinks and went away again.

"But what will Monk do to you?" Father Din asked, after a pause. "I mean, he was in a pretty bad temper when he left."

"Oh, he won't hurt me. At least he never has. Maybe just slap me around a little. He's not simple. He likes to use one person to hurt another. It's all a kind of a game with him."

"And you're going up there tonight?"

"I told you, I have to. If I don't, he won't give Jack his stuff. Jack picks up from Monk once a week. He sells him a whole week's supply at a time. Can you imagine what it would mean to be cut off?"

"Then, if you'll let me," Father Din found himself saying, "I'd like to go with you."

"Oh, Sam, no! Monk would just love to see your face again tonight. Especially somewhere out of public view."

"But I don't want you to go alone."

"I can't let you come with me," Toddy said, shaking her head negatively. It appeared that this was her final decision. Father Din decided to let the subject drop for the moment. But he was stubborn, and he had decided that he would not let her go without him.

Strange, at three o'clock this afternoon he had entered this place with no clear idea of what his purpose was, rather like some hypnotized subject of a night club act, and in less than five hours he had become involved, absorbed, in someone else's life. Now, he thought, all he wanted to do was to protect a beautiful woman. Suddenly he felt a wave of nausea.

"What's wrong?" Toddy asked, looking at him with alarm.

"I don't know. I feel uncomfortable. My stomach . . ." In a moment he found his way to the men's room and was vomiting into the toilet. He ran some cold water into the dirty sink and dowsed his face with it. "Warnings, warnings, warnings," he muttered to himself: for in his mind warnings were being sounded through the medium of Father Ryan's

54

voice. But Father Ryan was like a desperate parent with no argument at his command but that of an incommunicable experience, like the father who doubts the success of the project upon which his son has embarked, but, when asked what the basis of his doubt is, can only explain his feeling by saying that the project doesn't sound right.

"I think I know what is in the back of your mind," Father Ryan said, the last time they talked, "and let me assure you, Michael, that the pursuit of any such course of action can only lead to great heartache and suffering, both for yourself and for others. You'll wind up a spoiled priest." Father Ryan meant women, but was afraid to say so in so many words, as if saying what he feared might make it real. He had seen it before—the disaster of the young priest and his Eve.

"But, Father Liam," lied Father Din, "my only intention is to try to make more outside contacts. I'm a parish priest, not a monk. Look at Father Corrigan—"

"Outside contacts! You have a parishful of outside contacts to make. What are you talking about? Outside contacts, indeed! What nonsense! Michael, I don't mean to say that you haven't done your duty—you have—until lately, anyhow. And as for Thom Corrigan, look at the trouble he's causing—the publicity! His books. His television appearances. Openly flaunting a mistress. Why, he talks like a communist. He's a disgrace to the Church."

"He's doing good works . . . ."

"That is highly questionable. But, leaving all that aside, you are not Thom Corrigan, you are Michael Din, and a different kind of man. Thom Corrigan is a sophisticate. No man more appreciates your particular talents than I—but, Michael, you

55

are a very naive young man. My advice to you would be: hold back, wait, let time happen to you, graduate into the world."

"Warnings, warnings, warnings," muttered Father Din, dowsing his face with cold water. He looked at himself in the mirror over the sink. The new fresh face of a collegiate. "Maybe he's right," he said. "But," he added, raising his eyebrows, "I swear, I look drunk." He laughed. "I wish I could lie down for a few minutes." He stumbled out of the men's room and rejoined Toddy at the bar.

"Are you all right?" she asked.

"Look," he answered, "didn't you say that you had to be up at your place at ten?"

"Yes."

"Well, it's only a bit after eight now. Would you let me go up to your place and lie down until, say, nine or nine-thirty?"

"You'd be taking an awful chance. Suppose Monk were to show up early?"

"I'll take the chance on feeling better before he arrives."

"Are you sure?" she said. She knew it wasn't the best thing to do, but she wanted to stay with him. "Only if you promise to leave by nine-thirty," she said, knitting her brows. "Remember, it's you I'm thinking of."

PART TWO

WHIRLIGIG

Chapter 1

WAITING FOR TROUBLE

The vestibule was too small to hold them both, so Father Din waited on the sidewalk, holding the outer door open, while Toddy fumbled for her keys.

Looking back from her building, one of those tenements that materialized in long monotonous rows in every large eastern city around the turn of the last century, Father Din could see the multicolored glow of the signs of the rock clubs along the Strip, and beyond that, above an indefinite dark void, and casting a much greater, though less intense, glow high into the night, the uneven lights of the mid-town skyscrapers. Overhead the sky lowered like a taut black sheet. Occasionally, suddenly, it tore, revealing jagged, twisting light. Long, low, slowly-building rumbles, as of some cosmic drummer, preceded each flash. A storm was coming; its harbinger, the wind, had arrived, beating Father Din's coat against the backs of his legs, flashing through his hair like grazing bullets of ice.

Directly across the street was the building that housed Jack Muir's loft. It was a large, characterless edifice. Probably before being converted for studio use it had been a factory or a warehouse. Now, on the second and sixth floors, long rows of windows were lighted, so that they looked like great toothy smiles across its face. "And," thought Father Din, feeling the forced suspension of conscience which he must maintain, else concede his own error, "did a mocking laughter really emanate from the dark gulf between them?"

58

He wondered from behind which row of windows Jack Muir might be watching; wondered, instantly, what kind of man Muir was. Would he like him, despite what he had been told about him? Muir had problems; but then, so did he. The deeper he had sunk into his own problems the more responsive was his charity for others. Again, he found himself trying to believe that he was not being a fool. Nevertheless, he followed Toddy into the dismal, oily-green halls and stairwell, up stairs of deeply grooved white marble, turned peppery, braced in stiff metal. The wooden handrail of the metal banister was carved with hearts and initials, doubtless by turn-of-the-century immigrants, and resembled, to him, the long sticks upon which medieval stewards kept records. A commingled odor of life, death, and decay assailed his nostrils. His stomach heaved again. The sudden heat caused him to break out with perspiration. His head pounded. When he reached the fourth landing, he had to sit down at the top of the steps for a moment, while Toddy went on to the front to unlock her door. She came back and pulled him to his feet. "Oh, Sam, I'm sorry you feel so rotten," she said, as she led him to her door.

"It's just that I drank too much," he said, stepping behind her into the apartment.

"The cold air made me feel much better," she said, taking Father Din's great black overcoat and hanging it on a clothestree inside the door. She hung up her own coat, and then excused herself, laughing, saying: "But my kidneys can't hold anything in this kind of weather. You make yourself at home. I'll be right back. Go into the livingroom and sit down."

While she was gone Father Din surveyed the apartment. The hall door gave into the kitchen, a medium-sized room with the standard equipment, plus a bathtub. The tub was sunk inside of a plywood cabinet that had been decorated with painted daisies. The enameled cover, similarly decorated, and looking rather like a legless tabletop, stood leaning against a wall. Some clothes were soaking in the tub. The livingroom adjoined the kitchen. The marks of demarcation between the two rooms were the indications of a wall, and a brass rail-groove over which, upon a time, rolling doors had glided. However, the livingroom was much narrower and somewhat longer than the kitchen. An oriental screen stood at an angle between the two rooms, blocking part of the front room from view. This room was furnished with two easy chairs, a couch and a coffee table. An imitation Tiffany lamp hung in the middle of the room. The walls were decorated with posters. Kurt Cobane & Nirvana. Generation X. Greenpeace. There was a large poster of Madonna, hair flying. Father Din walked to the windows and opened one a crack. Another set of teeth had been added to the face of the building across the street, lending it an even more grotesque appearance than it had had a few minutes before, when seen from the street.

To his right, a door stood ajar. He stepped over to it and looked in. It was the bedroom, a small oblong, hung from ceiling to floor with purple velveteen drapes. A canopy bed, baldaquined in a satiny rose-colored material, filled the room but for a space around it just large enough to permit of a pair of legs. He retreated back to the window, and was posed, looking out, when Toddy returned.

"I'm sorry I was gone so long," she said. "I stopped across the hall to borrow a bottle of Scotch from my neighbor. She always has one. But when she doesn't, I do, so we're neither of us ever stuck when we have company."

"But not for me, I hope," Father Din said. "I've had too much already."

"No, I'll make you a cup of tea. That's the best thing in the world for an upset stomach. You just lie down on the couch. I've been thinking it over. I can handle Monk. So, you've got to be on your way before nine-thirty at the latest. That gives you an hour."

"I need it. I feel awful. I've never drunk so much in my life as I have today." He sat on the couch and took off his shoes.

"Then why today? Is today something special? Did you have a fight with your wife?"

"I'm not married. But maybe today is something special, I'm not sure yet." Father Din closed his eyes.

Toddy stood looking at him for a moment, a big, youthful fellow, sprawled on her couch. There was the shadow of a clean, fine beard appearing at his chin and jaws. She reached down and touched his damp cheek with her finger. His mouth twitched. She wondered who he was, really. Surely he was no salesman. Or it was a strange salesman who was so ill-at-ease and clumsy with strangers. But what was he then? Who was he? He was lonely, she knew. And why should such a nice-looking young man be lonely? Had he fallen out with his girl? He was attracted to her, that was plain. All she possessed, it seemed, was trouble. Was it trouble, then, that he was after? She was re-arriving at that one remove from sobriety that is a gift if going and a penalty if coming.

61

Chapter 2

TWO SAD NOTES

My dear—

*What can I say—I cannot live—I love you, my
darling girl—but I cannot live—Aunt Sybil
will look after you, won't you Syb—Be lucky—
I'm sorry—I can't explain—*
Daddy

Syb—

Please—

*Toddy has a trust fund—check with Morgan
and Atley, 400 Madison Avenue. Not much
but will allay your burden and take care of
educational expenses. Call super &/or
police. Don't let Toddy come home.
Further info. among papers in my desk.
Will included.*
Thank you

Toddy had read both of those notes hundreds of times—so
that she could recite them word for word—trying to penetrate
through to the state of mind of her father when he wrote them;
but she couldn't, not really, not so that she could finally understand—though she thought she understood his loneliness—and she ended, always, as she began, feeling deserted. People were such enigmas—you never really

knew. But she thought that he must never have loved her with anything like the love he had for her mother, in spite of the fact that she gave him every ounce of her love during those terrible years when her mother was dying and he and she were alone together, and she was growing up. She didn't count, that was all . . . not enough to keep him alive . . . . And now it was the same with Jack.

Chapter 3

RUSSIAN ROULETTE

Jack Muir paced back and forth behind the row of large casement windows that fronted his fifth floor loft.

His pale-blue eyes were set wide apart, and were slightly downcast at the outsides: and now, somewhat sunken, they gave him the appearance of a man engaged in hopeless prayer. He wore a pair of tie-dyed thermal long-johns, which bagged at the behind and knees and hung loose at the ankles and a baggy threadbare football sweatshirt, from which the name, number, and school had been removed, leaving only four gold letters—HIGH—to indicate its origins. His sandals flip-flapped as he made his stalking panther rounds inside the barless cage of his casement windows. Outside the wind was battering the loose panes of glass like an injured suppliant wanting in. One extraordinary thud brought a curse from Muir's petulant lips.

Suddenly he desisted from his pacing and maneuvered the fifty feet to the rear of the loft, overcoming an obstacle course of littered work tables, stacked canvases, and easled paintings. At the rear he bent over a small, paint-stained sink that was a mere afterthought affixed to the wall, and hastily brushed his teeth and rinsed his eyes with a damp washrag. He poured himself a glass of water, popped two big methadone tablets into his mouth and washed them down, gulping. He half filled a saucepan with water, threw a handful of Bustello coffee into it, and placed the pan on an electric single-burner in a corner which was already giving off heat from its glowing orange ring. Now he stumbled toward the front of the loft and threw himself down on the bare mattress that rested there and lighted a cigarette. He smoked for several minutes, staring up at the cracked ceiling through the changing cloud-patterns of smoke above him; then, hearing the coffee boiling, he got up and went into the back and returned with a mug and stood drinking the steaming brew and smoking the butt-end of his cigarette while staring down at the two fourth floor windows of the building directly across the street.

He had often stood behind the windows at which he was now looking, in a similar attitude, contemplating these casement windows behind which he now stood—behind which waited his work, his unfinished paintings: almost, one might say, adding the appropriate state of mind to this proposition, his destiny as an artist. Now, for several months, things had been quite the reverse: of late he had been standing as he now stood, contemplating the windows of what was once his apartment, his home, and wondering as to his destiny, not as an artist, but as a man.

Monk was his Mephistopheles, to whom in his blindness he had sold his soul. For knowledge! What kind of knowledge? Was it truly, as he had at first thought, for the knowledge that is the experience of profound creation? The sensations of genius without genius—can they be had, bought? No! He saw now that he had been like a child who demands that which he cannot properly use.

But was it truly for that that he had sold his soul? Or was it out of fear of failure? Doubt, doubt, that was all he had known for years. But a year ago he had had everything for which a wise man should have been grateful. Most important, he had had Toddy, who loved him. He stopped and looked down at the two black squares, like blind, lonely eyes, across the street. His nose was running badly, but he had no cold: it was withdrawal. He itched. But it wasn't bad at all, getting straight, kicking, being clean: the methadone made it easy. But one had to be careful to use as little as possible, or be hooked on it as well. He sniffled, dug in his pockets for a handkerchief or a piece of tissue, found none, and blew his nose between his fingers, farmer-style. He pulled his shirt up and wiped his nose on it, all the time keeping his eyes on the windows across the street.

He put down his empty coffee mug, which had been hanging, all the while, like a monstrous-odd jade ring, from the little finger of his left hand, and pushed up the sleeve of his football shirt, exposing a thin pale arm with a riddle of red dots and blue bruises at the crook and tracks up to his shoulder and down to his wrist. He jerked the sleeve of his shirt down to his wrist and turned to face his work.

The easled canvases stood about the huge room like so many accusing ghosts in the twilight. The room was like a moonlit graveyard. Ghosts, or headstones, beneath which were buried the aspirations of a young painter who no longer lived.

Suddenly he strode across the room to a small bureau and removed from the top drawer a dully glinting object of gun-metal blue. In the still, dark night of the enormous room there was only the clickety-clackity-click of the cylinder being rolled: then, as the hammer fell on an empty chamber, a sharp metallic snap.

Muir crossed the room to the mattress and threw himself down, breathing heavily. In a few moments his breathing became more even, and he lighted a cigarette, blowing the smoke up into the dim opacity above him. The loneliest of all moments had been overcome, survived. Inside, he glittered with ecstasy. It was better than dope. He was convinced, now, that he could live. For fifteen minutes he lay in the now thoroughly darkened room and smoked and enjoyed this overwhelming sensation of euphoria. Then he snuffed out his cigarette and fell asleep.

Chapter 4

COLD TURKEY

Fifteen minutes later Jack was awakened by a call from the street. He stood up, and something thudded to the floor at his feet. He took a step in the dark and kicked something. He heard the revolver slide weightily across the bare boards of the floor. He groped about by the mattress, found the flashlight, and then turned on a floor lamp that stood nearby. Muir went to the window and opened it, looking out. A cold blast snapped him awake. He looked down and saw Dedi Pavon's upward-tilted, wedge-shaped face atop a crazily foreshortened body, and, below the body, peeping out like little blue birds, two pointy, blue-tipped feet.

Dedi called up: "Hey, Jack, lemme in! She's freezing out here."

"Hold on," Muir called back. He searched for and found his trousers, and groped in them for his keyring. He found his keys and dropped them down to Dedi, hearing them hit, tinkling on the sidewalk below, and then pulled on the trousers. He looked across the street. Those enigmatic windows were still dark. He closed his own window and went into the rear to re-heat the coffee. In a moment, Dedi burst in the door, shivering and wiping his drizzling nose on his sleeve.

"Ay, it's cold as a dead fish out there!"

"Want some coffee?" Muir asked.

"Not that black mud you make, mon—no thanks. I got a weak stomach."

"It's P.R. coffee," said Muir, bringing two mugs despite Dedi's objection.

"I know it's P.R. coffee," said Dedi, who had received a mug into his hands and was now eyeing its contents suspiciously, "that's why I no want it—it's too strong. I only drink that weak gringo slop. You know I'm a sick boy." Nevertheless, he drained off half the coffee from the mug. He settled down, taking a seat on the mattress, and lighting a cigarette. His small, pocked, lesioned face assumed a lugubrious expression. "Hey, Jack," he said, challengingly, "why you not been around to see us, eh? Pilar think you don't love her no more."

"I've been kicking," Muir said, "I wanted to be alone. Tell her I'm sorry." He sipped his coffee, nervously.

"Kicking! No shit? What you wanta do that for?"

"Lots of reasons."

"No shit? Well, what you on? Meth? Or you been shooting tranks?"

"Shooting nothing," Muir said; "I don't intend to go out shooting. Besides, you can get an abscess from shooting tranquilizers, if you miss the vein. Shit, I'm through with needles. I'm sick of the whole scene."

"You taking methadone, eh?"

"Taking methadone," Muir affirmed.

"What, you at a clinic?"

"No. I traded my smack for the meth."

"Good deal?"

"Even Steven."

"You serious, eh?"

"I'm serious. I mean to get straight."

"Oh," Dedi said, rubbing his cheek and looking away, "you start again. Everybody starts again." He looked quickly back at Muir. "But, you know," he said, "like it's a good thing to get yourself clean out inside. I kicked lots of time. Pilar, she kicked. Everybody kicks. It's a good thing."

"It's not going to be that way with me," Muir said, his face assuming a determined expression, "I'll never start again. Anybody can kick if they've got the will. That's the body habit. The rest is in the mind."

"That's cool, mon," said Dedi, nodding his head up and down, "that's real cool. I know you mean that. But, you know, mon, that's pretty tough. Once you know what stuff is like, you always want to do it again. Hey, mon," Dedi exclaimed suddenly, "what's that? Is that real? What's you doing with that gat?" He pointed across the room to where the revolver lay.

"That's not what they call them anymore," said Muir. "You're out of touch, Dedi."

"Lissen, that's what Humphrey Bogart calls them in the old flicks, and if it's good enough for that cat it's good enough for me. What you want with that thing anyhow for?"

Muir went over and picked up the revolver and brought it back to the mattress, where he sat down. He hefted the pistol, looked it over, and then put it on the floor at his feet.

"What you gonna do?" asked Dedi. "You gonna kill some-body?"

"I use it in a game I've been playing," was Muir's enigmatic answer.

Dedi looked at him suspiciously. "I don't like to use no gat," he said, after a contemplative pause, "that way is too easy to kill somebody." He gave Muir a meaningful look. "That's big trouble, mon." He pulled from his belt a foot-long iron bar thickly wrapped in electrician's tape and hefted it admir-ingly. "Don't even break the skin if you use it right. But that—" he jerked his small, underslung knob of a chin at the revolver and grimaced.

"It was good enough for Bogart," Muir said.

"I dig, mon: but you ain't no classic. Look, Jack, what'sa matter with you? You make me worry about you, mon, and that ain't good, 'cause I'm a sick boy, see; I ain't supposed to worry."

"You know what's the matter with me," Muir said, lighting a cigarette, "I'm a crazy artist, you told me so yourself."

"No joke, mon! I know what you into again: you into that killing Monk shit. That's a bad scene, mon. Dig! Leave it

71

alone. You gonna get your ass in a sling, then what's you gonna do? Monk'll get you—he's a bad cat. But if you get him, your ass still in a sling. It ain't no good either way."

"What am I supposed to do, let him keep my wife? Besides, I don't intend to kill anybody. I'm just going to go over there and break it up, that's all."

"Get broke up, that's what you gonna do. And if you go over there with that gat, Monk'll kill you." Dedi shook his head. "How come a smart cat like you is so dumb? Eh? Lissen, mon, let them people alone. If you wanna get straight, you do that, mon, just don't go back there no more. Go see my sister; she in love with you. You and me, we could be brothers. Why you not marry my sister? Hey, why don't we do that, bro, that sounds real good?"

"And let that bastard get away with what he did to me?"

"Oh, yeah, I dig," said Dedi scornfully; "you a real macho, big mon, look at me. But that mon gonna eat you up. That geek bite off your head like you was a chicken." Dedi stuck a thumb in his mouth and jerked it out, folding it into his fingers. "Look, ma, no head."

"It didn't happen to you, you don't know how it feels."

"Look, you a real bright guy, but you been alone too much. That makes things get into your head. What you gotta do is get a real nice woman, bro, who like you, and then you go some place with her— You know what a good place to go is? Like Puerto Rico, see? Your old mon is rich. He would send you to Puerto Rico— "

"Lay off, Dedi," Muir said, getting to his feet, "you're pushing me, I can't think."

"Don't think, bro, that's the trouble with you. Same thing with all you gringos, think, think, think, and never do."

Muir went to the rear of the loft and came back with two more mugs of coffee. He handed one to Dedi. He remained standing.

"I seen Toddy just now with some new guy," Dedi dropped casually. He sipped his coffee, slurping.

"Where? Who?"

"At the Saints and Sinners. Some guy name Sam."

"Sam?"

"Si, Sam something. I don't know. A real dude type. I almost sold him a watch. Toddy and Tiger messed it up."

"What were they doing?"

"Just drinking. They was pretty high. You know this Sam guy?"

"I don't know anybody named Sam."

"Toddy said he was a friend of yours, I think."

Muir looked blank; then he said: "Were they— I mean, did they look . . . close?"

"Well, you know, bro, hard to say—they was high, like I said. Anyhow, what's you care? You got Pilar. She love you. What you going on about Toddy for? That bitch only make you unhappy, anyhow."

"Shut up, Dedi, you don't know what you're talking about."

"Hey, bro, don't get uptight. I'm only trying to help you."

"Don't try so hard. Drink your coffee and tell me what you want. I don't need a watch, if that's what's on your mind. Have you got a TV set under your shirt? By the way, where's your overcoat?"

"I fucked up, mon. My overcoat is at the scene of the crime. I busted a warehouse last night. Watchman almost got me. I had to split, pronto, dig? I got two boxes of watches that nobody will buy, and I lost a good overcoat that I really needed. What a life!"

"Can the coat be traced to you?"

"Come on, bro. It was just a coat."

"And you talk about me getting into trouble—"

"That ain't nothing. Nobody going to get excited about a couple of boxes of watches. Trouble is, see, I ain't got no way to fence nothing since they busted my guy. What I'm gonna do? I'm a sick boy! I gotta buy medicine tonight."

"Take some of my paintings down to the corner and peddle them. They ought to bring a couple of bucks for the canvas alone. Take that portrait I did of you—anybody'd pay a grand for it."

"Hey, you sure think you funny, Jack. Mon, you a scream. I only wish—shit, if you had a TV I'd steal it from you."

"I was offered two grand for it at the show."

"Sure. At the show. That was a year ago, bro. Where is that cat who offered you the two Gs? You tell me where he is and I'll go take him the painting. If he still want it."

"So, you think I'm a has-been, eh?"

"You said it, bro." Dedi laughed. "Hey," he exclaimed, "how 'bout that gat? I could get some nice change for that, I bet."

"I told you, I need that for a game I play."

"I think you loco, bro, you know that?" Dedi got to his feet, kicking his trousers down at the cuffs of his pants. "I guess you ain't gonna give me no bread, eh?"

"I haven't got any to give. My check doesn't come till the first of the month. I'm flat. Tap City."

"How come you broke already?"

"I had to buy the revolver to play my game, didn't I?"

"And that's what you spend your bread on? Shit, you worse off than me. Well, that means I gotta pull a job."

"Don't go getting yourself into trouble, macho," Muir said.

"Well, I gotta have my medicine, don't I?"

75

Muir shrugged. "Where are you going to meet Monk? Over there?" He indicated Toddy's apartment with a jerk of his head.

"Yeah; he'll be there at ten."

"Maybe I'll be over," Muir said.

"Well, I tell you what, bro," Dedi said, pulling open the door, "you wait till you see me come out before you go in, O.K.? 'Cause I got a weak stomach, Ace."

Chapter 5

HIS SISTER'S HONOR

Dedi worried about the fact that, for the first time since he had used heroin, Jack was trying to kick it, and he worried about the revolver. He worried as he walked with the wind at his back toward the center of the Strip. On the opposite side of the avenue Toddy Muir, one hand holding her tam in place, the other gripping the collar of her coat, and the man whom he had met a little while before under the name of Sam Hopkins, who slouched in a great black overcoat and heaved his long legs before him like a man climbing a steep hill, came fighting their way against the same wind that was pushing Dedi forward, a wind that would have negated by scattering into the void any cry of recognition he might make. He saw them, and went on, virtually lifted and cast forward like a kite, or a small, outlandishly feathered bird, hapless in the wrong climate, tail to the wind.

He staggered on, jacket collar up, small frail hands sunk deep in pockets, probing thin, spasmodically contracting thighs for warmth, shivering, shaking, and thinking of Jack Muir, his friend, and of Pilar, his sister.

As Dedi reconstructed the past, Pilar was not more than eight at the time that he was born, and they had lived at some seaside shack in New Jersey. When his father appeared with a knife with which to cut the cord and sink him for good where no one would ever look, and found what Pilar had done—how, desperate to save him, she had gnawed the cord through—the father began to rage. She had picked up the infant and run from the house. He came following her through beachfront streets and along the beach, stumbling and waving the knife, and calling drunkenly after her that he would kill them both, until she found sanctuary for them at the home, another beach-shack, of her mother's brother. It was the uncle who drove their father away by firing at him with a rifle. Now Jack Muir was important to Dedi, and to his sister. And there was Monk. Even now, he, Dedi Pavon, was doing a dance macabre to Monk's music. Behind any dream of his triad happiness—he and Pilar and Muir all together and loving in a Screen Gem Classic movie-set existence—were other, more immediate thoughts, the former only as a false dawn, beautiful and insubstantial, when compared with these later ruminations, these actual fires of a sun which was necessary to existence.

Dedi had decided what he was going to do before he left Muir's loft. At the far-opposite end of the Strip from Jack Muir's loft and Toddy Muir's apartment—past the Saints and Sinners Club and the other dives that formed the thick, crusted, bright-colored patch, like the front-and-center zircons of a cheap costume choker, which was the center of it, and set apart from that gaudy center by a double row of dead buildings, blank dark warehouses and a scissors factory— there existed, like the mirage of a small oasis among the grey, night-desert tones surrounding it, a small hotel. Dedi Pavon had never been inside this hotel (which, thirty years before, some previous perhaps altruistic owner of it had dubbed the Saint Christopher, after the patron saint of travellers, but which was known along the Strip, as the Busy Nook, thus re-dubbed by some humorous errant sailor upon his return from it to the Saints and Sinners Club after an hour's hiatus) but his sister had heard of it, as he knew, having had the misfortune to have overheard her name mentioned in connection with it in his fourteenth year: and ever after he had felt the need to avenge himself upon it, perhaps by burning it to the ground (but this idea he relented of when it occurred to him that there might be other poor misused girls like his own sister in the hotel), or perhaps by some other means of destruction, or some injury which he could inflict upon it which would even the score: but never until now had two needs coincided so perfectly as did his need of money and his need of revenge to produce an action on his part which he could consider something of an artistic achievement, if it could be brought off . . . "Do or die," Dedi said.

Chapter 6

THE BUSY NOOK

When Felix Potter, camel-faced night-clerk of The Busy Nook, and Peeping Tom extraordinaire, saw the young, badly pocked "Spic" enter the small, dank lobby, he thought: "He wants some action, and I have nothing to do all night but let the working girls check themselves in and out. Maybe I can get the boy to sit back here with me." But he said, in a stern voice, not, however, unmitigated by a kind of twilit, violet-flavored mouth-cologne: "Yea-ahs . . ? And what might I do for you?" But the boy, somewhat disconcertingly, proceeded to walk up to the desk, lift its gate, and step boldly in beside the night-clerk.

"Well? What do you want?" demanded Potter, alarm pretending to be anger. And that was the last thing that Potter remembered about the incident when he related these truncated events to the police an hour later.

"He must have hit me," exclaimed the night-clerk, who seemed to find it hard to believe that anyone would have the temerity to commit such an act.

"Did you recognize him?" asked Lieutenant Figlia.

"I'm not certain." Potter was holding an ice-cube wrapped in a washcloth to his temple. "All those Spics look alike to me. But there was something about him . . . maybe I've seen him in the neighborhood. But I'm not sure . . . no, I'm not sure."

"Would you recognize him if you saw him again?"

"I believe so . . . But, as I say, I'm not sure. It all happened so fast. The thing was, he had no overcoat. It crossed my mind that he should be wearing an overcoat on a cold night like this."

"No overcoat?" Figlia made a note, commenting, "There was a small overcoat left behind in a warehouse burglary last night. Possibly the same man. Kid," he amended. "And you said he was small?"

"Quite," Potter affirmed. "And gay."

"What makes you say that?"

"AIDS! Written all over his face. Safe sex is the only way to go," he added, taking a package of condoms from his inside pocket and displaying it as if displaying his own virtue. "Or come." He laughed.

"How much did he get?"

"Oh, that's the awful part." Potter rolled his head and eyes in different directions. "Dreadful! I should have cleared the drawer an hour ago—ordinarily we clear it every two hours—but I happened to be busy doing something upstairs—an emergency, a toilet backed up—and I hadn't got to it yet . . ."

"How much?"

"About three hundred and fifty dollars."

"Three and a half!" The young Detective Third Grade, Verdi, whose case it was, blew between his teeth, and winked at

Figlia. "That's a big take for a little pimp-haven like this," he said. "The service must be terrific."

Potter looked away; then, looking back, said: "My boss'll kill me."

"You shouldn't spend so much time upstairs, Mr. Potter," said the young Detective, grinning. Everyone in the precinct knew of Potter's proclivities. The working girls brought stories in to the station house.

"I have my duties to perform," the night clerk countered, indignantly.

"I bet you do," rejoined the Detective. "I hear you have to keep an eye on your guests."

"I only check to see that nothing is going on that shouldn't be," Potter said, flushing.

"Well," said the Detective, chuckling, "tell that to your boss."

Figlia gave the Detective a sharp look that erased his grin.

"But what are you going to do about this?" Potter demanded to know.

"Whatever we can, naturally," said Figlia. "But if you're hoping to get any of that take back before your boss finds out, you might as well forget it. There must be five-hundred kids in any neighborhood who fit the description you've given us."

"It was probably some junkie . . ." said the Detective. "Or maybe one of the Bravos, the motorcycle gang. They own a building near here."

"Come to think of it," said Potter, "he did look kind of hopped up or something . . . his eyes were funny."

"Sure," said Verdi, "funny eyes. I'll put that in my report."

Chapter 7

CONNECTING THE DOTS

Lieutenant Figlia knew the streets of the East Village, but his forays had been random. Detective Verdi was local. These were his streets. He knew them club by club, alley by alley. As they maneuvered the late evening traffic, he acted as a tour guide for Figlia. The streets of the East Village were teeming with activity. "Rockers," Verdi said. Music thumped and machine-gunned from the doors of the clubs. "Painters, sculptors, performance artists," Verdi said; and more music blared from the gates of the galleries. "Junkies, dealers, rapists, celebrities of every sort—it's a freak show in a carnival." Verdi steered slowly through the traffic. "I thought we might go over and roust the Bravos."

"Tell me about them," said Figlia.

"They're two-tiered. Juniors and seniors. The juniors range in age from around twelve to sixteen, seventeen, the seniors go on from there, up to twenty-five or so. They're racially mixed. The juniors are just your ordinary juvenile delinquent street gang, the seniors are full-blown gangsters. They deal in drugs, extortion, prostitution, everything. The seniors are recruited from the juniors. They own a building over on Third, their headquarters. It's supposed to be a sort of club house, but God knows what goes on in there when we're not looking. Ownership of the building is listed as a corporation. One of the members of the corporation is listed as Martin Kent. We figure it's Monk Stolz. We figure he supplies the club house and they do errands for him. The seniors aren't as difficult to deal with as the juniors are. The juniors get hopped up every so often and go crazy. They rampage through the streets. The seniors stick pretty much to business."

"How many are there?"

"Oh, hell, all together—might be two hundred."

"What's the point of rousting them?" said Figlia.

"Let's them know we're here."

"I don't like wasting my time," said Figlia. "Let's go back to the station."

Verdi looked disappointed. He drove on in silence.

Figlia said, "So you think Monk Stolz owns the building?"

"Oh, yeah," said Verdi, "that building and half a dozen others around here."

"So he's a real estate tycoon, too," said Figlia.

"These dealers got to have something to do with their money."

"Was there a time when I never heard of that son-of-a-bitch?" Figlia asked, connecting the dots back to that day six months earlier when he pulled up in front of his daughter's building, summoned by Sergeant Purl of his old Chelsea precinct.

The Chelsea studio-apartment was alive with post-mortem activity. "I found the sheet in a drawer and put it over her," said Sergeant Purl. The middle-aged precinct detective held

Lieutenant Figlia by the arm with one hand and lifted the sheet away with the other.

"Yes," Figlia said, "that's Rose. That's my daughter." He saw broken glass, and the powerful odor of Scotch rose from the bed.

"Sit down, Lieutenant." Purl swung him a straight-backed chair.

Figlia sat down.

"You don't know anything about this, then?"

Figlia shook his head. How would he, as a cop, want this story told? "Rose's mother died two years ago. Rose knew I had been seeing another woman—my present wife, Gena. When Gena and I got married, Rose resented it, and moved out of the house. That was a year ago. She came back here. I guess she wanted to be near her mother. I mean, where she grew up. She's only just eighteen." He leaned over, his hands on his knees. "Hell, I spent fifteen years in this precinct—at your job, in fact—before I transferred to narcotics. Chelsea was like a hometown to Rose. She was baptized here at St. Saviour's. God, Purl," he said, "leave me alone."

"Sure, Lieutenant. You just sit tight for a minute."

Chapter 8

THE WOMEN IN FIGLIA'S LIFE

Figlia had married his first wife, Cynthia, a frozen saint, when they were both eighteen. When he returned from Viet Nam, a bemedalled hero with a battlefield commission, he became a policeman, and they began to part ways.

Several factors contributed to this parting of the ways. For one thing, Cynthia, who had been an undemanding fiancee, made a demanding, jealous, and possessive—if not sexual—wife. She had no family of her own of which to speak, and she was jealously hostile toward Figlia's, which at that time consisted of his mother and his two sisters. Cynthia tried to drive a wedge between himself and his family, and his resentment of this became a factor in their dissolution.

Still another problem was that Cynthia, and he as well, had desired children, and none were immediately forthcoming. Then when he joined the Police Department all of these factors conjoined; for Cynthia had opposed his becoming a police officer, her true anxiety in this matter resting in her neurotic belief that he would meet women who would tempt him, and that she would lose him to one of them. She knew that he was not deeply religious, as she herself was, at least in the formal sense, and would not hesitate to divorce her and marry another, one who could get on with his mother, and who could bear him a child.

Over the first few years of their marriage, Figlia became, in the course of doing police work, increasingly worldly, while during the same years his wife became an embittered, semi-mystical hermit. Then, the child came, the product of cold, but required sex, his daughter, "little Cynthia," or Rose, the lynch-pin of their marriage.

In spite of his wife's wilder imaginings, Figlia had always honored his marriage. Now, with the child, with his work, which he loved, he felt that his destiny was decided. Two out of three was, to a worldly, rather fatalistic man, not a bad score. He did his job (and was steadily raised in rank and importance) and took good care of his family (but regretted that his duties kept him so much from his daughter, who was growing up), and nearly twenty years later his wife, grown into a veritable harridan, dropped dead at her prayers.

Figlia was sorry about his wife. He felt a low-keyed remorse that they hadn't loved each other. Looking back over their years together, he had also to admire her for her prophetic skill; because, in the long run, she had been right. At forty-three, loneliness had won out over good intentions, and he had acquired a mistress. Indeed, it was a youngish widow whom he had met during an investigation of an apartment house burglary, at the old precinct, in Chelsea. Gena had had nothing to do with the case. It was the apartment next to hers which had been burglarized, and he had only questioned her as to whether she'd heard anything. They immediately liked each other; he saw her again, then frequently; and soon they were in love. He was thinking of divorce. Then, as if on cue, Cynthia died. He was shocked, giddy, happy, guilty; and three-months later he introduced Gena to Rose.

Perhaps it was too soon. Perhaps it would always be too soon. Rose had belonged to Cynthia. Rose had been Cynthia's consolation prize. When, several months later, he married Gena, Rose, now eighteen, moved out. On several occasions, seeing how this estrangement was hurting her husband, Gena went to see Rose, only to be rebuffed, or to be abused as a homewrecker. They had killed her mother and ruined her own life. She hated them. Gena advised her husband to wait, not to push. He waited. He didn't push.

Finally Figlia felt free to transfer out of the routine of precinct work, something he had wished to do for years, and into the Narcotics Division, which allowed him a free-roaming life. Occasionally, when near it on some business or other, he would drop up to Rose's apartment. If she were at home, she'd open the door a crack, look at him contemptuously, and shut it in his face. He had heard vague neighborhood rumors, most emanating from activities centered at St. Saviours, that she had acquired a boyfriend. Once, after having the door slammed in his face, he returned to his car and sat in it for a long while, remembering those past years when she would run for half a block to leap into his arms, and he almost cried with his arms hanging on the steering wheel and his face buried in them. But one thing became a greater certainty each day—that he had been right to marry Gena. This he could not doubt even in the face of his daughter's death.

Chapter 9

THE NIGHTMARE OF FOREVER

Figlia had been present at dozens of scenes of death, and this one was typical, except for the fact that the dead girl was his daughter. He wondered why he didn't feel more, why he didn't find himself rolling about on the floor and screaming. Delayed reaction. He'd seen it before, and now he knew how it felt: the numbness of it. But the pain would come. He had seen people break down hours, days, even months later. He hung on to being a cop.

"I tried to see her," he said to Purl, "but it was no go. I've never been in this apartment. Can you imagine? But I thought she'd get over it."

"She would have," Purl said. "I got a teenager myself. It's hard for them. A lot of stress, but most of them get by."

"How do you read it?" Figlia asked.

"No indication of a habit. No tracks. No other needle marks."

"Then she was murdered."

"Not necessarily. Could have been her first time out."

"I know," said Figlia. "But isn't it murder just the same?"

"I know what you mean," said Purl. "She shared the place with a boyfriend. Did you know that?"

Figlia shook his head.

"A junkie. Three months out of rehab. He claims to be clean. About eighteen. There's an outfit on the bed by the—by her. Needle mark's in the right arm. Was she left-handed?"

"Yes."

"She was? Well, see, I thought maybe the kid could have shot her up. Nothing's too clear yet. She wasn't suicidal, was she?"

"No. God, I don't think so. What's the kid say?"

"Says he went on an errand for another guy who waited here. When he got back he found her."

"And he called in?"

"Right."

"Where is he?"

"At the station. Couple of the boys are going through the files with him. He says this other guy's name is Kenton."

"There has to be an autopsy, doesn't there?"

"You want to know for sure, don't you? It could have been a simple O.D., or it could have been bad stuff—poisoned, or God knows what. And if there's bad stuff on the street, you'd

91

want to know. Or it might have been an accident. Then a coverup."

"I want it done fast."

"Of course. It'll get priority." Sergeant Purl put a comforting hand on Figlia's narrow shoulder. "Let Homicide West handle this, Lieutenant."

Figlia flushed. "What am I a cop for, if not for this? Besides, this is a narcotics case, isn't it? That's my beat. I'm going over to the station and talk to the kid. What's his name?"

"Billy Sawyer."

Figlia watched blankly as the Medical Examiner's people removed the sheet from Rose's body. Later, he saw them zip her into a plastic bag.

Dusk settled on the hot city as Figlia walked the two blocks to his old precinct house. He knew the detectives who were questioning Billy Sawyer behind a big one-way mirror. He wiped sweat from his brow with a folded handkerchief held in a shaking hand, and studied the face of the skinny, frightened boy. He tapped on the one-way mirror, and one of the interrogators stepped out.

"What have you got?"

"He says it's this bird." He handed Figlia a thick manila folder. "Says this one sent him up to Penn Station to pick up a package, and when he got back—"

"Stolz!"

"You know him?"

"I know of him. A dealer. I broke up a party of his. He said he'd even the score. Maybe he has."

"Yes, sir."

"Is the boy on anything?"

"No, sir. He's clean."

"What was in the package?"

"A porno film. 8mm. A good-looker, maybe black, kinda pale; a white dyke; and a black guy. They're circling a bald headed, naked white side of beef with whips. They really lay it on him," he added.

"That would be the illustrious Mr. Kenton—Stolz, himself," said Figlia. "I've heard he's kinky. Know any of the others?"

"No, sir."

"Does he?" He pointed at the boy.

"No, sir."

"No drugs?"

"No drugs."

"What's it look like to you?"

The young detective looked nervous. "I think he's telling the truth."

Figlia crossed the room to his old desk, the one he had when he first got his gold detective shield. He draped his suit-coat and hat on the coat tree and sank into the swivel. It felt like the same chair. Everything seemed the same but for the computer that had replaced his old Remington. He shook off a sense of déjà vu, and phoned Billy Sawyer's parole officer. Billy appeared to be drug-free. He was a religious boy, acting as a sort of acolyte at St. Saviour's. His association with Stolz was a parole violation; but, in the current climate, not likely to be acted on.

Figlia talked again to the questioning detectives, who told him that, after Billy Sawyer graduated rehab, his first contact with Monk Stolz was for the purpose of borrowing money. He was to pay off this debt and to receive fifty dollars extra for his trip to Penn Station. This angel would have to wait a while for his wings. Two hundred and fifty dollars is a good deal of money for an errand. Surely he should have suspected that what he was doing wasn't kosher. Figlia saw the possibility of the kid spending some time in the slammer; but it wasn't likely, if nothing else came up. He went in alone to talk to the boy. The boy rose, then sank back into his chair.

"Are you her father?"

"Rose was my daughter."

"She talked about you. She said you were on the outs."

"Did she?" Figlia eyed the boy coldly.

"But she was proud of you."

"Was she proud of you?"

94

The boy stared at his knees, where his thin red hands rested.

"Where did you meet Rose?"

"At St. Saviour's. The drug rehab center."

"Rose wasn't on drugs, was she?"

"Oh, no, she just went to Mass there."

"Since she was a little girl . . . How could you bring a pig like Stolz to my daughter's apartment? How could you? And then leave him alone with her!"

"I didn't know about him. Honest, I didn't know what he was like. I didn't even know his name was Stolz. I thought it was Kenton. I got H from him a couple of times when I was on it, and I did a couple of odd-jobs—just pick up and delivery —when I got out. He seemed all right. He loaned me money when I needed clothes, so I could look for a job. If I'd known he was that kind of creep . . ." Figlia reached out and pulled the boy to his feet, shaking him. The boy went limp in Figlia's hands and let his head bob. Tears flew from his face. Figlia let him sink into the chair.

"I loved her," the boy said. "Honest I did."

Back in the squad room, Figlia telephoned Gena, who was waiting at their Long Island home for a second, confirming call.

"Yes?"

"It's true."

95

"No . . . Al, are you all right?"

"I'm all right. I want the funeral as soon as possible. We'll have Father Ryan here at St. Saviour's. He christened her. I'll go around and see if I can talk to him tonight. I need a drink. See you later." Now, six months later, the nightmare continued, and Figlia lived with it.

Chapter 10

SOMETHING LOST

A golden glow of light emanated from the front windows of the Mid-East Gardens Restaurant in Greenwich Village. Inside, Camilla, Ansar, and Mahmoud were surrounded by a three-walled mural describing in elaborate Arabic calligraphy outstanding events in the life of the Prophet Muhammad. The murals were in subdued, rich colors and gave the large diningroom filled with moving waiters and seated diners an atmosphere of coziness. They were led to a table, passed the extremely beautiful calligraphic description of Muhammad's Marriage to the Rich Widow, the Vision at Mt. Hira, and the Flight to Abyssinia. Ansar stood behind his chair, in front of The Plot to Murder the Prophet, bouncing on the balls of his horny feet. Camilla and Mahmoud were seated, and looked up at Ansar from their places at the table. Mahmoud said, "Aren't you going to sit down, my friend?"

"I have no appetite. I have things I must do. You must instruct me how to find this address," he said, throwing a scrap of paper in front of Mahmoud.

"Horatio Street," read Mahmoud. "Just walk north three blocks. Uptown. You can't miss it."

Ansar grabbed up the paper. "I am welcomed any time, I am told. I must go. I will rejoin you here in not too long. Camilla, you eat! Mahmoud, my friend, keep her safe. Allah be praised!" Ansar was such an energy that he did not seem to leave them, but to vanish before their eyes, leaving a stir of particles in the air.

Mahmoud ordered couscous and lamb for Camilla and himself, and, among several sharable dishes, a bean pie. He turned to scrutinize the young woman while they waited. "Camilla—that's a pretty name."

"I'm a freeborn girl. That's what Camilla means in Latin. My mother chose the name. She told me never to tell my father what it really meant. He has no idea." She frowned. "Also—one in attendance at a sacrifice. Scary, uh?"

Mahmoud had sensed that all was not well with her. "Is there anything wrong?" he said, after a moment's reflection.

"Everything's wrong," she said. "Mostly him."

"What do you mean?"

"Can't you tell? There's something wrong with him. I've always known who he was, but until yesterday I'd never laid eyes on him. My family and his are tied together from way back. My folks gave me to understand that I was—well—sorta promised to him, in the old country style. Growing up, I had two ways of looking at it. One was, that someday this romantic figure out of the Middle-East, like Sinbad, was going to come and claim me for his own. I liked that one. The other one was, that the whole notion of a real Ansar was a figment of my family's imagination. That I would never really meet this guy, that the whole thing was fantastic, like the Arabian Nights, which I read in State Street High School in Toddling Chicago. The whole thing seemed crazy as hell to me. And I really couldn't believe that my Mom and Dad

98

could possibly have meant it. Fundamentalists, strict, O.K., but my mom and dad, nonetheless. I've been thinking about taking off on my own for a year or so now. I couldn't take the atmosphere around the house anymore. But I didn't know anybody on the west coast—I'd thought about Hollywood—or on the east coast either. Then a couple of weeks ago it got to floating around the house that Ansar would be in New York—Brooklyn, Atlantic Avenue—so I took my chances that he'd turn out to be Sinbad. He ain't. More like Arafat."

"You have run away from home?" said Mahmoud, disapprovingly. "Young lady, what you have done is very, very wrong."

"Gimme a break," said Camilla, ruffling her hair with both hands. "That kind of stuff is the reason I ran away in the first place. Do you know what this jerk did when he first laid eyes on me? I went down to Brooklyn to meet him. He says, 'I claim you hereby in the name of Allah.' Here's this little beer barrel—that I never laid eyes on—and he claims me! I said to myself, from the frying pan into the fire, but I figured what the heck, I'll see where it leads for a day or two. After all, I don't know anybody else around here and I don't have much money."

"Do your parents have any idea where you are?"

"They might think that I came East to meet him."

"We must phone them sometime tonight and let them know that you are safe. I can only imagine the anxiety you must be causing them."

"Is that other guy we met really your brother? The hip guy?"

99

"Tory? Yes, he is my benighted brother."

"He seemed real cool to me."

"You are very young," and, he thought, "very attractive." Mahmoud wondered if she might have some Ethiopian blood. In any case, she was a jewel that must be kept safely hidden from thieves.

Camilla liked the bean pie. "I've never had anything like it," she said, just as Ansar came up to the table. He was carrying a shopping bag from Saks Fifth Avenue. It bulged with clinking paraphernalia. Emanating from it was the foul stink of rotten eggs. He clanked it down beside his chair, and threw his coat over the back, where it hung like a dead baby camel. He sat down. "All has gone as planned. I'm hungry now."

Mahmoud called the waiter. He wondered if he should tell Ansar what Camilla had told him. He decided for the moment on discretion. He would wait and see. Ansar had begun to disturb him as well.

They sat through Ansar's enormous meal sipping coffee and making small talk, Camilla and Mahmoud locked in a conspiracy of discretion, Ansar fingering food into his face as if there might soon be no more on the planet. Suddenly Ansar was finished eating. He rose without consultation. "We must go. I have much work to do," he said. He looked at Mahmoud. "You will leave us. We will go to Brooklyn." He heaved on his Loden coat, patted its big pockets, and a look of sheer terror came over him. "My book!" he exclaimed. "My book! Where's my book? I must have it. I cannot do my work without it." Now he was looking under

100

the table, now like an Indian scout he followed the trail of the Persian rug out to the cash register, to the front door, then back to the table, desperation replacing terror.

"It probably dropped out at the Saints and Sinners Club," said Mahmoud. "You threw your coat over the back of the chair there, too."

"Of course!" said Ansar. "We must go back!"

Chapter 11

"MY NAME IS MICHAEL"

BILLIE HOLIDAY MEETS LAST CUE. Under the bold headline was a photo of the beautiful, black jazz singer; beside it, "She Died Game" heading three columns. The framed page of a "Daily News" article, a strange gift from Monk, who insisted that it be hung on the wall over the table, confronted Toddy as she entered the kitchen. She took two steps to the kitchen table and filled her glass with Scotch. Then she remembered that she had offered Sam Hopkins a cup of tea to soothe his whisky-corrupted stomach. It was quarter past nine. Soon time for Sam to be moving on. Maybe it was time for her to move on, too. Just pick up and walk out the door with the unknown Sam. Soon time for Monk . . . . She got out a battered tea-kettle, half filled it with water, and placed it over a flame. In a few minutes, the tea-kettle whistled. She put a tea bag in a cup and let it steep. She glanced at the clock. Soon, it said, soon. Sam must go soon. She banged her empty glass down on the counter-top, and went into the living room. Sam turned on his side in his sleep, away from her. She snuggled down close beside him, spoon-fashion, slipping her right arm around his chest. There was barely enough room. She closed her eyes and pressed herself to him, balancing on the edge, squeezing herself closer and closer to him, flattening her breasts against his back. She put her lips to the back of his neck, kissing lightly, searching around the base of his skull to his ear. She shoved her hips closer and lifted her right leg over his, her long mossy-green tweed skirt sliding upward, revealing black underwear and a strong firm rounded thigh. Her right hand with its tapered translucent little fingernails unbuttoned his shirt and slipped inside into the valley of his chest beneath the undershirt.

The wind outside gusted at the glass panes in their ancient sashes nearby and produced a muffled rumble. The sound seemed to come from far away, muted and dangerous, like that of a distant approaching army.

Toddy felt her heart beat on Sam's back like an accompaniment to the prickly nerves tingling from her calves up her spine and through her shoulders and arms. Her searching hand reached down to Sam's waist, moved along the belt to its buckle, undoing. She gently but firmly rubbed his crotch. He turned toward her with a groan, his left arm encircling her waist, pulling, his right arm lifting her onto him, her long legs astraddle. Toddy sat up, and, grasping her orange sweater, arms crossed, she pulled it up, up, revealing lacy black, creamy white, and then honey blonde hair, falling, falling, as she slung the garment to the floor.

Father Din was full awake. His sexual experience had been scant, and had left him bewildered and ashamed, longing for absolution in order that he might live the life that had been chosen for him. But this beautiful woman who sat astride him in the dim light exuded such a power, compelling, drawing him to her—closer, closer. She was real. And she wanted him. Her tenderness, the sweetness of her being, were all powerful. This was communion. *This* was what he had dreamed of without knowing the meaning of the dream. That part of himself which he had struggled to hide, which had hitherto been his mystery, had connected. She leaned toward him a little, eyes closed. He drew upward, toward her, reaching up, his hands molding her breasts, inching inside their black lace cover, freeing one pink nipple. He looked at her closed eyes and whispered, not in confession, but in a soft

103

declaration, "My name is Michael." But Toddy heard only the couch creak as he raised them both slowly, to stand, shedding their clothes like leaves in winter.

With their arms entwined they stepped together crabwise, to the bedroom door and nearly stumbled onto the big bed. Toddy spread over him in a relief of passion. She pressed a liquid tongue between his lips, his teeth. Little beads of sweat formed on her forehead. "Oh, Sam, Ooooh," she crooned. Like a baby being comforted, he heard her breathy lullaby. Toddy reached under a pillow and withdrew a small packet, a condom. She handed it to him and then wiggled herself onto him, feeling the heat from him thumping inside her. She was alive! Oh, bloody hell, she was singing in her veins. The long nights of misery and loss which had submerged her, left her bereft of spirit and companion and communion, pushed away as if pulled by the magnet moon.

Chapter 12

HARD COPY

Name: STOLZ, KENNETH

Criminal Identification No.: X112857

F.B.I. No.: LL2456

Date of Birth: 4/18/60

Known Aliases: Kenneth Stark, George Kenton, Harry Kent, Thomas Paterson, Duane Lewis (last two names of former associates). Sometimes uses nickname: Monk.

History of Arrests:

First Arrest: Dec. 19, 1971

Charge: Pettit larceny.

Disposition: Charge dropped.

Second Arrest: April 21, 1974

Charge: Grand larceny (auto).

Disposition: Charge dropped, changed to Juvenile Delinquency (general detainment, due to age of subject). Subject released in custody of Juvenile Court, probation five-years.

Third Arrest: May 12, 1975

Charge: Robbery (mugging). Parole violation.

Disposition: Remanded to Boys' House of Detention until his sixteenth year.

Fourth Arrest: August 5, 1977

Charge: Aggravated assault.

Disposition: Charge dropped (insufficient evidence: victim withdrew complaint).

Fifth Arrest: Oct. 16, 1977

Charge: Homocide (suspicion of murder).

Disposition: Indicted, tried, found not guilty. Remarks: The victim here was the same woman who brought the charge of aggravated assault against Stolz (see above). However, there was not enough evidence to bring a conviction.

"Vengeful bastard, ain't he?" said Captain Hubbard, who was reading Monk's file over Lieutenant Figlia's shoulder.

Figlia's straight black hair was thinning and through it his scalp gleamed. "So am I," he said. Hubbard took his hand from the back of Figlia's chair and came around the desk, seating himself on its front edge. He was a bulky black man in his early fifties with white hair, and tired, half-masted gray eyes. He was drinking coffee from a plastic container. "The man is criminally insane," he said, his half-hidden gray eyes contemplating Figlia's large brown ones; "you could go on reading his file for a week. But that file is just the tip of the iceberg."

106

"He's an animal," Figlia said, pushing away the file on Kenneth Stolz with his free hand: his other hand was rubbing the back of his neck, massaging loose the cord-like muscles there, that had grown rigid as steel cables as he'd sat reading the printout of the man who was responsible for his daughter's death. "He has to be hunted down and . . ."

". . . brought in?" Hubbard finished Figlia's sentence.

Figlia's eyes grew hard. "What else?" he challenged.

"I don't know . . ."

"Look, Hub," Figlia snapped, "You think I haven't heard the stories that circulate about me? Of how I'm supposed to be on a vendetta? Obviously you believe they're true. I thought I could expect more from someone who's known me as long as you have. I thought I could expect—"

"Hold on, hold on," Hubbard said, breaking in, "take it easy now. It was you—only a moment ago—who said 'So am I' when I called Monk a vengeful bastard; isn't that so? That's the only reason I said anything."

Figlia stared at Hubbard for a moment, then wearifully dropped his head forward, inserting his chin into the open V of his collar, and closed his eyes.

"You're tired, strung out," Hubbard said. "Why don't you lie down in back for an hour?"

"When I finish this," Figlia said without opening his eyes.

"You've read it before."

107

"I want to read it again. I want to know how he does it. How he always gets away with it."

"He's a smart cookie and he's got plenty of money to play with. More than we'll ever see in a lifetime. But he doesn't always get away, as you can see."

Figlia opened his eyes. "But he gets away with the big things, the worst things," he said bitterly. "How come?"

"He either bribes or scares anybody who could talk against him—or else they disappear . . ."

"He bribes cops too," said Figlia.

Hubbard shrugged. "What can you do?"

"What can you do? Is that anything to say?"

"O.K. then," said Hubbard, ruffled, "what should I say?"

"Well, he's been around here for some time, Hub, from what I can gather. Why can't you get anything on him?"

"You want me to pick him up for jaywalking?"

Figlia closed his eyes and corrugated his forehead. He was only vaguely aware of Hubbard's short, sharp curse, of his getting to his feet, walking away. He looked up in time to see Hubbard's white head nodding, a door being pulled to, shutting it from view. He cupped his hands over his eyes and leaned back in his chair, staring into sudden pools of blue.

He swiveled into an upright position. Suddenly the room seemed to be filled with clatter. What time was it? Almost eight. He pushed aside several pages of the file until the came to one marked SECOND SHEET. He read:

Name: STOLZ, KENNETH

Criminal Identification No. . . .

His eyes drifted down the page.

Height: 5'11"

Weight: 225 lbs.

Hair: Dark brown. Note: Subject shaves head.

Eyes: Gray.

Nose: Thickened at bridge; medium length; narrow at nostrils, sharp at tip.

Mouth: Wide; thick lips.

Chin: Round; prominent. Note: Subject sometimes wears beard or goatee.

Bone Structure: Heavy.

Unusual Marks: Tattoo, center of chest. Hanging man with Latin word "Nullus" on forehead of figure. Executed in green, red, and blue. Pierced right earlobe. Note: Subject sometimes wears small earring. Bullet wound scar on right side of chest near shoulder, upper pectoral. Knife or razor-slash scar across left upper arm, at bicep. Shrapnel wound scars scattered on outer right thigh, inner left thigh.

Note: See SUPPLEMENTARY REMARKS.

Figlia pushed several more sheets aside and found SUPPLE-MENTARY REMARKS. He read:

PSYCHIATRIC REPORT, BOYS' HOUSE OF DETEN-TION, PHILLIPSBURG, NEW YORK: Kenneth Stolz is a boy of above average intelligence, but is wracked by inner conflicts stemming from a childhood spent under the dominance of an autocratic/authoritarian father and a neurotically submissive mother. The result: the sado-masochistic syndrome is prominent. The psyche is torn between . . . however, the id . . .

Figlia turned the page on this psycho-babble.

Stolz is possessed of a highly dangerous, vindictive . . .

Figlia turned the page. He read:

HABITS/CHARACTERISTICS: Kenneth Stolz is known to be a periodic alcoholic. There is no evidence, however, that he has ever taken hard drugs. He is known to have dealt in drugs (spc. heroin, opium, morphine, cocaine, and crack cocaine) but it is believed that he holds users in contempt. It is believed that he spent some time in Africa, employed as a mercenary soldier (details are lacking). His political affiliations, if any, are unknown. According to earlier records he was baptized as a Catholic, but religious affiliation is probably nominal. He is of German stock and speaks the language. His English has the perfection of a second language: he probably heard a good deal of German spoken at home as a child. He is a good talker, and has been employed as a salesman. He uses current slang. It is believed that he has some pretensions as a writer, and is fond of bohemian circles. He is interested in the occult. He is known to engage in unusual sex practices. Should be considered unpredictable, highly dangerous . . ."

Figlia gathered up the pages scattered over his desk and put them into a neat stack, and re-clipped them. He picked up a glass ball full of drifting snow, Santa Claus and reindeers, and placed it on top of the file. Then he got up and staggered into another room, rubbing his sore eyes. Monk equated with death. The thought of death gave urgency to life. He needed Gena. He found his topcoat and left for Long Island, home and hearth.

Chapter 13

TRAPPED!

"What's that noise? Toddy?"

"Mmm—what noise?"

"*That.* That banging."

"Oh, my God!"

"Who is it? Is it Monk?"

"Yes, probably."

They sat up, stung awake.

"What time is it?"

"Nine forty-five," Father Din said.

There came another round of rapid pounding at the door.

"Now you've done it," Toddy said. "I warned you."

"I knew what I was doing," Father Din said. "I wanted to see you through this evening."

"You're crazy. You don't know what you're getting into."

"Don't tell me you didn't want me to stay. Not after what we've just done."

"Maybe I did. I did and I didn't. I wanted you to stay but I was afraid for you."

"We both wanted it this way. We'll face him down together. You'd better let him in before he breaks the door down. Hasn't he got a key?"

"I locked the door from the inside."

"Then he knows you're here . . . ."

Toddy nodded.

"What will he do?"

"I don't know—anything—nothing."

"Would it be better for you if I stayed out of sight until he's gone?"

"No. The apartment's too small, and once he comes in he won't leave for hours. It's no use; you have to meet him and get away as soon as possible. I'll try to head him off and explain before he sees you."

"Suppose you try to take him out with you?"

"He won't go. He's meeting people here."

"Then suppose you don't let him in at all?"

But as if in answer to this, the door gave a splintering gasp.

"No, no—nothing'll work now but making it up with him."

113

The door gave another gasp.

"Pull yourself together," Toddy called back as she ran into the kitchen, pulling on her sweater; and—"O.K., wait a minute; I'm coming."

Father Din stood up, and pulled on his clothes. He quickly ran a comb through his hair; then shrugged his shoulders, trying to re-shape his jacket. He heard Monk's voice sounding in the kitchen. "Where were you? I've been pounding on that damned door—"

"I fell asleep. Monk, listen . . ."

"—*Well?*"

"My friend is here—Sam Hopkins, the one in Tiger's. He was drunk, Monk—he got sick. I brought him up here so he could lie down. He's been sleeping." She was breathless.

Father Din, following Toddy's lead, moved into the middle of the livingroom, clear of the Oriental screen, so that Monk could see him.

Chapter 14

THE BRAVOS

"What can I *do?*" cried Ansar, outside the Mid-East Gardens. His question, more of a plaint, was directed above to the unanswering sky. "Suppose I lost my book on the bus . . ." he posited, turning back, as Camilla and Mahmoud caught up with him.

"We'll wait for the same driver who brought us over to come round again," said Mahmoud, "but I think you probably lost it at the Saints and Sinners Club. I don't see how anything could drop out of those pockets when you were wearing the coat."

"I must be sure. We will wait here for the same driver to come around."

The three huddled at the bus stop, a treacherous cold corner, under a street lamp. The dull stars were being chased across the planetary night sky by an invisible force. Small, wicked eels of lightning wriggled down the sky. The street was quiet, but they could hear the traffic rumble from the broad avenue two blocks away. Finally a big rattling box of light came toward them, pulled to the gutter, snorted, and opened its doors. Ansar stepped up to the door, inspected the driver, and turned away, shaking his head. "Not this one," he said to Mahmoud. "This driver is a female." Then they heard a doggerel rhythm floating out of the dark toward them. And now they could distinguish a crowd of shadowy figures emerging into view. A gang of rappers, singing: *If you can, then kill a cop, cut his belly, make him pop! A cop is full of ugly gas, rip his belly, save his ass!*

Camilla whispered, "Oh, my God!" She hid herself between Ansar and Mahmoud and hunched down in her coat as if trying to become invisible. In a moment, they were surrounded by chanting rappers who wore on their black plastic coats logos of knives stabbing through bleeding hearts. They continued their chant of *A cop is full of ugly gas, rip his belly, save his ass! The Bravos say it with a will, you got to learn to kill, kill, kill!*

Ansar looked nervously about him at the dancing, chanting figures who had formed a circle around himself, Mahmoud and Camilla. Mahmoud was worried. He thought they might be mugged. Camilla was terrified. Back in Chicago she knew which streets to avoid. Just then another brightly-lighted bus emerged from the darkness and pulled up at the curb. There was a human traffic jam at the door, with one of the Bravos up front by the driver arguing that he was paying for all. He paid for himself and at least twenty others followed him aboard, ignoring the driver. The driver ignored the fact that no one else paid. It was the right driver, the one who had brought Ansar, Mahmoud and Camilla over from the East Village. "We must get on," said Ansar. "I must find my book." He grabbed Camilla's hand and dragged her aboard. Mahmoud reluctantly followed.

The Bravo chorus had fallen apart while boarding. Now, seated, or hanging from straps, they gathered their syncopation up and began to chant in unison again—*If you can, then kill a cop! Cut his belly, make him pop!*

Mahmoud and Camilla sat down close to the driver and the front door, but Ansar wandered back through the bus and through the Bravos, looking under seats, asking the chanting gang members if they saw a book anywhere.

His crazy indifference to danger worked a small miracle. The gang members, used to causing fear, treated him with a degree of respect, breaking their chant to help him look. Mahmoud observed that a number of the gang were bandaged, bloodstains showing through gauze. He ventured to ask one sitting next to him what had happened. "We-comin-from-St.-Vincent's- Hospital," chunked out the surly face. "We been wilding, man!" The sullen face turned to him. "Who is your friend look like Arafat?" he asked. "He's cool. He's chilled out. He's ice."

"That's Ansar the Great," said Mahmoud. "He can do magic. Watch out what you say to him. Be careful."

Mahmoud had turned to face his interlocutor. He was trying to hide as much of Camilla as possible. She shrunk behind him, shaking. The bus driver made no stops, but stared grimly ahead, foot down on the gas-pedal. Ansar wobbled back to them, saying, "My book is not here. That Zionist must have it." Mahmoud saw their stop ahead and called to the driver. The driver pulled to the curb, opened the doors, jumped out, and ran up the street.

The Bravos began to cheer his disappearing form. Mahmoud pulled Camilla behind him off the bus. Ansar followed. The Bravos followed Ansar, as they might follow a Messiah. Mahmoud, who rarely cursed, said, "Oh, shit," under his breath, and pulled Camilla toward the Saints and Sinners Club, which seemed at the moment an oasis of safety. Ansar came directly behind them, chanting something about his book, and the Bravos followed Ansar, chanting, *The Bravos say it with a will! You got to learn to kill, kill, kill!*

117

Even to the bohemian denizens of the East Village, this was a sight to see, and they stopped in their tracks to gape. Some took up step and followed along. Now the whole augmented mob burst into the Saints and Sinners Club. "I want my book," cried Ansar to the startled Tiger.

Tiger looked about him in dismay. His seated customers half-rose from the bar and the tables. He was afraid this gang would chase them out. "You mean the bomb book?" he said to Ansar. His face hardened. He was not a man to be easily intimidated. "What does anybody need a book on making bombs for?"

"If you have found it, you must return it," said Ansar. "The rest is none of your business."

"Bomb book," said one of the Bravos. The sullen faced Bravo from the bus said, "Ansar the Great is making bombs. *To blow them up, he cannot wait! He's the man, Ansar the Great!*

Mahmoud pulled Camilla back through the crowd and into a corner.

> *He's the man, Ansar the Great!*
> *To blow them up, he cannot wait!*

Tiger went to the cash register, picked up the book which rested beside it, and threw it on the bar. "There's your damn book," he said, "now all of you get the hell out of my place."

"Hey," said one of the Bravos, "speak with respect to Ansar the Great!"

"He is a Zionist," cried Ansar. "He knows no respect!"

A local sculptor, a powerfully built man, got up from his table, where he was surrounded by drinking buddies. "Tiger told you guys to clear *out*. Now clear out!"

Mahmoud could not see what happened next. The crowd was too thick. But there was a scuffle, several female screams, and a thud.

Like a plasmodium, one of those multinucleate masses of protoplasm that can separate into many cells and then rejoin itself, the Bravos regained their gang form and flowed out the door. But once outside, they disintegrated again into separate entities and formed a half moon around the corner bar. Somebody heaved something heavy and metallic through one of the plateglass windows. Inside, Mahmoud and Camilla could not find Ansar. Outside, Ansar was stuffing his book into his Saks Fifth Avenue bag and stuffing the bag into a garbage can. The Bravos renewed their crack-induced chant, Kill, Kill, Kill! Now they were joined in their chant by some passersby, who had no idea what was going on, but loved the excitement. Several garbage cans were thrown about, cars rocked, random sounds of broken glass punctuated the long moans of the cold, windy night. A police car and a mobile television unit materialized out of nowhere. The police stayed in their car, looking nervously about; the television people plunged into the scene, their cameras rocking.

PART THREE

RAPPING HORSE

Chapter 1

R.S.V.P.

Monk's massive bald dome shone like a full yellow moon under the raw glare of the kitchen light, his tin-white eyes seemed aglitter with reckonings, and the smooth skin of his face was opalescent, ghostly and ghastly.

Father Din felt dishevelled and ridiculous, but summoned his dignity, and pulled himself up to his full six feet three inches. Monk studied him coldly.

Acting as if nothing could be more natural than the present situation, Toddy said: "You remember Sam, don't you, Monk?"

Monk turned on her scornfully. "Don't be a fool. Of course I know who he is." He returned his attention to Father Din. "Maybe you'd like to explain why you've chosen to ignore my warning?"

"I got sick in the bar and Toddy brought me up here to rest."

"And now I guess you think you're just going to be on your merry way, is that it? It wouldn't be very polite of you to come to my party and leave just when I arrive."

"You mean, if I wanted to go, you'd try to stop me?"

"Not try! What caused the trouble between us earlier, if you'll remember, was that I asked you to leave and you refused. Now I'm inviting you to stay. I know you're not going to refuse me twice in one day."

"Why do you want me to stay?"

"By now you know more about me than I do about you, and I don't like that."

"There isn't anything to know about me."

"There's always something to know. For instance, I'd like to know what you know about me."

"I don't know anything about you."

Monk gave Toddy a baleful look. "You remember what my priestess said in the bar." He looked back at Father Din. "You know that."

"What do you mean?"

"Come on, Mr. Hopkins, you know exactly what I mean. That's why I've got to know who you are. Let's set aside for the moment our earlier difference. That was an unfortunate situation provoked in part by this young lady, who has seen fit of late to turn herself into an irresponsible lush. But consider how your being here must look to me. When I saw you down in the bar I thought you were just some jerk trying to pick up a woman. I was and I still am certain that you heard and understood what Toddy said about me; but, assuming you were just what I took you to be, it seemed safe enough to let it go. You were slumming. Drinking. Something like that would add vague color to your memories of the night before, if you succeeded in remembering anything at all. Then, too, I had a hunch that you

123

were somehow in the wrong yourself, and not likely to cause trouble. With your wife maybe . . . or on your job . . . a runaway or an embezzler . . . perhaps you were wanted by the police . . . There was something in your attitude . . . guilt. And that gave me a certain sense of security. He's not likely to run to the police, I said to myself. But now, finding you here, makes me wonder if you aren't some kind of agent. You could be D.E.A. You must see how curious you've made me. I can't help thinking: either he's courting disaster or he has a good reason for being here . . ."

No one had moved. Monk stood in the middle of the small kitchen, between Father Din and the door. His stance was erect, military, but he seemed quite at ease, his powerful, heavy body resting in an absolute gravitational relationship with the floor under his feet. It seemed that he could stand that way for hours, tireless and dominant. Toddy stood aside, near the kitchen table, with arms folded under her breasts in the attitude of a woman suffering a winter chill. She looked from Monk to Father Din and back. Her torso seemed to sink into her hips, and her face was pale and pinched, like a tired housewife's. She shifted her weight from hip to hip and sank deeper.

Father Din remained in the livingroom, just clear of the Oriental screen, not ten paces from Monk. He also appeared to be, and felt he was, sinking. Again he pulled himself up. For the first time today, as a result of hearing Monk's reasoning, he realized the irrational nature of what he had done, was doing. Was his really a compulsive personality? It was as though he were some kind of wheeled machine with a jammed gear, heading at an accelerating speed toward a precipice.

Outwardly, however, he insisted on the case as Toddy had put it. "I tell you I simply got drunk. I'm not a drinker; I'm not used to drinking. I threw up in the men's room of the bar. Toddy mentioned that she lived only a few blocks away, and I asked her to let me come up and rest until I felt well enough to go on my way. She told me that I'd have to be gone by nine-thirty, but, the truth is, Toddy fell asleep herself and didn't wake me. That's all there is to it. Most of what you've said sounds like some kind of double-talk to me. I don't know what it is that you keep saying Toddy said. I don't know anything about the police or agents or the D.E.A., whatever that means . . ."

Monk thought for a moment; then, slowly, decisively, with narrowed eyes, he said: "You know that I'm a—dealer." Quickly he flipped the pink palm of a thick hand up, stopping Father Din before he could refute the statement. "Don't you see, Mr. Hopkins," he amplified, "that whether you picked up on it in the bar—which, I can see now from your lack of surprise, you did—or not, the only way I can know for certain is to force the knowledge upon you and then to decide how to deal with you. I know that you know and that knowledge eliminates confusion and doubt. Now it's your turn. It's up to you to convince me that I can let you go."

"But how can he do that?" Toddy asked.

"I want to know who he is, why he came up here, what he wants. Maybe you're just a damned fool who got himself drunk enough to walk in where angels fear to tread; still, I have to be sure that it's safe to let you walk out again . . ."

"I'm going to sit down," Father Din said. He looked weak in the knees.

125

"Just a minute!" Monk commanded, before Father Din could seat himself. He stepped up to Father Din and frisked him from shoulders to ankles so rapidly that Father Din did not understand what was being done. For an instant he thought Monk was going to hit him. Then Monk was standing back again, an unreadable expression on his face, three feet away. "Go ahead, sit down," Monk said.

Father Din sank into a chair. "You didn't actually think I had a gun?"

"Why not? I have one." Monk turned and threw off his black leather trench coat and hung it over Father Din's overcoat on the clothestree. Then he sat down at the table, across from Father Din. Seated, he looked like a squat, malevolent god.

"Suppose you decide that it isn't safe to let me walk out," Father Din said. "What then?"

"Fix me a drink, Toddy," Monk ordered.

"Straight on ice?"

He looked at her.

"Sam, I'll fix you that tea I promised you."

"Make it coffee, would you? What I want to know is," Father Din pursued, "what are you threatening me with?"

"I have a question for you, Mr. Hopkins," Monk countered. "Were you two making it when I interrupted you?"

"No, Monk!" Toddy exclaimed.

126

"Sleeping," Father Din said definitively, and with a tone that was meant to erase suspicion from the air.

Chapter 2

TABLE TALK

Monk took out his cigarette holder, prepared a smoke, and lit up. "But I'm inclined to believe you," he went on, exhaling a mixture of words and smoke. "I don't think you'd have nerve enough to do it, either of you, knowing that I was going to show up." He sat at the table across from Father Din.

Toddy placed a drink before Monk, and a cup of coffee before Father Din. She sat down, holding her hands in her lap and her drink between them. From somewhere in the house seeped the distant music of a Latin rhythmist. In front, the windows rumbled softly with outer turbulence.

Monk said, "I've known the Priestess for a long time and I've never heard her mention you. Where do you know each other from?"

"Just from the bar," Father Din said, before Toddy could entangle herself in another lie. "We only met this afternoon."

"So, my Priestess, then you don't know any more about our friend here than I do. Old friends . . . that's what you said in the bar, wasn't it? You've become a pathological liar. I'm proud of you."

"I'm a fool," Toddy said warmly.

"Yes, I know," Monk responded. "I haven't met anyone in a long time who wasn't . . . unless perhaps Mr. Hopkins is not what he seems to be." He checked his watch against the wall clock. "Where are the little lambs of my congregation? It's after ten. Hopkins, don't ever deal with junkies; they're the most undependable people on earth, even worse than drunks." He shot down the remainder of his drink.

"*Noch ein*, Toddy; fix me another. Not so much ice this time. Leave room for the Scotch." He lighted another cigarette. "Hopkins, this is the way it's going to be—you're going to spend the evening with us as my guest, and I'm going to decide what's to be done about you . . ."

"Does that mean that if you thought you could trust me you'd just . . . you'd let me leave?"

"Why not, in that case? There must be a hundred people around here who know who I am and what I do. Some of them wouldn't have anything to do with dope—using or peddling—but neither would they have anything to do with the cops. That's the kind of neighborhood it is: live and let die. Maybe you belong in Needleneck. I'll know before the party's over."

"Let him go now, Monk," Toddy urged, serving him a fresh drink; "he won't cause you any trouble."

"Let me remind you, Priestess, that if you had learned, like a good girl, when to keep your pretty lips puckered, Hopkins probably wouldn't be in this situation. However, you're right in saying that he won't cause me any trouble. I'll see to it that he doesn't." Another mirthless laugh pictured itself with a gust of smoke. "You see, Mr. Hopkins, you've been brought to this impasse by the ancient evils of alcohol . . . or, specifically, by a drunken, loose-mouthed woman . . ." He gave Toddy a mocking nod. "Now, that's one thing about dopers: they don't talk. Drunks talk: but dopers just keep

129

nodding off. I'm talking about heroin users. Have you ever tried talking to one?"

"I don't know much about dopers."

"So—" Monk said lightly, "I've discovered nothing. You remain an enigma. You're either an innocent, or too clever to be taken in by so obvious a gambit. Which is it, I wonder?"

"You enjoy playing games, don't you?"

"Oh, very much," said Monk. He removed a Manilla envelope from an inside pocket of his suit-jacket, caught a longish thumbnail in the corner of the flap, ripped it open, and dumped the contents, several small glassine bags, containing a whitish powder, on the table. He tapped a stubby index-finger from one to the other, pushing them about, making patterns. "This is heroin," he said. "It's not a sexy drug—like coke, like crack, or the designer drugs. Journalists don't go on about it. But three times as much of it is being used now than was twenty years ago. For a junkie, this is food, sleep, sex, love, heaven, and hell, all in one."

He looked at Toddy. "Have you told Hopkins about your husband?" he asked, and went on without waiting for her answer—"She's married, you know. Her husband is a member of my congregation. A moral freak, like herself. A weakling, a beggar, a whiner, and a groveler. He traded me the use of his wife and his home for the privilege, revocable at my amusement, to buy his stupor of dreams from me. I own his soul. I bought it with this stuff. But the funny part is, he paid. Do you understand the economics of heroin, Mr. Hopkins? Opium poppies, which are its ultimate source, are cheaper than daisies on site. The growers sell 'em for next to nothing. Why should the drug be worth millions on the

130

streets? Because to bring it in you have to climb the Wall. The Wall is everything that tries to keep it out. The Wall is what makes it expensive on the streets. The Wall is supposed to stop it from coming in, but, because it makes it expensive, it encourages people to bring it in. To stop it from coming, you tear down the Wall."

"Legalize it, you mean."

"Of course. Take the incredible profit out of it, and who would bother to bring it in? The junkies would have to go cold turkey then. I've worked for and made deals with the C.I.A., the D.E.A., and state and local narcs. They're part of it—the Wall. The Wall is as much a part of the drug trade as the growers and the dealers. Everybody makes a buck, including high government officials, here and at the source. None of us want drugs legalized. Who would, when we're all doing so well?"

"Some would still come in. I mean, individuals would send their friends . . ."

"The dribble. Of course. But nothing like now. I'd have to go and find another gold mine."

A knock came at the door. Monk lifted an open hand in a gesture of "Don't move."

"Who is it?" he called.

A woman's voice answered indistinctly.

"It's Pilar," he said. "Let her in."

Chapter 3

FIRST COME, FIRST SERVED

Toddy opened the door and a young woman stepped into the kitchen. She was of middle height, with wide, high cheekbones, large ebony eyes, and full, beautiful lips which twisted scornfully down at the corners as she gave Toddy a cursory nod of recognition. "Who this?" The young woman spat the words challengingly, eyeing Father Din from head to foot. Her face had a satanic cast to it, and her whole attitude was aggressive, pugnacious even; yet Father Din saw the dark hollows under the light-washed bones of her upper face, and the tension in her thin, erotic body, and felt an affinity for the young woman.

"Sam Hopkins," said Toddy, "he's a friend of mine."

"My name is Pilar. Are you a friend of Jack, too?"

"No, I'm not. I only met Toddy this afternoon."

Pilar's expression, which had become for a moment less severe, revealing a face that hinted of submerged generosity, resumed its harshness. "How you know he ain't a cop?" she shot at Monk.

"I *don't* know," Monk said, enjoying her state of upset.

"Then why you let him be here?"

"He's my special guest."

132

"I'm not a cop," said Father Din. "You don't have to be afraid of me."

"Ha!" Pilar exclaimed. "*Afraid*! You think I'm afraid of a cop!"

"*Silencio!*" Monk snapped. "This is none of your business. Now! Let's see your dinero, Pepperpot."

"I've got it. What you think, I come to ask you any favor?"

Monk winked at Father Din. "Now, that's a smart dame for you. You see, she understands me." Then, down to business: "Get it up, then. You're late as it is."

Pilar opened her pocketbook, whipped out a roll of bills, and handed it to Monk.

"Give me the stuff," she demanded.

"Why don't you fix here," said Monk, counting the bills with deliberate slowness. "I like to watch dames shoot up."

"I got to go. Give me my stuff!" Pilar reached out for the several glassine packets of heroin which Monk had set aside.

"Easy," he said, pushing her hand away. "Can't wait to turn yourself into a zombi, can you?"

"For God's sake, Monk, give them to her," Toddy urged.

"Give me that!" Pilar cried, trying again to seize the packets.

Again Monk pushed her away, this time roughly.

"Damn you, gringo bastard!" Pilar cried.

"Give them to her, please," Toddy begged him.

"You stay out of this," Pilar shouted, "you *bitch*! I no need your help, you no-good *bitch*! What you done to my Jack! I take my Gem blade out of my cheek and I cut off your nose! You no look so good then, ha!" She was moving on Toddy now, and Toddy, sudden fear in her eyes, was backing up. "You think you *some*thing. You think you too good for spics. You even think you too good for Jack, and he better than you, way better . . . Everybody know what *you* do to him. You give him the *horns*. You give him the horns with this bad man. I fix you—" and with a click of her cheek she spat a glinting object into her right hand and raised it up, menacingly. Toddy screamed. Father Din caught Pilar's wrist and drew it down, wresting the object, which was indeed a single-edged Gem razor blade, from her hand.

"Please, don't do this," he said, gently. She fell into his shoulder, and buried her head there, and sobbed.

Toddy was ashen. She went over to a chair and sank into it, slowly shaking her head.

Monk let out a plangent horse whoop of laughter, the first instance of true hilarity of which Father Din had observed him to be capable. "Animals," he cried, with true if somewhat diabolic mirth, "beasts! Ho-ho, hoo-hoo." He appeared to be more than a little drunk. Almost immediately, however, his mad laughter went into diminuendo, ending in a last sharp nasty cackle, and ceased abruptly. "Here, get your junk and get the fuck out of here," he said.

"I'm sorry," Father Din whispered into Pilar's ear, "I didn't mean to hurt you . . ."

"I know," she whispered back, "I got a bad temper . . . But that—"

"Shh! Hush . . ." He patted her shoulder gently. "Don't . . ."

"Si, I don't." She withdrew from Father Din's embrace, and stood apart, rubbing her eyes.

"Well?" Monk spat. "What are you waiting for? Get out!"

"He *such* a nice man," Pilar said contemptuously.

"Go on, split," Monk said, "before I break your little fingers."

Undaunted, Pilar ignored him for the moment. Addressing herself to Father Din, and not without a certain hauteur, she said: "These people are no good. They are bad people. I warn you." Her eyes darted to Toddy, who had regained some composure. "Has my brother been here?"

"No," said Toddy.

Pilar looked at Father Din. "You . . . thanks," she said.

Father Din nodded.

"Go!" Monk cried, and made as if to rise.

Pilar took a hurried step to the table, scooped the glassine bags into her pocketbook, and went to the door, pulling it open. There she paused, looking back, then said, her eyes molten, "You will please to do me one big favor, Mr.

Monkey," gritting her teeth, "you will go to live your days in hell with the witches and burn forever," with which she disappeared behind the slamming door. They could hear the quick, nervous tapping of her high heels going down the hall.

"Stupid!" Monk said. "They don't think. She'll have to come back next week. I'd take it out in trade, but she probably has AIDS from screwing her brother. But she'll pay. Stupid people always pay."

"You're a miserable S.O.B.," Father Din said. "Did you ever ask yourself why?"

Monk considered. "The weak always try to convince themselves that the strong are unhappy, Mr. Hopkins, because it makes them feel better to believe it. But go ahead, tell me, why do you think I'm miserable? Toddy, bring that bottle over here."

"Because you've stripped yourself of humanity—or you've tried to. There's nothing left of you but the beast."

"Ha, no, that's where you're wrong. I'm psychologist enough to know that that can't be done." He was quite drunk now. "No, Mr. Hopkins, I have to disappoint you—I am a happy man. But come to think of it, there is one thing that could add to my bliss . . . I'd like to see Toddy hooked, like Jack Muir is. That's one of my ambitions. I'd like to see her crawl and beg. If she makes me wait much longer, I'll shoot her up myself."

"He's only trying to frighten me," Toddy said to Father Din. "He says that every time he gets drunk."

"You don't think I'd do it?" shot Monk, lighting a cigarette.

136

"Oh, you'd do it. But you don't."

"And so I won't?"

"No. Because you don't want to."

"And why do you think I don't want to?"

"Because it would spoil your fun. If I were as sick as Jack, I wouldn't know when he was suffering."

"Very acute, Toddy. She has brains; that's why I like her. That's why she's my Priestess . . . my Priestess of the Church of Moral Freaks. And she understands the way my mind works. She's partly right, you know. But there's another reason too. I'll tell you what that is in a few minutes. I want you to know. But, do you know, Toddy, I might do it anyway. I might do it some night, and we'll see what you do about it, how you decide to avenge yourself upon me. A nano-second after that needle's in, you'll be in another world, and that's a world that it isn't easy to come back from. Ask Jack if he knows how to come back from it."

"But people *do* come back," said Father Din.

"Hopkins, I may just keep you here all night. In my business I don't get many opportunities to talk with an educated man— or at least with one who isn't nodding off with an imbecilic expression on his face, like some grunge rocker after a concert. I hope it never becomes your misfortune to deal with the kind of scum I'm often forced to deal with. Illiterates, many of them—clowns of a low order, even if some of them drive big black limousines. That's the reason I like to work in an area like this, where there are painters and writers—

intellectuals. But, as to addicts being cured—yes, you're right, there are ways to come back; but those who go are seldom strong enough in the first place to be able to come back, otherwise they wouldn't have gone. That's one reason I won't force the Priestess into it—she's not ready yet. I couldn't stay with her to see to it that she got enough to get her hooked. That'd take several shots a day for a while. While I was gone, she'd come off. She's still too strong. She doesn't *want* to be hooked. But she has one weakness; she knows it—and that's her weakness for Jack Muir. Now, starting there, I begin a program of conditioning. The groundwork hasn't been laid yet—she isn't as yet perfectly predisposed to addiction, the way Muir was—but when I get through with her, she'll be perfect addict material. I'll turn her into Needle Woman."

"You'll never do that to me," Toddy said with resolution.

"Oh, yes I will, Priestess. Then you'll be just like your Jack of Hearts." He paused. "I threw Muir out of here myself. I told him that if he wanted any more smack from me, or from anybody, he'd have to go across the street to that loft of his and be a good boy and stay away from Toddy. I even gave him a boot in the ass on the way out the door. Then I took the Priestess into the bedroom."

"Please stop, Monk—"

"But that's what happened, isn't it?"

"Yes yes yes!" Toddy wailed, clenching her fists.

"Now be careful," Monk persisted, heedless, "or I might decide I need you tonight." He winked at Father Din, who sat staring stonily at him. "I get these moods," he said.

"For God's sake, man," Father Din said, "isn't there any limit?"

"Limit? What limit? Does she know any limit of degradation? Do you?" He snorted. "Look at you—you sit there like a little tin god of self-righteousness, but still you sit—because I've ordered you to. I could make her do anything tonight. Do you know why? Because her Jack of Hearts would beg her to. What limit are you talking about? Isn't that true, Priestess? Tell the simple-hearted—not to say -minded—Mr. Hopkins—tell him!"

Toddy refused to speak or move, but sat with her arms folded on the table and her face buried in them.

"Leave her alone," Father Din commanded.

Monk, who had been slouching a bit over his drink, pulled himself up and raised his dark brows. "Oh," he said, "are we going to have trouble with you?"

"Leave her alone."

"If you and I are going to get along, you better wipe that self-righteous smirk off your face. And keep it off."

Chapter 4

HAUNTED

"Something has to be done," Father Din thought, looking at Monk. He recalled a scene as if he were reliving it—his mother and father playing their parts as they once had, himself standing outside the kitchen door, on the backporch of their cop's second-mortgaged house in Jersey City, listening. He must have been about seven years old.

"Something had to be done," his father said. His father had brought a bottle of whiskey home and was sitting at the kitchen table, taking drink after drink as if his intention was to drown something from his consciousness. Young Michael had never seen his upright father in such a condition. He leaned back against his suit jacket, which hung over the chair, exposing the compact snubnosed Police Special on his belt, his tie pulled loose, his hat on the floor next to his chair, and his dark hair in disarray. His mother sat close beside his father at the round oak table. She made no fuss, as she usually did at his homecoming, but sat quietly, fingering his shirtsleeve. His father's partner was named Mike, after whom Father Din had been named. "Mike," said his father, "Mike and I—we just couldn't help it. Eventually, he would have killed her. There just wasn't anybody on Earth to help her. He'd nearly killed her twice before. She was afraid to leave him. He had her terrorized. Hell, he had everybody terrorized. We've taken him in a dozen times. As fast as we bring him in the system lets him out. He was evil, I tell you, evil! I know I've sinned—Mike and I have sinned—but something had to be done."

140

Then Father Din's mother spoke the electrifying words: "But couldn't you just frighten him? Warn him? Scare him off? Did you have to kill him?"

"We didn't mean to. Honest to God! I swear! It just went too far. Don't be afraid, no one will ever know."

"We will," his mother had almost whispered.

Ever since that evening Father Din had prayed to forget what he had heard, and, until this evening, he almost had. But Monk had brought the terrible scene back, more vividly than ever.

Chapter 5

MAYHEM

Casually, Monk reached under his left arm and drew out a big Uzi automatic and placed it on the table. "What do you think this is," he said, "amateur hour?"

"Put that away," said Toddy, gripping the edge of the table.

"Don't worry," Father Din said, "he wouldn't fire that in here. The whole neighborhood would hear it."

"And what good would that do you?" said Monk. He laughed, a mad cackle. "But the truth is that you're right, I wouldn't let this off indoors. It might disturb the neighbors. It just isn't done, is it? I was only trying to shake you up. Tell the truth now, you were frightened, weren't you?"

"Only a fool would pretend that he isn't frightened when a man who's had too much to drink takes out a gun."

"You're a sensible man, Mr. Hopkins. You deserve a reward for being such a sensible man. Listen, have you ever seen this?" He made a V-for-Victory or Peace sign with the first and second fingers of his right hand. "Do you know what this means?"

"Peace?" essayed Father Din.

"No, no, no no no," said Monk. "Look, let me tell you in your ear; this is not for the ladies." He and Father Din were sitting cater-cornered from each other at one corner of the table, and

were only about two feet apart. Monk leaned forward, looking at his V-ed fingers, leering, like a man with a dirty joke
to tell, and put his thick, fin-like left arm over Father Din's
shoulders, pulling them into a conspiratorial huddle. Father
Din had no desire to listen, but the fraternal arm pulling him
in was heavy and powerful and apparently benevolently determined, and he thought it wise to appease it, so he leaned
forward into it, let it take him, his right ear to Monk's mouth
to hear, his eyes focused on the two thick V-ed fingers that
hovered below them, waiting for the promised illumination,
when suddenly it came.

The arm over his shoulders slid up to the back of his neck and
suddenly evolved into a headlock. He tried to pull away, to
stand, but Monk's weight and power held him in place, as if
in a stock. "What are you doing?" he cried through clenched
jaws, as the arm about his neck became a tremendous weight,
and he felt that his neck would snap. For a moment, light
faded from his eyes. His ears roared. Then he could hear
again, as the pressure slackened a little, and he heard Toddy's
excited voice, Monk's calm, deliberate tone, but he could not
make out what they were saying, and then light came back
into his eyes like a vortex starting at a distant point and
coming at him with great speed, and colors flashed, took
shape: he saw Monk's bulky knees—apparently both he and
Monk were still seated—and then he saw the thick V-ed
fingers, like some disembodied incarnate fork, hovering,
threatening—Monk whispered wetly into his ear: "This'll
clear your head"—and the fingers rammed up and back into
his nostrils till his whole face seemed about to split open. His
head fell backwards, cradled on Monk's arm, so that he was
like a man in a dentist's chair, his mouth gaping, gagging, the
two-pronged fork searching out his brain.

143

Chapter 6

TRIAGE

Father Din saw a small pool of blood on the floor where his head had rested, before being gathered into Toddy's arms. Then he passed out again. When he woke the second time, he was lying on Toddy's bed, his nose, still flowing, like a double-tapped keg. He tried his jaw. It worked. Then he felt the back of his head. The hair was sticky and matted. Toddy came in with a basin filled with ice and damp towels.

"Don't try to get up," she ordered.

"I'm all right," he said.

"No you're not," Toddy said emphatically. "You should be in the emergency ward. Now lean back."

Father Din did as he was ordered. Toddy put cotton in his nostrils to stop the bleeding, and held ice-cubes to the bridge of his nose to retard the swelling. "What's the damage?" he asked. "Is my head bleeding in back?"

"No. You bumped it, but it's not cut. The blood is from your nose. You rolled in it. And there's a small cut under your chin—one of his rings made that. He punched you. It's your nose that's hurt, but I don't think it's much more serious than a bloody nose, really. It feels solid. He said he could have ripped it off. Oh, what a horrible thing to do! I've never seen anything so awful. My God, I tried to make him stop, but I couldn't budge him. He's made of iron."

144

"Where is he?"

"In the kitchen, finishing up my Scotch. He doesn't seem to think anything of it. He wants me to make him something to eat. Can you imagine it? He's hungry. Just as if a minute ago he hadn't sat—doing that."

"Wasn't somebody else here? For a minute back there. . ."

"Dedi Pavon—Pilar's brother—the boy you met at the Saints and Sinners. He helped me bring you in here. Monk wouldn't lift a hand."

"I'm surprised that he let you help me. That man is insane, you know."

"Whatever he is, I hate him. Oh, Sam, I feel so terribly guilty. I feel responsible for dragging you into all this. I'm so sorry."

"Nonsense," said Father Din, touching her cheek, "I got myself into this. I insisted on coming up. You warned me. So, for that matter, did Monk. But I wanted to come."

"But if I had watched the time, you'd have been gone now."

"I didn't really want to be gone. No one's fault—except mine. But I've got to get you away from him," he said, getting to his feet, his rigid muscles tearing over his long bones as they straightened them. His head roared with the surf of an inner sea, and he stood holding the bedpost for a moment, waiting for his vertigo to pass. Toddy watched him, shaken, trying to fathom his mind. Then he staggered into the livingroom, swaying like a drunken man, on rubbery legs. Toddy followed him, wondering, frightened.

Monk and Dedi looked up from their business in the kitchen.

"Hey, mon," Dedi called, "you O.K.? Need any help?"

"No . . . thank you," Father Din answered. Toddy came up beside him and took his left upper arm in her own arms and helped him on. Father Din hesitated at the threshold of the kitchen, and stood studying Monk, again the image of a squat, malevolent god coming to mind.

Chapter 7

THE DICTATOR

"Come in here and sit down," Monk ordered. "If I haven't made this clear before, I'll make it clear now. I'll kill anyone who tries to get between me and the Priestess, here. If you've got any ideas about running off with her—remember this—" he tapped the table with thick fingers— "I'll track you down and kill you." Kaleidoscopically, his mood altered, and he said, not unpleasantly, "I want to tell you about my book. I told you that I was writing a book, didn't I? I'm going to call it Priest of Evil, and subtitle it The Autobiography of an Honest Man. Come on. Sit down. I won't hurt you." He had a waterglassful of Scotch in front of him, and was smoking a holderless cigarette.

On the table was an "outfit," an open tin pillbox containing a disposable plastic hypodermic, extra needles, cotton, and a pink birthday candle. Dedi, quick to observe Father Din's interest in the outfit, beamed proudly. He said, "That's my outfit. Nice, uh? It ain't chrome or silver or platinum, though, like I heard Keith Richards and other rich rockers got; but I sent away in the mail for this glass-type hypo, and when she comes I get me a new box, maybe a gold cigarette case— take it off some rich old lady in the street, wow, ha."

Father Din looked pity at the scarred boy. His head was clearing now, and he was able to stand, with reasonable steadiness, on his own two feet; and so gently pulled his arm free of Toddy's support, thinking it unwise for Toddy to stand too long holding his arm while Monk looked on.

147

"Monk," Toddy began to plead, "please let Sam go now. He ought to get to a hospital. You might have broken his nose. And besides, none of this has anything to do with him. He won't talk —"

Neither Monk nor Father Din paid her any attention. Father Din sat down at the table, holding his head with his left hand, and began to stare at Monk from under it, like a man trying to see into the distance. He knew now that Monk was not an ordinary criminal, but a true sociopath, a soul-less unreachable creature.

"Here," Monk said, pushing his glass of Scotch across the table to Father Din, "you look like you need this more than I do."

"—and I'm gonna get me a needle made out of a diamond someday—" Dedi picked up, like a boy in a trance, "and I won't ever have to sharpen it, like with these—"

Father Din drained off a large shot from the glass, coughed, shuddered, and shook his head. Toddy came behind him with a washcloth and began washing the blood out of his matted hair. When she was finished with that, she placed a Band-Aid under his chin. "There," she said, "how do you feel?"

"Better," he said. "I'll be fine."

"You know," Dedi wandered on, heedless, "it's pretty weird, mon—sometimes you poke the needle in your arm and you see that needle push the vein away, you dig? 'Cause she's dull—you know? Maybe only ten, twelve times stay sharp, then you gotta start sharpening them. If you don't, you get the black-and-blues—"

"Shut up, Dedi," Toddy snapped. "I don't want to hear about it."

Dedi looked at her with big brown amazed eyes. "What'd I do?"

"Just be quiet," Toddy said, kindlier.

"Who are you talking to?" Monk said. "Can't you see that he just got off? He's not there."

"Only did half a bag," Dedi said dreamily.

"Would you believe it," Monk said, ignoring Dedi, "I really didn't mean to hurt you that badly, Mr. Hopkins. That trick looks more ferocious than it is, if you do it right. A good subduer. I learned it from a Dutch African mercenary, a regular Zouave, one of the best fighting men I've ever known. He's in prison now. Once you get your fingers in, if a man doesn't struggle he won't get hurt, but if he does, you can pull his nose off his face. You were struggling, that's why I popped you off the way I did. An uppercut under the chin to calm you down."

"I'm very grateful," said Father Din.

Monk chugged his drink. He re-filled it from the bottle, which was now two-thirds empty, and gulped down another drink.

"Go on," he said to Toddy, "sit down, nursey. I hate it when women fuss over a man like that. Get out of the way," he shouted. "I want to talk to Mr. Hopkins about my book." He looked drink-mad, frightening.

149

Dedi said: "Hey, mon, I bet your head don't feel so good, eh? You know what you need, mon? You need a fix. Hey, Monk, why you no give heem a fix?"

"Shut up," Monk said; then: "Have you ever seen anybody shoot up, Mr. Hopkins?"

"No, thank you."

"Well, you've got to see that." He refocussed glassily on Dedi Pavon. "Dedi, get ready; I want you to fix for Mr. Hopkins."

"I don't want to see it."

"I don't care what you want," Monk said softly. "It's very difficult for me to make that clear to you, isn't it?"

"Hey, Monk, I ain't ready yet," Dedi said.

"Do as I say!" Monk said. "You only had half a bag," he added after a moment, "so this time use a whole bag."

"That's too much," Dedi protested, "and it's too quick for me. I'm a sick boy. I ain't got no strength. Lemme just shoot the other half of the bag—"

"No," Monk said, "a whole bag. You love it so much, then use it."

"I don't like to shoot with strangers watching me," Dedi said.

"Strangers?" Monk looked around. "Oh, do you mean Mr. Hopkins? Why, he's no stranger anymore; he's one of us now. He's been baptized. Haven't you?"

"In blood," said Father Din.

Chapter 8

THE FIX

Dedi poured the contents of one of the glassine bags into a spoon, added water, stirred, and held the solution over the flame of the pink birthday candle (Monk said, "That's to liquify and purify the stuff"—); when he had "cooked" the heroin, Dedi rested the spoon containing the solution inside the open pillbox; then he took up his plastic hypo, and previously having sharpened the needle, attached that to it; next, pumping the plunger, he rinsed the hypo with water, squirting long, miniature garden hose streams on the floor. He placed the hypo on the table; and, tearing off a small piece of cotton, added that to the contents of the spoon. ("They draw the stuff up through the cotton," Monk commentaried, "to filter it.") Then he stood up and took off his jacket and rolled up his sleeve. His arm showed under the harsh kitchen light like that of a skinny boy's, but for the red rash and blue bruises at the inner elbow, the arm's crook, and the strange long jagged scars, or "tracks," where veins had collapsed along the forearm.

Monk, enthusiastic for this kind of sport, urged the boy to get to it: "Mr. Hopkins is waiting." The boy looked around him—at Monk, imploringly, then at Toddy and at Father Din. "I should wait . . ."

"Go on," Monk ordered.

Father Din sat in grim silence, feeling that it was hopeless to try to intercede. It was not for himself he feared, but for Toddy, even the boy. Monk was crazy drunk. The Uzi automatic lay on the table. He now believed Monk capable of anything. And everyone present knew more about the use of the drug than he did. Nonetheless he ventured: "Why not let him wait, if he wants to . . ."

"Because I say not," Monk cried. "He's shot two bags at a time before—it's not that that's bothering him. It's that he's shy. He doesn't want to give a performance. But I say now, Dedi—for the last time, I say *now*."

Dedi gave in; he shrugged his thin narrow shoulders, pulled the tie from his neck, drew a length of iron pipe (the same that Mr. Potter of The Busy Nook never saw, and which Jack Muir had examined earlier, with its bands of black electrician's tape around it), and fashioned a tourniquet, which he held— he was standing—by locking it into position between his knees.

"See the veins pop out?" said Monk, his eyes obscene, as the big blue veins showed in bas-relief from the skinny arm like long balloons.

Dedi, with the efficiency of long practice, drew the pale fluid up into the hypo through the soggy cotton, and began roughly probing, apparently quite impervious to any pain, among the veins at the crook of his arm—"See!" Dedi cried, suddenly excited, "see the way she pushing that vein over . . . dull—" and indeed it was quite ugly, Father Din thought, to see the living tender vein being pushed about beneath the almost transparent skin—Toddy had turned away from the sight— "There's one; I got a good one," Dedi cried—What was he doing?—"That's what they call 'registering'," Monk said, as Dedi drew his blood up into the hypo, clear to be seen, through the plastic, sloshing about, mixing a little with the heroin solution—"uuuuuuuooohgg," Dedi moaned in

153

something like pleasure: twisted in his Quasimodo-like position, and under the cruel glare of the kitchen light, the boy looked like an obscene monstrosity—but the needle was in, and his thumb was closing down on the plunger with a steady pressure, as Father Din watched in a kind of stupor of unbelief—"More!" Monk cried, his voice thick—"More," Dedi repeated; then, rhythmically, like a musician: "More, more, more, more, more, more, hey, more, hey, more, hey, hey, more . . . ah, ah, ah . . ." —"Boot it, boy, boot it," Monk cried, and suddenly Dedi drew back the plunger, filling the hypo to the top with his blood—"Washes the last drop of dope out of the hypo," Monk sang—"Boot it, boy—that's it"—and back down went the plunger, driving the blood before it into the veins, out of the plastic—and Dedi tugged the needle away from his arm—"Hey, good!"

"Look at him!" Monk cried excitedly—"Look at him!"

"Hey, mon . . . I wanna go rest . . . Toddy . . . I'm gonna lay down, eh . . ."

"Go in my bedroom," Toddy said.

"Is he all right?" Father Din asked.

"He's O.K.," said Monk. "Toddy, I want something to eat."

Chapter 9

A CONFESSION

"She ain't got no right to do this to me."

"Fuck you, Tory!"

Monk picked up the pistol from the table and stuck it in his belt, buttoning his jacket across to hide the weapon. Then he stood up and walked across the room to the door and pulled it open. Outside stood Tory Amsterdam and two women.

"She can do any damned thing she wants. You don't own her, Tory." This rebutting remark came from a short-haired, putty-faced woman of about forty. The woman wore an elaborate, deadly looking ring on the second finger of either hand, and at this moment both hands were fists.

The apparent object of this altercation was a cherub-faced, gold-eyed beauty with an elaborate Egyptian hairdo of woven pigtails. She wore a multi-skinned Kaross that came to her upper thighs. Black tights showed shapely legs down to her boots. She smiled gleamingly at Toddy and sighed "Hi, baby;" then, seeing Father Din, who rose from his chair, she asked, "This the boy you was talking about?"

Toddy said: "Sam, this is my friend, Opal Nearing. Opal, this is Sam Hopkins . . ."

"Hi. Oooh! What happened to you?"

"He ran into an old friend," Monk said. "What the hell do you care? Shut up and get in here." He slammed the door.

"Oh, you here, Monk?" said Opal casually. "Funny, I never seen you when I came in."

"Let me give you a piece of sound advice, Supi-yaw-lat: start looking."

"Who?" asked Opal.

"Theebaw's queen. That's Kipling."

"I don't know no Kipling. He a dealer? You think you're the only dealer in town?"

"The only one for you," said Monk, "and don't ever make the mistake of forgetting it." He looked at Father Din. "Here's a whole nest of hopheads for you, out of the woodwork . . ."

The two antagonists stood silently boiling, waiting.

"What's he doing?" Opal said, tossing her head, indicating Monk. "On a toot? Having a party? Somebody die?"

"Shut up, you black slut!" Monk exclaimed, eyes bulging.

"Hey, man," put in Tory, "you don't supposed to talk to her like that."

"You be quiet, too, hornblower," ordered the putty-faced woman. "Can't you see he's out of his skull?"

"What?" said Monk, not quite hearing this last.

156

"That still don't give him no call to talk to Opal like that."

"Be quiet, Tory," Opal said. "I'll speak for myself."

"So what are you going to do about it?" goaded the woman. "Go ahead, get your head split. That'd be great. What do I care, anyhow? Go ahead, stupid, get busted up; see if I care!"

"Oh, you goddamn old ofay bulldyke! You old white bull-cow!"

"Tory, don't you ever—"

"I said for the two of you to shut up, damn it!" Monk roared, and the room fell silent. Monk paused; then said: "Yeah, Supi-yaw-lat, I'm giving myself a party tonight. And do you know why? Because I'm being stalked. There's a hunter out in that jungle, and I'm his prey, and he's getting too close this time. This time he's only a few blocks from this room. This is the big one—the big moment of my life. This is the gunfight at the O.K. Corral. This is Armageddon."

"That nark?" asked Tory.

"Figlia," said Monk. "He's going to hide behind that gold shield of his and blow me away when I'm not looking."

"Well, what do you know?" said Opal. "The great man's scared."

"No, I'm not scared," Monk said. "I'm preparing for my greatest adventure. This thing with Figlia means a lot to me. He's what they call an honest cop. Well, I killed his little girl—did you know that?"

157

"Are you talking about Rose Figlia?" blurted Father Din. He realized now who Figlia was. Father Liam had handled Rose's funeral. He had helped.

"What do you know about Rose Figlia?"

"Just something I saw in the paper," said Father Din.

"Oh, fuck it," said Monk. "I have more important things to think about—anyway it can't be proved—let's see what his honesty amounts to." He thought for a minute. "On the contrary, this is one of my greatest opportunities . . ." He dropped his sentence and looked around, as if coming out of a reverie. "You, Tory, I've got a job for you. Come in the other room for a minute." He got to his feet and lumbered into the livingroom, swaying like a shot bull, with Tory following.

Chapter 10

TORY GETS HIS ORDERS

Tory's raised voice was audible in the kitchen: "I CAN'T!"

"You CAN and you WILL," came Monk's voice.

"Oh, man . . ." Tory groaned.

"Wonder what that's all about," said Opal; then, smiling at Father Din, "Say," she said, "Toddy told me she only met you this afternoon, but that she think you O.K. I think she kinda goes for you, you know?"

Father Din looked at Toddy, who was standing at the stove, cooking eggs for Monk. He looked at Opal: "Is that what she said?"

"Well, you know . . . sort'f. 'Course, she's married—you know that?"

"Yes."

"Good, then it's all square. See, I don't like nobody to get cheated. I tell them two fools"—she indicated the other woman and Tory with specific rolls of her eyes— "that I like 'em each—see I'm honest—for what I get from 'em—Elga, she buy my stuff for me; and Tory, he—well, never mind what he give me—ha!—but what I mean, I play square, you dig?"

Father Din nodded.

"What happen to you?" she said. "You look all swollen."

"An accident."

"But, you know, Sam—O.K. if I call you Sam, ain't it?—Toddy been lonely. I told her before she should let that fool Jack of hers go and forget him; get her somebody new, and get out, you dig?"

Father Din nodded.

"'Cause this is no good no way. You understand?"

Father Din nodded.

"'Cause that man of hers ain't never going to be like he was, you know?"

Father Din nodded.

"'Cause Monk got him right under his evil thumb."

Father Din nodded.

"Now you come along, nice stud like she said you was . . . maybe she got herself a chance. She and me is old friends. Used to model together. That's how we met. That's where she met Jack. I used to pose for him, too. He done lots of pictures of me. Studies . . . I thought he was a pretty good artist, but I don't say I know much about that stuff. But now he ain't. Monk took his manhood away."

"Hey, bitch!" said Tory, coming into the kitchen behind Monk. "What're you up to? You trying to add somebody new to your list?"

"If I am," Opal turned on him, "it ain't none of your business, big mouth." She grinned at Father Din. "That big mouth of his is only good for blowin' out blue and cool on that sax, and kissin', but he can't talk with it and make no sense, that boy. Can you, big mouth?"

"You gonna push me too far someday, Opal," said the musician, solemnly shaking his head.

"I thought you were on a break," Elga said to him. "Shouldn't you be getting back? You know, there aren't many people who like your kind of music anymore—you shouldn't keep them waiting."

"Don't worry about it, bull-cow!"

"She's right," Monk said. "You've got your stuff—you know what to do—so get out. Go blow your brains out. But, Tory, remember: I want that done, and done just as I told you to do it, or don't let me find you, do you get me?"

Tory nodded gravely.

"Hopkins, did I tell you that I produce my own movies? Produce, direct, and star in them. These three are my cast. Now go on, get out! I'm tired of listening to your stupid argument."

"Are you coming?" asked Elga of Opal.

"You go on across the hall, I'll be there in a minute."

"No you ain't," said Tory, "you ain't going back in that apartment with that old bull-cow. You going to come to the Cuttlefish with me. You going to sit right there where I can see you while I play."

Opal arched an eyebrow, defiant. "I go just where I please to go, boy, and right now I'm staying here."

"Don't call me no boy. I'll slap you up 'side your—"

"Try me *first*," said Elga, making fists of her hands and jutting her massive bosom against the skinny black man's stomach.

Monk got suddenly to his feet and, taking Elga and Tory each roughly by an arm, hurtled the argument into the hall. Slamming the door after it, he came back to the table and sat down heavily. In an instant, the musician's voice could be heard in a piercing scream, then a curse. A door was slammed, and fast, angry footsteps diminished down the hall.

Chapter 11

!ALERTE!

"Opal," Monk suddenly commanded, "go get me another bottle of Scotch."

"I'll have to go to the store," Opal protested. "It's cold out there, and maybe ain't none open. It's late."

"I don't care where you get it, just get it. Here." He threw a hundred dollar bill on the table.

Opal picked it up, saying, "Be right back," and went reluctantly out the door.

"Where's my food?" Monk demanded.

Toddy swung around, holding her forehead with her right hand and a frying pan with her left. "Here it is," she cried, "burnt on the stove! I can't cook with all these people running in and out. I can't stand much more of this!" She threw the pan back on the stove with a clang and, holding her face in both hands, began to sob hysterically.

Monk looked at her, drunkenly amazed.

Father Din had started to his feet to comfort her when the door burst open and Opal re-entered, a quart of Scotch in hand.

"What's going on here?" she asked, seeing Toddy. "Why you cryin' like that, baby?"

163

She threw the bottle of Scotch, with a "Here," to Monk, who caught it, a surprised look on his face, and went and put her arms around Toddy.

"What!" she exclaimed, looking at Father Din. "You another one? Why isn't you up here holdin' this girl?"

"Shit!" said Monk, twisting the top off the new bottle.

Father Din stood up, reflexively.

"Don't pay any goddamn attention to that little whore," Monk said. "You, Opal! Where did you get this liquor? I know you didn't go to the store that fast. Who do you think you're putting one over on? Where's my change?" But this train of thought was interrupted when a loud moan came from the front of the apartment.

"What's that?" asked Opal, glad for the distraction.

"It sounds like Dedi," said Toddy.

Opal, surprised, still holding Toddy, said: "You mean little Dedi in there all this time?"

"He said he wanted to rest."

"He shot up?"

"Yes."

"He O.K.?"

"Of course he's O.K.," said Monk. "The little sewer-rat is dreaming about old time movie stars. You know what he's like."

"That little boy is very weak, you know," Opal said, a look of concern in her big-eyed, doll-like face.

Just then came another moan from the bedroom, as if to punctuate Opal's words.

"Is something wrong?" asked Father Din.

"Sure could be," said Opal. "That don't sound right to me."

"He's just dreaming," Monk said.

"Let's take a look," Opal said. Toddy nodded assent, and the two women went through the livingroom and disappeared into the bedroom.

"I wonder where Jack is?" Monk mused.

"Maybe he couldn't get the money," Father Din ventured.

"Maybe he's dead," Monk said. He looked at Father Din. "I suppose you think this is pretty small-time for a man like myself?"

"I don't know what you mean. I suppose there's a great deal of money in drugs."

"Oh, there is," Monk said. "But what I pick up here is only chickenfeed, a matter of a few grand. You don't think that a man like me would trouble himself for the price of a suit, do you? This suit I'm wearing cost more than what I pick up here. No, this is my—my hobby. This is my rest and relaxation."

In a few minutes Toddy came back from the bedroom, her face pale.

"There's something wrong with Dedi, Monk. His face is all twisted, and he's drenched in sweat."

"What?" said Monk, who had nodded off open-eyed for a moment. "What's that?"

"It's Dedi," said Toddy. "He's sick."

"So?" said Monk. "What am I supposed to do?"

"Well, you've got to do something. I think it's an O.D."

"An overdose?"

"Yes, I think so. We ought to get him to the E.M."

"A doctor?" said Monk, suddenly alert. "That's out. No doctors, got it? Wait a minute, I'll take a look at him." He got up and went to the sink and washed his face with cold water.

Father Din went into the bedroom. In a moment, Monk and Toddy followed him.

Chapter 12

O. D.

It was impossible for all of them to get into the small, bed-crowded room, so while Father Din slid in beside the bed, Toddy and Monk remained in the doorway, looking on. Opal sat on the bed, beside Dedi. The boy was having difficulty breathing, and his face was bubbling with sweat. There were great damp rings under the arms of his limp cha-cha shirt. His legs twitched about. His skin was a mottled blue.

"This boy has O.D.-ed," said Opal grimly. "It look bad to me. He oughta go to a hospital."

"That's out," said Monk. "Got any naline, Opal?"

"I haven't got nothin'," said Opal, looking at the boy, slowly shaking her head.

"Then get some ice cubes and rub on him. Open his collar. Do whatever you want, but he doesn't go out of here and nobody else comes in either. That's the way it's going to be."

"This little boy'll die, Monk," said Opal, wiping Dedi's forehead with a handkerchief. "You gotta let somebody get him some help."

"Then he'll just have to die," said Monk. "He's got AIDS anyway. He's not the first junky to O.D. Nobody cares. The cops don't even care. Around here the street-cleaners pick up their bodies like so much garbage. But listen, all of you: the first person who tries to go out that door will find out how

167

serious I am." His grogginess of a few moments before was gone. He seemed again in firm control of himself. He turned and left the doorway, calling back from the next room: "Besides, the little freak irritated me."

"I'll go get some towels and ice," Toddy said, following Monk into the kitchen.

"You said he could die," said Father Din to Opal.

"Happen all the time."

"Isn't there anything we can do for him? Will the ice really do any good?"

"Do I look like a doctor?"

Father Din widened the boy's collar.

"If that man in there let us get him to the hospital maybe he be O.K."

"But he won't."

"Well, maybe that's up to you. You the only man here."

"He's got a gun."

"Yup."

"I know you think I should do something," Father Din said, uncertain whether to kneel and pray or ball his fists and fight. "He might shoot somebody . . . you . . . or Toddy."

"Or you?"

"Believe me, that's not what I'm worried about."

"Don't matter what I believe."

"You'll have to think what you like," Father Din said, unsure of his own stance. "Is he always like this?"

"When he get drunk he bad. But he in a real fit tonight. I think he kinda scared of that Lieutenant Figlia."

Father Din wondered aloud: "Wouldn't it be safer for him if he got the boy out of here?"

Opal nodded in the direction of the kitchen with mixed contempt and awe: "That devil know what he doin', drunk or sober. He got a plan already. He thinkin' all around our heads. I seen it before."

Toddy came back, squeezing in beside Father Din, bringing ice cubes wrapped in a towel. She brought a dry towel also, and with it she wiped the perspiration from Dedi's brow. "This isn't going to do any good," she said, only saying what they all knew.

Dedi moaned. He opened his eyes, but did not seem to see any of them. "Oh . . . *hey!* . . . Jack!"

Toddy winced at the sound of her husband's name.

The boy struggled to raise himself up on his el- bows. "Jack! Pilar! Hey! I no feel so good, mon . . . Hey!"

"Try to rest, boy," Opal said. "Rest."

169

Chapter 13

LAST RITES

Dedi was ghastly bluish pale, mottled like marble. His skinny, chickenboned hands tried to open, tried to shut. And it seemed that the thick air could not be sucked down into his lungs. As his little cage of a chest struggled to expand, his back arched; then, as if exhausted with the effort, the whole pathetic structure, a mockery of inspiration, would again collapse. Each word came hissed on a small sigh: "Pilar . . ." he uttered: then, with an effort terrible to see: "Bogie . . . he . . . the . . . mon . . . Pilar!" He tossed for breath. "Pilar! . . . hey . . . help . . . me . . . ."

The three near the dying boy looked helplessly at him. Then, decisively, Father Din said: "Leave me alone with him for a few minutes, would you?"

"What are you going to do?" Toddy asked.

"I have an idea. Maybe I can . . . save him. Let me try."

Opal climbed off the bed and took Toddy's arm. "Come on, baby," she said, "we can't do no good. If the man thinks he can do something, let's do what he say."

"But *what* . . .?"

"Come on, baby," said Opal, and led Toddy out of the room.

Father Din sat on the edge of the bed and took one of Dedi's small hands in his own.

"Can you hear me, Dedi Pavon?"

And somewhere in the deep reaches of his mind Dedi understood he was receiving the Last Rites of the Catholic Church, as they were sometimes given on the battlefield; that a prayer was being spoken over his floating, swaying self. Oh, that Jack and Pilar could share with him the incredibly sweet, incredibly sad music of the words! And Dedi could see Jack, now, in the small, cataracted, half-blind eye of his mind, as through the opacity of a vague and meaningless light. Jack was holding Pilar's hand: everything was going to come out right! Oh, it was all coming true! It was radiant, now, with fine, clean truth! Oh, why must it be gone! Jack's smiling face was gone! Pilar, a Pilar who was truly happy, was gone! *"Donde esta mi hermana? . . . Alquien tragame mi hermana . . . Pilar?"*

Father Din prayed for his own forgiveness in hope of God's forgiveness of Dedi. Had he the right to give Last Rites, he wondered.

"Wait, my son . . . my brother . . . ."

Wait?

In a few minutes Father Din came into the kitchen. His face was gray and damp. His mouth hung open.

Monk and the two women looked at him.

"Well?" said Monk impatiently.

"He's dead."

Monk got up and started to pass Father Din on his way to the bedroom. Father Din grabbed his arm.

"Now that you've killed him," Father Din said, "what are you going to do with him?"

Monk looked at him, hard-eyed. "He killed himself," he fairly hissed. He jerked his arm free and went on into the bedroom. In a moment, Monk came back into the kitchen with the boy in his arms. Monk laid the boy's body on the floor and went through its pockets. He found several cheap rings. He then removed the boy's wrist watch. There was nothing else to take.

"Where's his suit jacket?" Monk asked. "He gave me a couple of hundred dollars; he must have got that someplace. I know he's got more on him."

Opal found the jacket down behind a chair, handed it to Monk, and stood by in silence. Monk went through the jacket, finding a wallet with a hundred and fifty dollars in it, and saying, "The kid must have knocked over a piggy bank this afternoon." He emptied the wallet of money and threw it on the table. Surreptitiously, Father Din took the wallet from the table and went through it. In a moment he found what he was looking for: Dedi's address, on a clinic card. He replaced the wallet on the table. Monk was then pulling a half a dozen watches from where they were pinned to the lining of Dedi's jacket. "I can pass these out to the Bravos like tips," he said, putting the jacket back on the corpse. "Punk," he said, eyeing the tape-wrapped pipe which the boy carried, now stuck in his belt. "Give me that wallet." He stuffed the wallet into Dedi's inside jacket pocket. He threw the boy's body over his shoulder, its limp arms and legs hanging like those of a ventriloquist's dummy.

"What are you going to do with him?" Father Din repeated.

"He's dead. Monk said. "I'm going to take him to the poor people's morgue. Open that door."

Opal pulled open the door and waited.

"Anyone coming?" Monk asked.

Opal stepped into the hall.

"No," she said.

"Where are you going?" asked Father Din. "What are you doing?"

"Get out of my way," Monk said.

"Not until you explain."

"All right," Monk said, "I'll explain. How's this for an explanation?" He reached into his belt and drew out the huge automatic pistol and set its cold muzzle to rest in the middle of Father Din's forehead. "Now get out of my way," he said, "and remember, nobody leaves this apartment. Anybody leaves, I'll track you down and kill you."

Father Din blinked, and stepped aside. But when Monk could be heard lumbering up the stairs to the fifth floor, Father Din followed after him. On the fifth floor, Father Din saw Monk climbing the stairs to the roof, and when Father Din reached the roof, he saw Monk, silhouetted in the oddly gleaming moonlight, marching across the roof with Dedi Pavon's body draped over his hand as a shotputter holds a shot, and, in exactly the same way that a shotputter puts the shot, Father Din saw Monk put Dedi Pavon's body off the roof and into space, down which it fell six stories to be pulped in the alley below.

The icy wind whipped at Father Din's hair and face, but he could feel nothing save the weight of the blank sky upon his mind.

PART FOUR

SERIOUS PURSUITS

Chapter 1

FIGLIA IN LOVE

Outside, the seventy mile per hour gale from off the chopping, tumultuous Atlantic deracinated a delicate tall poplar which had grown for twenty years overlooking the headland, two-hundred yards from the bursting surf, and sent it, a whirling, root-feathered spear, crashing into a weekend-fisherman's deserted shack, which, upon impact, vanished, like a house of cards in a wind tunnel, its thin, weathery boards blown scattering wildly into the night. For the force of the gale the shrub-like conifers that dotted the cape lay in flat obeisance and the rocks of the promontory roared. Then the big wind began to push a dazzling whirl of fine white flakes before it, and from the land it seemed that a gossamer curtain had been lowered far out at sea. When it woke in the morning, Long Island would find that it had slept under a blanket of snow.

Inside, warm and snug on the cushiony couch in the living-room of his ranch-style house, far from the cape, but still on Long Island, in the town of Beachberry, which grew no berries and which was some distance from the nearest beach, Detective Lieutenant Albert Figlia watched a televised weather report . . .

". . . the possibility exists that the storm will change its course and be blown out to sea. However, at best it's certain that much of the metropolitan area will see some snow. At worst," the dapper-looking, striped-shirted weatherman said, smiling sheepishly, "I'm afraid we're in for a blizzard."

"And how in hell am I going to get back into the city in the morning if we have a blizzard?" Figlia demanded of the weatherman, who shrugged his shoulders, as if in reply, and said, "This is meteorologist Herb Kline reporting," and vanished.

"I'd better drive back in tonight," Figlia said, "just in case he has it right for once. I don't want to be stranded."

"You talking to yourself again?" asked Gena, his wife, who had stopped at the threshold of the livingroom on her way through to the kitchen. "When you start talking to yourself, I know you're tired. Why don't you go into bed, Al? I'll be right along."

Figlia, still in his rolled-up shirtsleeves and day-rumpled trousers, argyle-stocking-footed, looked quickly up at her from the silly mythology of an Old South Plantation House, a picture of emerald lawns and white fluted pillars, before which the florid face of Colonel Drummond of Deep Down Done Chicken fame, his white locks wafting in a gentler breeze than that which rumbled the windows of Long Island, his chicken-fat yellowy mustaches parting for the insertion of a gooey drumstick, floated like a redneck's conception of a fatherly god.

"I was just thinking aloud that I'd better drive into the city tonight," he said. "There's maybe a blizzard coming."

"Oh no!" Gena exclaimed, frowning. She was a tall, slender woman, taller than her husband, and in her middle thirties, over a decade younger than he was. She stepped back into the livingroom, pulling the belt closed around her long satin dressing gown. "Well," she said, brightening, walking toward him and giving him a wink, "I'm glad you were able

177

to visit the homefront and relieve me of these! She bent over, grabbed up from the carpet the lacy lingerie that Figlia had lovingly removed from her an hour before, and shook the lavender handful at him.

He stood up, facing her. They were almost eye-level and his sad, brown-eyed gaze invited her closer. Of late, whenever he left for the precinct, she saw that dark, Monk-thinking look, like a shadow. He knew she saw it; knew he could not keep it from his face. He averted his eyes and buried his head on her shoulder, kissing her neck. "Fair lady, we do have world enough and time," he whispered, and led her out of the room, across the hall, into the dim bedroom where a small bedside lamp shaped like a lily shone like a beacon.

They lay naked beneath a comforter. From the livingroom came the faint dazzle and hum of unattended commercials and sitcoms. Nearby the tiny ticks of ice that shot through the wind tattooed upon a window pane. Figlia was certain that the mixed blessings of life had taught him something, had taught him what love is. He had shaken in the hopper of his mind the ingredients of life. He was a quietly contemplative man. He believed in God, but he thought that organized religions were human creations, anthropological stuff and nonsense, bred in the lonely, primitive heart. It was his opinion that God's will had been withdrawn from nature and humankind was on its own. He had come to believe this in war, and on the hard streets of his patrols, come to believe that the war of good and evil was between connectedness and dis-connectedness; or, on a lower plane, but symbolically the same, between social and anti-social behavior.

The ultimate in anti-social behavior was loveless sex, he thought, as in prostitution; the ultimate in social behavior was sexual love. The sparks of the heart's warmth he felt with

Gena were the stars of the universe. He thanked the God that made the universe for having set him free from a loveless marriage, for giving him this chance to know what love was. Gena could feel her husband's heart beat upon her chest. He wiggled his torso down between her legs, and rested his head on her stomach, just below the rib cage. He hugged her around her upper thighs, squeezing hard. He inched his way back up, leaving a trail of warm kisses.

Afterward, the comforter at their feet, Gena lay in Figlia's arms. "I guess I will have to make that coffee, now, won't I?" she whispered.

"Yes, and make it strong. Then I'll go." Neither of them moved. There had been world enough, but now there was no more time.

"I hate to see you take that long drive back tonight. Where will you sleep? At the station house?"

"I'll take a hotel room."

"Good."

Figlia sat up, stretched, yawned, and began to grope about under the bed for his shoes. Gena pulled her robe on and went to brew coffee. When it was ready, she found Figlia seated on the couch in the livingroom, lacing his shoes. "Turn it off," she said, meaning the TV, and placing a tray holding two cups of coffee on the table. "It's so distracting."

"No wait," said Figlia leaning forward. "What's that?"

SPECIAL REPORT

No picture came, only a voice, filled with newsman urgency: "We have as yet an incomplete report of a disturbance in Manhattan's lower East Side. The disturbance could be of a racial nature, but nothing has as yet been confirmed. More as information comes in. We return you now—"

"What's that?" said Gena.

"Maybe a riot," said Figlia. "It's down where I am."

"And now here's Kathy Field downtown on the Lower East Side." Kathy Field stood, mike in hand, on the sidewalk in front of the Saints and Sinners Club.

"That's right on the Strip," Figlia commentaried, "only a few blocks from the station. I passed by there at least twice today."

"This is Kathy Field reporting from the East Village, where what police spokespersons have referred to as a serious disturbance, but what looks to us more like a riot, is underway. There are crowds of East Villagers out here, some seeming to participate in the disturbance and others merely rubber-necking. From what I can discover, it all started here, in this grunge-rock bar that you see behind me—the Saints and Sinners Club—when a teen gang, called the Bravos, invaded the place, which is habituated by artists and musicians and other bohemians. The owner, a man called Tiger—and we think his last name is Hartzmann—an ex-wrestler, tried to evict the gang single-handedly. Others joined in to help him, it appears, and we believe there has been a stabbing, the seriousness of which we are not as yet certain. Oh, I believe this is Mr. Hartzmann. Step in, Mr. Hartzmann. Would you care to tell us your version of what happened?"

180

Tiger stepped before the camera. His breath steamed from the cold. His wall-eye was rolling.

"I think I remember him from wrestling matches on TV," said Figlia.

"Well, that's what happened," said Tiger, "just what you said. I don't want no big-mouthed trouble makers in my joint."

Kathy Field nodded, non-commitally, and pushed the mike forward, almost into Tiger's mouth. "Then you don't view this as a racial incident?"

"Naw," moaned Tiger, disgustedly. "Chrissake, I don't see what all the excitement's about. I just trew out a few loud-mouths. Now everybody's running up and down, TV cameras . . . Christ! It's the media, that's what it is. It's you!"

"But a man was knifed, wasn't he?"

"Stabbed. Yeah. But it happens down here. Nothin' new." Tiger looked cold. He wore only a gray cardigan sweater over his starched white shirt, collar open. His hands were plunged in his trousers pockets. His teeth seemed to chatter.

"Mr. Hartzmann when you leave us, do you intend to close the Saints and Sinners Club for the night?"

"No. I don't close shop until four in the morning and unless the police ask me to close earlier, that's when I'll close. Why should I have to close my bar because a gang of bums start causing trouble?" Behind Tiger a teenaged girl stood staring

181

dreamily into the camera, mittened hands over her ears. Behind her, floating in space, was a large placard. On it was written:

MINORITIES COALITION LIBERTY PARTY
MEANS FREEDOM!

Kathy Field dropped Tiger cold, and, with a wave of her hand toward the placard bearers, signaling her camera person, plunged into the crowd. The camera caught up with her, sticking her mike into the face of a pale, blue-eyed, good looking young man with a Fu-Manchu mustache, who held one end of the sign. "And what do you say happened here tonight?" she cried. The young man said, "A very basic thing has happened here tonight. We were denied our basic right of freedom of expression . . ."

"It doesn't look like much yet," Figlia said. "Looks like the media is trying to blow a mole-hill into a mountain. Must be a slow news night."

"Yes," said Gena, "but a man was stabbed, maybe killed."

"Honey," said Figlia, "it happens fifty times a night and nobody shows up most of the time. Ms. Field there probably thinks she can get some racial divisiveness into it. Trouble is, she might succeed. Maybe it's a good thing I'm going in. Hubbard will need all the help he can get."

"It's not your job," Gena objected. "You go to a hotel and get a good night's sleep. Now, that's an order, Lieutenant."

"Yes, Ma'am," said Figlia. He drained the coffee from his cup, finished tying his shoes, and went looking for his suit jacket and overcoat.

"Wear your scarf," Gena called after him, "it's freezing out."

"That's why I don't think that business'll get very big," Figlia said, returning. He was dressed for the outdoors. "It's too damned cold for much outdoors mischief."

Within five minutes, Figlia was pulling onto the Long Island Expressway, beginning his third trip of the day along that drab, curving commuter run. He focused his thoughts with his eyes fixed upon the dark, forward, cloud-scumbled sky. Occasional auto-lights glared that from view. At the beginning of a long, sweeping curve, he passed a tree that stood on a hill in high tableau against a section of cloud-pale, electric sky. Its bare boughs were like skinny, gnarled fingers, clutching the clouds.

Chapter 2

FIGLIA IN CHARGE

Forty minutes later Figlia pulled up in front of the station house. He went directly to Hubbard's office and knocked. "Come in," called Hubbard. Hubbard's sleepy eyes opened happily. "Al!" he exclaimed, "I'm glad to see you back. I've got my hands full and I need some experienced help." For a quarter of a century Hubbard had been losing more than his share of sleep—thus the eyes, perennially at half-mast—and tonight was no exception. "I just spoke with your wife. I think I woke the poor girl up. For nothing, as it turns out. She said you were on your way in." Hubbard leaned back in his swivel chair, lighted what must have been a cheap stogie, judging from the face he made, and spat dryly several times. The whites of his eyes were red and he did not look well. He said, "Gena told me you saw the trouble on TV. These racial entanglements can get messy. I guess I should know, being black. It's already all over the media."

"What happened out there?"

"I've heard all kinds of things," he said, coughing. He cleared his throat. "Look, I'm not feeling so hot. I think I'm running a temp." He coughed again, and spit up into his handkerchief. "I mean, I don't know exactly how the trouble got started. Anyhow, some sculptor is making it over at St. Vincent's. One of the Bravo punks shoved a shiv in his belly. There seemed to be a couple of other jerk-offs involved, but they don't seem to have anything directly to do with the violence. We're going to run them out of here. We

184

need room for the real thing. The gang stays, though, until we can sort out which one of them did the knifing. Hell, you know it won't stick to charge the whole bunch of 'em. We know there's drugs going in and out of their place—you know they own a building just a couple of blocks from here?—their 'headquarters'—but the guys we've got in the tank are clean. How 'bout you taking this thing on, as a favor? Pull all the tangles out of this baby, O.K.?"

"Do you think I should shut the club down? There was a stabbing . . ."

"I tell you what, I wouldn't want to be the one to tell that cock-eyed old wrestler I'm shutting him down." He thought for a moment. "Why close him up? It's not that kind of situation. Nobody's dead. We know the stabber is one of the Bravos. The guy who did the knifing was wearing a Bravo coat, you know, black plastic with a knife and a bleeding heart. We got him in the tank. We just have to sort them out. But do what you think best. Close him down, if you want to. But it wasn't his fault. As for me, I'm going home and go to bed. My night chief is out sick, or moonlighting. It's hard to tell the blue flu from the real flu except that I think I've got the real thing. I may not come back for a day or so. I'll put young Verdi in charge, officially. You keep an eye on him." He rose from his desk, grabbed his trenchcoat, and pulled open the door. "See you in a day or so. I'll keep in touch by phone."

When the door was shut behind Hubbard, Figlia called Gena. He promised he'd get some sleep. He hung up and sat for a long time, holding his head in his hands. Now, unofficially, he had a whole precinct to worry about.

185

Chapter 3

PROCRASTINATION

Jack Muir cupped his hands around a lighted match and dipped his cigarette into them. He puffed with numb-cold lips until smoke came, keeping his eyes on the windows of Toddy's apartment.

He was standing, hunched and shivering, in the doorway of his own building; across the street, slightly cater-cornered from him, was the doorway of Toddy's. No one had come or left by that door for the past half hour.

He was certain, however, that persons whom he knew, or of whose existence he was aware, had entered the building before he had taken up his windswept post; because perhaps a quarter of an hour earlier he had seen Monk's unmistakable bald dome and thick body pass in front of the window next to Toddy's bedroom; and he had seen Toddy, too; and he had seen another man—a big, dark fellow—probably the man whom Dedi mentioned having seen with Toddy earlier in the day, at the Saints and Sinners Club.

Another woman—he believed it was Opal—was up there, too.

Once, Monk passed in front of the window carrying something, but Jack had been unable to make out what it was: the other man had followed Monk, obscuring the view. Muir drew his head, turtlewise, down into the high collar of his khaki army-surplus overcoat. He wore a woolen-knit ski-band of bright yellow pulled down over the tips of his reddened ears, and a long scarf of the same color about his neck. Below the long, flared skirt of the army coat, a short length of grungy, torn jeans could be seen, disappearing into a pair of down-at-heels Wellington boots.

A large, bloodstone-and-pounded-copper brooch was pinned to the coat, over his heart. He avoided looking at the brooch. The gleaming copper, which he kept polished, made him feel even colder than he was, as did the touch of the icy pistol in his pocket.

How would he appear, he wondered, to a stranger who passed and saw him there. No one would guess that his parents were wealthy, and that he himself might have been, might still be. A passing stranger might take him for a half-starved hippie derelict—or for what he was, he thought bitterly, a dumb junkie—with his hollow, haunted face, and Dachau eyes.

Afraid? Yes, he was afraid Afraid of what, though? Only a few hours earlier he had conquered his fear of death in a game of Russian roulette. But he knew that his wife was the distance of that building across the street from him, and that he wanted to go to her but was afraid to do so. Now the wind went by, a ghost rolling a garbage-can lid. The thing clanged down the middle of the street, passing in front of him, then veered off toward a parked car, crashed into a fender, and clattered into silence. The racket scared out from under the car a pair of hair-on-end, courting cats, who scurried off into the alley next to Toddy's building, bushy-tailed. A few moments later, from out of sight, Muir heard their screams of conflict or lust. His teeth chattered. He spit out the butt-end of his cigarette and stamped on it, as much to warm himself as to put it out. The sparks scattered across the sidewalk to the gutter and spun off in miniature dying flares in the wind. It was no good. He couldn't bring himself to do it. He stepped out of the doorway and into a wind that felt like a heavy hand on his chest, and started walking toward the Strip. As he walked, he took the pistol from his pocket and put it inside his coat, in his belt. It had become almost too cold to touch.

Earlier, he had heard the Martian wail of police sirens sounding from the Strip. Now, as he approached its center, he was reminded of them. Obviously, there had been trouble. He counted five police cars, most of them double-parked, their beacons slowly turning. A truck from one of the television networks was on the scene. The remainder of what must have been a crowd wandered about, occasionally being shooed from here to there by police. Some of these, upon being told to move on, or to "Break it up," went into the bars, which, along the Strip, on week-nights, were often open until four in the morning, their late-night customers being mostly mug-of-beer-drinking or white wine Bohemian types, artists and would-be artists, long-drawn-out-talkers. By day the whisky-drinking set held sway.

A cop strode toward him, and Muir knew that he was going to be told to move along, so he turned and started back toward his loft. He had no deep interest in whatever was going on— or had gone on. He also had an unauthorized pistol tucked in his belt, and many old needle-tracks on his arms. He glanced back over his shoulder and saw the cop lose interest and turn away.

Then he ran into Tory, who came plunging out of one of the bars. Stoned on heroin, Tory was drunk as well, smelling potently of gin. The skinny black jazzman with the poodling locks grinned when he saw Muir. He was toting his battered tenor-sax case in his left hand. He flapped out his right hand flat for Muir to slap, saying:

"Hey, man, what's happenin'?" He didn't wait for an answer. "You missed a bad scene," he went on.

"You mean all this?" Muir said, throwing a look back at the police cars. "What happened?"

"Naw, man," Tory said thickly, "Up at your old lady's."

"What happened?" A sharp look came on Muir's face. "Is anything wrong?"

"Wrong?" Tory shrugged a skinny right shoulder; his left hung like part of a rope that was tied about his neck on one end and to the handle of his sax-case on the other. "What's *wrong*? I never heard of *wrong*. It's just that bullet-headed, ofay—beg pardon—mother Monk."

"What's happened, Tory?" Muir urged. "Get to the point."

"Aw, nothin'—nothin' happened, man. You worried 'bout your old lady? Sheee-it!" He waved that aside. "No, man," he went on, "he just drunk. But you know how he get when he get like that—bad-assin' all over the place. It's me, man. He's drivin' me out. You know what he tried to tell me that I should *do*?"

"What?" Muir asked, momentarily relieved.

Tory widened his glazed eyes. "He told me he want me to burn old Tiger out. He told me I gotta pop a Molotov cocktail in on that old man. Now why I wanna do that?" he asked, tucking his chin in and raising his eyebrows. "Huh? You tell me."

"Are you going to do it?"

189

"Shit, no! He got the wrong man for that kinda gig. I'm strictly an artist. You know me, man. Huh-huh," he grunted, shaking his head in the emphatic negative, his dangle of curls flapping on his forehead, "not *me*."

"What's he got against Tiger?"

"How'm *I* s'pose to know? What he got against everybody?"

"Toddy's all right, then?"

"She's all right."

"But he's drunk."

"Aw, Jack—*man*, you know she's been with him when he was drunk before . . . I mean, I don't wanna hurt your feelings, man—but what could you do about it, anyhow? You'd best forget that scene."

Muir knew Tory meant well, but his remarks still stung. He changed the subject, reverting to Tory's problem: "What are *you* going to do?"

Tory laughed pathetically. "I dunno, man. It's like this: I'm gonna hope that he's drunk enough so he don't remember telling me to do that thing." He looked a question mark down his nose at Muir. "Mmm?" he added.

"Suppose he does remember?"

"Then I'm gonna tell him that I thought he was too drunk, and that maybe I shouldn't do what he said till he was sober."

"That won't work," Muir said.

"I know," said Tory, shaking his head sadly. "I don't know what to do, man . . ." He threw his arms out, helplessly. The heavy case held the one close to his side. He set the case down, and repeated the gesture with tremendous emphasis. "I just don't *know* . . . ."

"You better go hide," said Muir.

"Dig, man, I think that's what I'm gonna do. See if my brother will put me up. But first, I'm gonna find Opal and take her with me. And if I get a chance before I split, I'm gonna break that bulldyke girlfriend of her's neck."

"What happened here?" Muir asked, indicating the situation on the Strip.

"Oh, man, everything. Looked like there was gonna be a riot. I ain't heard how it started." He rolled his eyes. "Say, man," he said suddenly, "I'm freezing. Think I'm gonna round me up my old lady, and Goodbye, Tory! Trouble is, I got another session to do tonight, but then I'm gone . . . up where they got soul-food and hot-sauce. Bury me not on the lone prairee . . ." He grinned a little sadly. "Dig you later, man," he said, and picked up his sax-case and started off, calling back: "I'll meet you right on this spot in one year, Jack . . . but don't wait!"

Muir stood for a moment, watching Tory reeling off as if pulled by the weight of his saxophone case. Then he entered the bar from which Tory had plunged. He needed a good, stiff drink. One—and then he was going up and take Toddy out of that apartment, away from that—what did Tory say?— mother, Monk.

191

Chapter 4

ESCAPE

Upon re-entering the apartment, Monk had demanded to know where Opal had gone. Toddy had shrugged for answer. "I knew she'd run," Monk had said. "But I don't have to worry about her. She won't say a word. *You* might talk, but she won't. On the other hand, you wouldn't run. I knew that when I went up to the roof. I knew Hopkins would follow me, and I knew that you wouldn't leave without him. You see, I know my congregation." Monk had taken his seat, grinning with self-satisfaction, and had poured himself a drink. After a pause, he'd said: "Nothing's a chance when you know what you're doing."

But now it seemed to Father Din that Monk had been silent for a long time. He was thinking this when he felt himself being nudged in the ribs. Toddy indicated Monk with a slight dip of her head. Father Din looked at him. He sprawled in his chair, his small goatee pressed into his jutting chest, his eyes half-masted.

"Is he . . ."

"Shhhhh!" Toddy leaned toward Father Din, putting her mouth to his ear and her hand over it, and whispered, "Opal put veronal in his bottle."

"When?" asked Father Din.

"Before Dedi . . . We've been waiting for it to hit him."

192

"I wish it had hit him before he did that to Dedi," Father Din said.

"So do I," said Toddy. She studied Monk's face. "I think he's out," she said.

"He might be faking."

"No, I don't think so, but there's only one way to find out. Come on, let's get out of here."

Toddy got carefully to her feet, and tiptoed to the door. She took her own coat from the clothestree, putting it over her arm, and got Father Din's out from under Monk's, and carefully opened the door. She held Father Din's coat out to him, saying, "Here. Hurry." Monk snorted, and Toddy froze, stock-still. In a moment Monk's mouth dropped open, he nuzzled his goatee deeper into his chest, and began to snore. Toddy stepped into the hall, again holding Father Din's coat out to him. "Come!" she urged.

Father Din followed her into the hall.

He started to pull the door to, but Toddy stopped him, saying, "Leave it. It might wake him." In a moment they had their coats on and were in the street.

Toddy looked up at Jack Muir's loft. "There's no light up there," she said. "Either Jack's asleep, or he's out. It's so quiet. Think it could wake Monk if I called up for him? I'm so afraid he'll go up to my place, and with Monk—"

"Try," said Father Din. "You should try. Your kitchen is toward the rear. Monk won't hear you, not with this wind." They crossed the street, their coats blowing, and

193

Toddy called up to the loft several times, but there was no response from the row of blank, black windows.

Father Din waited, the cold air having a beneficial effect on his mind and nerves. His head was clearing. But still, he felt weak. He had eaten nothing since that morning's breakfast. His nose was caked inside with dried blood, and ached. Occasionally, his stomach would seem to float upwards, uncomfortably, like a helium-filled balloon.

He pulled his collar up against the wind, and looked at the storm-ominous sky. He knew that it could not be more than a hundred yards from where he stood to where Dedi's body must be, cold and broken. The thought made him shudder. Toddy came up beside him and took his arm. "It's no use," she said. "Let's get out of here."

Chapter 5

MALADIES

An hour earlier, after turning a quick trick at the Busy Nook, Pilar had shot up, and now felt that she was basking on the golden shore of a great, warm sea.

Indeed, it would be so easy to drift into sleep in such womb-like, sun-warm comfort, that she must now draw herself up in the seat of the cab, and think hard of what she intended to do.

She and Dedi lived by night. This would be her night-time lunch—usually she'd go out again, after preparing and eating it—and Dedi's night-time supper. Pilar liked to believe that Dedi would stay home and go to bed. Now she tried to concentrate on the meal she would make, hoping, too, that Jack would share it with them. There would be . . . But the thought slipped away.

She tried to remember what she'd bought, and found that she couldn't. She would like to have some fried plantains! She looked into the tops of the paper bags that sat next to her on the seat. A loaf of bread . . .

Suddenly she found herself coming out of a kind of drifting sleep. It had been a delicious, eternal moment, but she remembered that she must stay awake. If she slept, the driver would go right on by Jack's building. She'd given him her address, but had not told him that she meant to stop and pick someone up. The fact was, she didn't know Jack's address— she knew the building, of course—but not the address. The only address she knew was her own, and it had taken her some time to learn it—not that she was dumb; she just hated numbers. She rolled down the window and let the icy wind blow in upon her.

Dedi was a sick boy. This horrible disease! But he had never been strong. *Ay!* She remembered the terrible night of his birth, when she herself was no more than a child. If it had not been for her mother's brother, who shot at their father with a rifle, scaring him off, neither of them would be alive today.

He was so crazy-drunk that he would have cut them up with his knife, that father of theirs, that prick! She had saved Dedi, gnawed him free of their drunken Mama's body with her own sharp teeth; and he would always be hers because of that—he was hers! But many times since they had laughed at how close he had come to being dropped down the hole. "You little wet-fur rat," she would yell at him playfully, "I should have let you go into the shit, where you belong." And Dedi would say, "Thank you for picking me out of the shit." Then they would laugh and laugh. He was a good little prick, Dedi, and he respected her, else she'd take a strap to him. But she liked best to rub his little belly, and to kiss his big ears.

She remembered how, when Dedi had rickets, she fed him pigeon broth until he grew strong again. Then he gained weight; but still, he had asthma. Then she cured him of that with a brew of manatee fish bones, ground into powder and boiled in water. Her spiritist had told her that she had the gift of healing. But Dedi was a bad patient; he would lie to her and say that he took the elixirs she made for him. "You little liar!" she would yell. "You did not drink that." And he would cry, and, crying, say, "But you can stab my sister in the tit if I lie!" Then she would believe him. But nothing could

196

heal him now from this new illness. Why did she not get the AIDS? It should have been her.

Dedi got everything—rickets, asthma, tapeworm, and as soon as he was old enough to stick his little thing into a woman, he got the white flower; but she cured him of that, too, with saluarron and bismuth. *Caramba!* that little dog would hump anything! He's a real *machisto! Mio tinayel . . .* Well, that's the way a man should be. He never got the AIDS from putting it in the wrong place. It was the needles, sharing them on the street.

She was sorry that Dedi was a junkie. That had been her fault. You can't cover the sky with your hand. He was a junkie because of her doing it. That made her feel very sad, so she tried not to think about it. She stabbed her own arm for the first time when she was only twelve. She'd made her first money from her first man a year before that. Now she'd been in the life, a whore, for . . . but she didn't like numbers. Numbers can be used to cast spells.

"What number did you say, lady?" asked the driver.

"Go on. It's a lot more blocks."

"No, it's no use trying to cover the sky with your hand," thought Pilar, "you can't do it. What's true is true. I'm a whore. But I am also a witch. I can do sorcery. It cost me many dollars to learn that, but my spiritist told me it was true. And today I found a broken medal. That's a sure sign that she was right. So nobody can treat me like a whore and get away with it. Monk will find out very soon that I have cast a spell on him and that he is doomed. When I talked to the dead, they heard me. He will see. I'll make his lungs fly out of his mouth and carry him away to hell. That *atomico!* That *chulo!* That *bubarron!* I don't let any big blubber lips like him treat me like that."

The cab leaped a bump in the road and Pilar had to save her groceries from falling to the floor. She searched her pocketbook for cigarettes, found one, and lit up. She pulled the cigarette from her violet lips and hissed the smoke out as if it were distasteful, acrid. She threw the butt out the window, sparks flying backwards like little comets. The Saints and Sinners Club rolled by like a gaudy package on wheels. She had just missed seeing Toddy and Father Din enter. She rolled the window up.

"Getting cold enough for you, lady?" asked the cabbie.

"You just drive," Pilar snapped back at him.

"No, lady," the cabbie tried to mitigate, "I only meant that it's starting to snow."

"I no care what it does," said Pilar, "you just drive."

Chapter 6

HOME FREE

Father Din pushed open the door of the Saints and Sinners Club and followed Toddy in. They were greeted by Opal, who sat at the return of the bar, near the door. "Oh, honey," Opal said to Toddy, "I'm glad to see that you two got outta there. I been scared! I didn't know what I should *do*."

"He passed out—*finally*." Toddy said. "What happened here? I mean the broken window."

"Some kind of riot," Opal said. "Nothing for us to worry about. We got enough trouble of our own, and he back there at your place. Oh, *man!*" she exclaimed. "Honey, that was a *baahd* scene. That poor little boy!" She looked at Father Din. "What do you think we should do? Did he throw that little boy's body off the roof? I figured him for doing that." She looked like she was going to cry.

"Into the alley," Father Din said.

"I knew he meant to do that. Then the police find him, and they say, 'Look, he fell. It don't matter, he's just another junkie.'"

"You don't think they'd investigate further?"

"'*Vestigate*! They don't care. 'Round Needleneck, they *always* finding junkies' bodies. In doorways. . .in alleys . . ."

"What about his sister," asked Father Din, "won't she go to the police?"

"Pilar?" Opal shook her head negatively. "She scared if she see a blue coat in a store window. 'Sides, one of us would have to talk. And I know you ain't gonna catch me doin' any talking. Tory want us to get lost up in Harlem—maybe stay with his brother at the Temple up there—and I think he's right. Till this all blow away. He said that Monk put a bad job on him that he don't want to do. So he got a reason for gettin' out of here, and now I got a reason too. Anyhow, you the main witness, Sam. What you gonna do?"

Father Din shook his head. "I don't know yet." He felt that he should go to the police, identify himself, and have Monk arrested. But then, tossing a corpse from a roof didn't sound like much of a charge. Monk would probably laugh himself free.

"Where's Tiger?" asked Toddy, growing impatient for a drink.

"He's in back," said Opal, "watching my two fools shooting pool."

"Tory and Elga?"

"Ah-ha. I had to get my coat outa my place, so I got Elga too. She was sittin' in there by her lonesome, sulkin'. Tory come staggerin' in here a few minutes ago. He said he saw Jack before, on the street."

"Jack wasn't going up to my place, was he?" Toddy asked in alarm.

"Tory said he wasn't. But he's all shot up and stoned. He don't know from nothin'. He had to do another session tonight, at the Cuttlefish, but he never went back. He still after Elga's head. And now it's worse. Elga just beat him at pool. He raised such a noise, Tiger had to go back and keep a eye on him. Jealousy! He won't go till he beats her, and I want to get out of here. Before Tory come in, I was only waitin' to see would you come in." She shrugged. "Anyhow, what if Jack goes up there? I give Monk enough of that dope to keep him out all night. He can't hurt Jack if he asleep. And Jack wouldn't do nothin' to a man like that, not who was sleeping. Monk would do that to Jack, or to anybody he felt like it. But Jack just ain't that kind of guy."

"But you can't tell about Monk," Toddy said. "Nothing seems to stop him for long. He might already be awake. And suppose Jack should—"

"Listen, honey," Opal reassured her, "he bad, but he human. He ain't gonna wake up till morning, and then he gonna have some headache. Wait a minute, I'll get Tiger." She slid like a big, sleek cat off her stool, and went to the back.

"God, I pray he doesn't go up there," Toddy said.

"If Opal's right," Father Din said, "I don't think you need be overly concerned. Monk was certainly out cold when we left." He had his own doubts, though.

In a moment, Opal returned, followed by Tiger.

"I told him to come on out here and take care of us payin' customers," Opal said.

"Toddy," said Tiger, "I had a lot o' trouble in here tonight. Some maniac calling me a Zionist. I'm not even sure what that is, but he made it sound bad. Did you see all the cops?"

Father Din and Toddy shook their heads, blankly.

"You didn't? They're all over the street."

"They got other things on their mind, Tiger," Opal said.

"I got a guy knifed in here tonight. A regular. A nice guy. He was trying to help me. Makes me feel lousy."

"In here?" Toddy said, unbelievingly.

"Right over there. Look." He pointed.

Father Din and Toddy looked. They saw the blood stains.

"God," Toddy exclaimed. "What a night!"

"It must be the last night of the bad world," said Opal.

"What hit you?" said Tiger to Father Din.

"I got at cross purposes with Monk."

"He's at cross purposes with the whole world," said Tiger.

Chapter 7

READING THE SIGNS

"I think, Toddy," Father Din said, hesitatingly, "I think you should check into a hotel. Is there one near here?"

"There's the St. Christopher," said Opal. "That's only a few blocks from here, right up the Strip. But it's a real dump. The nightstalkers turn tricks there. Everybody calls it The Busy Nook."

"What do you think?" Father Din asked Toddy. "At least it's close. Is it safe?" he asked Opal.

"What's safe? Safe as any place. They don't like trouble."

"I can't think," Toddy said. "I'll do whatever you think is best. But what about Dedi? We can't leave him . . . like that."

"I don't know yet," said Father Din. "There are other things involved. If a connection is made right now between Dedi and Monk, and Monk finds out about it, I don't know what the consequences will be for Jack, or . . ."

"Or for me," Toddy finished his sentence.

"Or me either," said Opal.

Father Din remembered Monk's vivid threat—I'll track you down and kill you! He said, "I think it would be best if you checked in that hotel. Then I'll go and get help—advice."

Tiger placed a cup of steaming black mud in front of Father Din, and drinks before Toddy and Opal.

"I put a good strong shot in the coffee," he said.

"I wish you hadn't done that," said Father Din. His head was just beginning to clear.

"Look," Tiger said, "I been in this business a long time, and I know when a guy should take a drink and when he shouldn't. You had a lot to drink when you was in here this afternoon, and if I ever saw a hangover, you got it. Go on, drink it. You need it. Do like I say, like I was your old man, O.K.?"

It was the first time that Father Din had smiled in hours, and it hurt. He took a sip of the laced coffee for Tiger's benefit.

"Attaboy!" Tiger exclaimed, pleased. "I think I'll have one myself. I need it after the day I've had." He threw his hands out. "Look at this place! Empty! Everybody's still scared to come in."

"Why don't you close up?" asked Father Din. "It's two-thirty."

"This is my home," said Tiger. "I live here."

He looked at Tiger, who had literally wrestled with life. He thought of his own father, who had seized the day against evil. Somehow he had entered the wrong tunnel when too young to have read the signs correctly. It was a fine tunnel for those like Father Ryan who were meant to go in that direction, but it was wrong for him, and he for it. For the right man it might have led to light, but it had brought him to this dark time and place. He was determined to back out of it and find the right entrance to the right way before it was too late.

Chapter 8

STALKING MONK

Instead of the one "good, stiff drink" he'd planned to have, Jack Muir had had three. First Opal and Elga, then Toddy and Father Din had passed by across the street from where he sat, but Muir had not been looking out, instead he'd been looking inwards, at himself, and not liking what he saw.

Now, determined, he climbed the first three flights of stairs leading to Toddy's apartment, taking the steps two at a time. But he took the last flight with less resolution and a great deal more caution. He edged along the hallway, his back to the wall that was on the door side, his revolver held out ahead of him, in his right hand. Halfway down the hall, he realized that the door to Toddy's apartment was open. The pool of light there was streaming from her kitchen. But there was no sound from the apartment. No one spoke. Nothing!

Perhaps, he thought, Monk had laid a trap for him, something humiliating, or perhaps deadly. Fear raced over his nerves as fingertips race over the strings of a harp. Still, he slid toward the open door, his back against the wall, tiny bubbles of cold sweat breaking on his forehead, heart pounding.

He stood next to the open door and waited for some sign from within. Then the thought came terrible upon him that he did not wish to hurt anyone, not even Monk. He breathed heavily, his heart fluttering. "I must be crazy," he thought. But now he was as much afraid to move away from the door as he was to enter it. Still, no sound. But this was it. If he did nothing now, he would damn himself forever. He eased

206

himself away from the wall, leaned forward, and looked in the door.

Monk lay sprawled back in a chair at the kitchen table, his head sunk down on his chest, asleep. Muir felt faint with relief. He dropped into a squatting position, his right hand hanging over his right knee, loosely holding the revolver, and his left hand to his forehead. He took several slow, deliberate deep breaths, trying to slow the pounding of his heart. When he resumed a standing position, the blood rushed to his head, and again he had to wait to get his equilibrium. Then, very cautiously, he stepped inside the apartment.

He went quietly into the livingroom, peeked into the bed-room, and returned to the kitchen. Two Scotch bottles, one empty, one nearly full, were ranged on the table. There was a bloody towel on the floor beside a chair. The broken wrap-per of a Band-Aid lay beside that. Whatever had happened, Muir reasoned, it couldn't have been very serious, or a Band-Aid would not have sufficed to take care of it.

He leveled the long-barreled revolver on Monk's slowly lifting and falling chest with a shaking hand. He thumbed the hammer back. He leaned into a step toward Monk. But just then Monk gave a grunt out of his sleep and Muir's trigger-finger reacted, in a reflex, tensing, and the hammer fell with a dull metallic snap on an empty chamber. Muir's heart nearly failed him.

Chapter 9

"STAY WITH ME"

His scalp was still tight and his hair still standing on end five minutes later. He had plunged from the apartment. He was leaning against the front of Toddy's building, still trying to calm the erratic beating of his heart, when he saw Pilar Pavon's taxicab draw to a stop at the curb.

Once Jack was settled in the cab, and the cab was on its way, Pilar asked: "What you doing, Jack, hanging around in front of Toddy's place like that, eh? You was looking for trouble, no? Oh, Jack, you a fool!"

"I guess I am," Muir said mechanically. He had forgotten to load the revolver. It held only one bullet in its cylinder of six chambers. But being a fool had its compensations. If the pistol had been fully loaded, Monk would be dead and he, Jack Muir, would be a murderer.

"Have you seen Toddy?" he asked.

"Don't speak to me about her," Pilar said, moving away from his side.

But Muir demanded an answer.

"Yes, I saw her," Pilar snapped. "When I picked up my stuff, before midnight. Her new boyfriend was with her."

"Was she all right?"

"Sure, she was O.K." Pilar stared straight ahead, coldly.

"Monk must have been pretty drunk tonight."

"I think so. At first, he wouldn't give me my stuff."

"How does he get along with this . . . friend of Toddy's."

Pilar shrugged. "I don't know."

"Do you know anything about this guy?"

"No."

They fell silent for a few minutes; then Pilar said: "You ask so many questions, now you tell me if you have seen my brother?"

"He was up at my place earlier, at around eight. Haven't you seen him?"

"No. He wasn't with Monk yet, when I was there. I hope he is at home. I worry so much. He always coughing. And where have you been? I no see you in a long time. Why you not come to see me? You no love Pilar anymore? You only like women who shit from up high?"

"I've been doing something."

"What? You painting a picture?"

"No."

"Well, what you been doing?"

"Something I had to do alone."

"What?"

"I've been kicking."

"What?"

"I've kicked, Pilar. I'm through with junk. I'm clean. I'm only taking meth. I'm going to kick off completely."

Pilar looked at him, uncertain. If true, what would this mean to her, she wondered.

Did you tell Dedi?"

"Yes."

"Did you meet Monk tonight? No, I guess you didn't."

"No."

"Then he will know . . ."

"Know what? For all he knows, I could be dead."

"Shhh!" Pilar hissed. "You must never say such a thing! To speak of yourself as dead . . ."

"Crap!"

"No, it's true. But tomorrow I will fix it up with my spiritist. Don't worry. But Monk; he is the one you do not want to know about it. He will come against you now."

Muir remembered the snap of the empty revolver. "He won't bother me," he said. "He's got what he wanted."

"Then you don't wish to go back to Toddy?"

"What does it matter what I wish," asked Muir, quietly.

"And what does it matter what I wish, either?" asked Pilar. "Nobody care what I wish."

"Maybe I better get out," said Muir, leaning forward to tap the driver.

"No, Jack," said Pilar, taking his arm, "please come home with me. I make you something good to eat. I no quarrel, I promise."

Muir sat back in the seat, feeling like a heel. His gaunt, tired-eyed face betrayed a profound exhaustion.

"You look terrible," said Pilar, after a pause. "Stay with me tonight, Jack, eh? I have a surprise for you. It is something I will show you tonight. I will show you how much I love you. Ah, Jack, *que bontos ojos blue tienes*. What pretty blue eyes you have. Please stay with me all night, Jack."

Muir looked at the young woman. "Yes," he said wearily, "I'll stay with you.

Chapter 10

CHECK IN

Camel-faced Felix Potter, a large blue welt on his left temple, sat behind the imitation-onyx-topped desk of the St. Christopher Hotel, in an old-fashioned oak swivel chair, his bulging eyes at half mast, dreaming of keyholes. The bell banged him awake. "Yes," he said, jumping to his feet. Dignity assumed him as a sheet assumes a ghost. "What might I do for you?" Not the type for the Busy Nook, he thought. *He* would never bring a young woman like *that* to a place like *this*. . . . "Do you wish a room?" He had decided upon cordiality.

"Yes," said the young woman.

Ah, it was *her* party. Of course, it would be. There was a dark, morning shadow on the man's jaws and chin. Big fellow, his face, across the bridge of his nose, seemed swollen. Barroom brawl? She, slumming, probably picked him up in one of the joints on the Strip. Been drinking all day, and now this: out-of-the-way, and what all. The man, who had been about to speak, fell back into silence. *She* had decided. Strange, too, for she would be easy to take.

"A double?" Potter persisted, amused.

"Yes." Again, *she* decided.

"Sign here," Potter said for the first time that day. He usually just handed a hooker a key and received it back a half hour later.

"That's a nasty looking bruise," she said.

"Yes," said Potter. "A most unusual thing occurred here this evening." His loquacity would get him in trouble one day. Why scare them off? They looked promising. But the Devil teased him on. "Most unusual indeed. We were robbed. First time since I've been in the hotel business. Twenty-five years. Some young hoodlum walked in here and knocked me unconscious. Could have killed me." He snapped his fingers. "Just like that."

"That's terrible," she said.

"Yes. Cleaned us out. A very unpleasant experience, I assure you."

"Oh, I should think so."

"'Twas. Terrible. Oh, well, that's the way of it nowadays. Here's your key. Room 22, second floor, to the left. You can walk up. I'm afraid the phones are out of order, something to do with the storm, but if you want anything—"

"That'll be all right," she said, snatching the key. She went up the stairs, the man following behind almost as if reluctant to go with her.

"Strange pair," thought Potter, popping a violet-flavored lozenge into his mouth, and sinking into his swivel chair.

Chapter 11

CONFESSION

In room 22, Toddy pulled off her coat and threw herself on the bed with a sigh of relief. She closed her eyes, shutting out a jagged crack in the ceiling plaster. "What a dump!"

Father Din looked about the room, more than a bit disheartened at the thought of leaving her in such a fleabag. "If you'd rather go someplace else . . . ."

"Where could we go? You know we couldn't find a legitimate cab in this snow at this time of night. And no car service will pick up anyone from this place." She opened her eyes and smiled at Father Din. "Really, this'll be fine until tomorrow. Besides, I can't move. I wouldn't go anywhere else if you offered to carry me. I'll tell you one thing. I don't think Monk would ever think to look for me here. He'd think I had better taste." She paused, and said, "Sam, come over here and lie down with me."

"No, no, Toddy—I'm afraid I can't. I have somebody I must see. Somebody I think can help us. I've never felt myself to be such a fool as I do tonight. I should have done something!"

Toddy sat up, looking at him. "There was nothing you could have done. You did what you could," she emphasized.

"But it's much more than just that, Toddy," he said. "Much more."

"Are you married? Is that it?"

"No . . ."

"Then you're not married?"

"No. I'm a priest."

"A *priest!*" She sat up, stared at him, unbelieving. "You're a priest?"

"Yes. My real name is Michael Din . . . Father Michael Din."

"*Michael* . . . that's what you meant. I thought—when you said 'My name is Michael'—I thought you were quoting something . . ." An ironic little smile shaped Toddy's mouth. "Well, I'll be damned!" she cried, slapping her forehead. She sat up on the edge of the bed. "If I don't have the craziest luck."

She looked at him. "You know, I've only known you for about—what?—twelve hours, but we've been through so much together . . . I thought I knew you." She turned away and sat silently for a few moments. Then she turned back, looking at Father Din. "Now I understand so much," she said. "But what were you doing?"

"I'm not sure I know myself."

"All right," she said decisively, "never mind that. But if you could just tell me one thing . . ."

"What is it?"

"Do you like me? Do you care about me? Do you want me? I have a right to know, don't I? I'm frightened. If I only

215

understood how you feel. You see, I'm ready to try something new. I don't want any more of what I've been having. Tonight was the end for me. I've had it."

"Doesn't my being a priest change any of that?"

"I'm afraid not," Toddy said. "Well, maybe," she added, "but I feel the same about you. I suppose I should feel badly about having been with a priest, but I don't. After all, I didn't know. And besides, I think the moral sense has gone numb in me. I need . . . love. Do you understand?" She threw up her hands. "Priest or not, I want you to keep on being Sam. Can you? For my sake?"

"Can you accept an honest answer, Toddy?"

"I think so."

"Then my answer is that I don't know yet. But I'm coming to a conclusion. Something's been building in me for . . . well, actually for years. It's the only answer I can give you now. But you asked me before if I liked you. I do like you. More than any woman I've ever known. That answers another question, too. Yes, I do care. But I won't be any good to you or anyone until I find my way."

Toddy's eyes filled; but she said: "You said that you were going to see someone who could help us?"

"Yes."

"Well, when you go, take this key with you, in your pocket. Touch it, think of me, and if you want to come back tonight, I'll be here."

216

"I'd better go now," he said.

"You're a man of principle, aren't you, Sam? Or Michael," Toddy corrected. "Well, Michael, remember while you're gone that principles are cold things. A woman is warmer than a principle."

Chapter 12

THE SHOCK OF RECOGNITION

Toddy was not able to sleep. When Father Din left, she'd got undressed and into a bed that sank in the middle like a hammock. Now she lay on her side, watching as the blue-and-red neon sign outside the window blinked its monotonous signal.

ST. CHRIST PHER (RED)

(————————————)

ST. CHRIST PHER (BLUE)

(————————————)

ST. CHRIST PHER (RED)

(————————————)

ST. CHRIST PHER (BLUE)

(————————————)

O.K., O.K.," she exclaimed irritably, "I believe you," and tossed over to face the semi-dark. But the sign appeared there as a shadow on the wall. Exasperated, she leaped out of bed, turned on the light, and lighted a cigarette. She began pacing up and down, barefooted, on a rug that felt like mouse-skin.

The room was warm, stuffy. Apparently, heat, needed by the naked, was the only convenience demanded at The Busy

Nook. She relived each moment of the previous day and of this morning in her mind. She knew that she wanted Sam Hopkins, Michael, and it was so wild an idea that she became even more agitated. A priest! Sam Hopkins. No! Father Michael Din. Mike, she tried the new name in her mind. No, he would prefer to be called Michael.

How long can a woman go on loving a ghost? It was as though Jack Muir had died long ago, and she had gone on, as if in mourning, like some wife of an ancient time, waiting for death, waiting to join him. Why hadn't Monk buried her with Jack?

Oh, yes, she had loved Jack. Patiently, she had waited for his return from his living death, his zombie-life. He had refused to return to her. Yet still she had waited. But there must be an end.

She stopped pacing abruptly. The hand holding her cigarette dropped to her side and her shoulders hunched to her neck. She stood frozen. Then the bulging eyes, the lugubrious camel-like face dropped away from the transom. She heard fast footsteps going down the hall. She didn't hear herself scream, but someone in the next room did.

"Knock it off in there!" came a cry.

Chapter 13

NIGHT LIFE

Now where are you tonight, Michael? Father Ryan wondered. Oh, my boy, you have given this old man a very difficult day. You have shown me how indispensable you have become to me, in practical affairs, and in the heart, too. For Father Din had a full and loving heart, as anyone could see.

Father Ryan opened his wallet and removed a tattered and folded page, on which Father Din had typed a poem he had written some years earlier. The poem had disturbed Father Ryan when he first read it, with its evidence of Father Din's early forays into the dark side, but he had come to see the compassionate disillusionment of the piece, its sadness for the sufferings of humankind. It was called "Night Life."

> *When I've gone out to walk at night,*
> *to tour the streets, mean-dark, false-bright,*
> *of this sick city that is no home*
> *but for the Giant and the Gnome,*
> *the Monsters of Despair, I've seen*
> *pathetic sights and sights obscene:*
> *The fat black man who has no eyes*
> *but two great holes from which he cries*
> *long hours, holding out his cup*
> *for Times Square crowds to fill it up;*
> *the woman with the bleeding leg*
> *who climbs the subway stairs to beg;*
> *the legless men who crabwise creep*
> *on wooden gloves to morning sleep;*

the varicosed, tumescent, sick,
already dead and yet still quick;
*   male hustlers, leaning in long rows,*
posed in mock movie-hero pose;
*   porn shops with tainted men inside*
some of whom have kissed a bride;
*   retarded vendors at their stands*
masturbating, hiding hands
beneath big stacks of filthy mags;
*   and drunks on jags, and hags in rags,*
asleep in doorways commandeered
from rats and stiffs; the other weird
displaying signs of coming doom
Hellfire and Brimstone in the tomb;
*   and faces stupefied by dope,*
expressionless of love or hope—
*   these sights and worse are near Times Square*
at night when I go walking there.

Yes, anyone could see that Father Din was a deeply caring young man, but that alone did not prove a vocation for the priesthood, the discipline and sense of responsibility required. Other vocations require discipline and responsibility, but they may also require a deep subjective involvement or a highly objective distancing. The priest should position himself at a middle distance, and maintain his equilibrium there. Michael tended to extremes.

At first, Father Ryan's new young curate had been a blessing. Father Ryan was in his late sixties and had little energy to spare. Father Din relieved him of calls for Last Rites and funerals, attended Boys Club meetings, helped with the parish drug rehab program (of which Billy Sawyer, Rose Figlia's boyfriend, was a graduate), and acted as minister to the many AIDS victims of the Chelsea parish. But that was during the

221

period of Michael's hyperactivity, a time when Father Ryan had begun to suspect that there might be something wrong with this piling on of labors. As when, for instance, in summer, when all else seemed to fail to distract the young curate, he'd plunge into the cold, blue rippling water of the Parish Athletic Club pool, and drive furiously from end to end like a trapped seal. Father Ryan thought that there was something desperate about this, because it did not appear to be an act of pleasure. And when the young priest assumed more and more things to do that simply need not be done, and did the things that did need to be done with such frenetic energy, things that by now seemed to be taxing his strength, perhaps even his emotional health, something, Father Ryan began to suspect, must be seriously amiss, and something must be done to find out what it was.

The confessional was no help. Father Din said nothing in the confessional that indicated a problem, and, outside the confessional, had ceased altogether to speak of personal things to the older priest, who now felt cut off from one for whom he felt no small affection.

Lately things had changed for the worse. Father Din began to drop duties and to go off by himself, neglecting his work to spend his time God knew where or how. And, if Father Ryan was not particularly adept at the finer points of scholastic philosophy, the years having robbed him of much learning, time and experience had given him a functional understanding of the major motives of humankind. He knew people and the signs of their discontent. Father Din had something on his mind. Father Ryan essayed that it was women. Yes, and Father Ryan knew women. How should he not, who had been raised amidst the caterwaul of seven sisters?

222

But where was Father Din now? Gone for long evenings, even overnight. He had sat up all night tonight, waiting to confront Father Din. He had read and drunk coffee and had had an occasional Irish whiskey and then more coffee. He was determined to stay awake until Father Din returned. He was reading Father Thom Corrigan's book, *Husbands of the Church*, and getting angrier and angrier.

Sipping from a large glass of Irish whiskey, he tried to think charitably, but found that he could not. He felt that it was wrong of him to think it, but think it he did—Thom Corrigan was a disgrace to the priesthood. He prayed the Lord to forgive him for his lack of charity; but it was a deep additional worry all that night, that he knew there to be some association between young Father Din and Thom Corrigan, the celebrity, the poet-priest and political activist, for they had been seen together several times and it had been mentioned to him, in the way of warning. Lord, it is Your way to try us constantly.

Father Ryan turned the lights low and sat smoking a lumpy green cigar. He would wait. He would wait. He would wait. The cigar ember died and went cold.

Chapter 14

SCENARIO FOR SCORSESE

Father Ryan was on a television talk show. He was debating Father Corrigan, who was defending situational ethics. The host agreed with Father Corrigan and was openly hostile to Father Ryan. The audience was hostile too, and booed him as he began to defend his position. "The only morality," Father Ryan shouted back at them, "is a shared morality. The only morality is a shared morality, the only morality is a shared morality, the—"

Father Din removed the dead cigar from Father Ryan's hand and shook his shoulder.

"Father! Father! You're having a nightmare," he said.

Father Ryan shook himself free of the horrible dream. "Michael . . . Where have you been? I've been worried."

"I'm sorry, Father."

"I'll turn on the table-light."

"I must talk to you, Father."

"Oh, my, what's happened to you? You look terrible." Father Ryan studied Father Din's appearance with deep shock. The young man was in blood-spattered civilian clothes, his nose and the front of his face near his nose were swollen and distorted. There was a dark, rather bluish tint under both of his eyes. "Have you been mugged?"

"Father, I've got to speak with you . . . about—I'm afraid I'm in trouble."

"Should we go to confession?

"No. I want to tell you things, but I must speak to you as a man."

Father Ryan went to his desk, sat down, and leaned back. Now he was tight-lipped, staring at his young curate. He felt that this was it. He was glad that the young priest wanted simply to talk, for now he might be able to get to the bottom of things, but he was also more than a little afraid of what he was going to hear.

"You're always offering me Irish whiskey, Father. I'd like one now."

Father Ryan said nothing, but rose, crossed the room, and returned with two tall glasses filled with whiskey. "In vino veritas," he said, clinking his glass against Michael's. "But I don't know if that applies to Irish whiskey. Sometimes I think that it causes much more blarney than truth. Go ahead, Michael. I've been expecting something like this for some time."

Father Din said, "I've got to begin somewhere. Let me begin with an only child who worshiped his father, who wanted more than anything in the world to be just like him, but that father wanted the child to be something else, something that he thought was superior—a priest.

225

"When those who led the Jersey City Archdiocese selected that little choir boy for the priesthood—robbing the cradle, as it were—they had no idea how they were distorting the dreams of a child. But when the child's father was proud, honored, what then could the child say? Could he go against the father that he loved? Anyway, everything seemed so distant and unreal then. It only seemed that the child had to go through this thing and somehow come out on the other end of it.

"At Seton Hall, I never doubted for a moment that all this would be over some day and that I would be what I'd always wanted to be, like my father, a cop. Yes, a cop! The rest of it didn't seem real. Then in seminary—all right, it was six lousy years of Latin—it was asking who should be saved, the woman or the child—but I was still going to be a chip off the old block. Once this was over, I would be me again, I would be like my Dad, somehow I would be a cop. But it didn't stop. I found myself here. What was I thinking? That, now, I couldn't disappoint my father's memory, that I must somehow remain a priest, that I must wear alien clothing and live an alien life? I am Michael Din. I am my father's son. He had no right to do this to me. Nor did the Church. And forgive me, Father—my dear Father Ryan—neither did you."

"You are in a crisis of doubt, Michael."

"Doubt! Yes! All doubt!"

"Why haven't I heard any of this in Confession? How have you managed to keep it secret?"

"Let me recite my newest poem. It's called "Scenario for Scorsese."

226

"Who is Scorsese?"

"A movie director, Father. This poem is a form of confession. It'll make things clear to you."

"Go ahead," said Father Ryan, chomping his cigar.

Father Din began to recite, his voice wavering:

> "There was a young priest
> who stalked the pornographic
> night of the X-rated
> movie houses and the
> prostituting streets
> outside them in what had
> become a sexual compulsion.
> Sometimes he felt that he had lost
> all control of himself and
> with that loss his very soul.
> But his soul was saved through
> the confession of his sins
> and their forgiveness
> by a fellow priest who
> was not his own publicly
> acknowledged confessor
> but a fellow sinner,
> an older priest who had had
> a twenty-year quasi-marriage
> and who would in turn ask
> the young priest for
> absolution after
> confessing to him. When
> the young priest made
> confession to his acknowledged

confessor and spiritual guide
a little later, he had only
to confess to the evil
thoughts of the days since
he last stalked the streets,
thereby keeping his
spiritual guide in the dark.
He behaves as if in a
dream when he is in the grip
of this compulsion, as if
he himself has become a
character in the dirty
movie he is watching,
and in this state of
disassociation picks up
the first prostitute he sees,
and, with release, becomes
guilt-ridden and disgraced
until he must seek out
his secret-confessor.
He will find a telephone
within minutes of the event,
plug in the number, wait,
and say in a voice
thick with mixed emotions
of shame and anger,
"I must see you."
His secret confessor
never refuses,
no priest does,
but he will take
the confession with a
heavy heart, for
his friend and
for himself. The

confession, it seems,
has become part of
the compulsion, as both
have come to suspect.
Advice is traded,
elements of which might
have proven helpful to
either priest, but none
has been acted on,
until . . ."

"Until what?" said Father Ryan.

"I don't know," said Father Din.

"Even your style has changed. You write like a hippie now. I
presume the other priest is Thom Corrigan, and I presume the
poetical influence is his as well. I won't presume to judge the
poetry, however, but the story it tells is an extremely hurtful
one to me, personally. It shows an ultimate distrust in me, an
ultimate lack of faith in my ability to understand, and it shows
a priestly dishonor in both you and Thom Corrigan. Do you
still believe in God?"

"Of course I do. I am and always will be a good Catholic,
like my father, but I was not made to be a priest. I'm wrong
for it. Perhaps not good enough. Definitely not good
enough.

"Do you know, Father, that until no more than a few months
ago I had never seen a woman naked? I have been counseling
people on their sexual problems when they know more than I
do. Old ladies know more than I do, or knew more. I wasn't
fit to talk to them.

229

"I know that you know what a priest-teaser is, Father, one of those women, or sometimes men, who try to titillate the priest in the confessional with lurid tales of sex, going into the most graphic detail. I don't know that this boy of whom I am about to speak was like that, but he would come to me constantly, and tell me about his visits to pornographic movie houses. He would describe in detail, though I would try to stop him, acts of which I could not even conceive. When I asked myself what it was that I was doing, I would try to believe that I was trying to help him. How could I help him if I did not under-stand—I would tell myself—what he was talking about? I convinced myself that it was my duty—though certainly, in-stinctively, I knew I lied—to go and actually see some of these films.

"But there had to be more than what I saw. The actual expe-rience must be different. I had to find out. I picked up a prostitute one day, but the experience was so ugly—I'm sorry Father—so ugly that I could not believe that it represented what I hoped for . . . longed for. Now I *had* to know. I had to find a decent partner—I had to. And again I lied to my-self. Somehow, I developed an interest in the most avant-garde art, and began frequenting the galleries in the East Village and SoHo and TriBeCa, the artistic haunts. I would tell myself that I am going to look at art. I am going to listen to music. Lies! Lies! Lies! I was looking for life, real life, not the phantasma of the church. I was looking for a *woman*.

"Now, in retrospect, it all seems clear enough. But I swear to you, Father, by Jesus Christ whom we both love, I did not really know what I was doing until tonight. Tonight I made love to a real, live woman, a woman filled with tenderness, with passion, and now I know another part of life that that young choir boy in Jersey City has missed; a part of life, God forgive me, that has been stolen from him. From *me*!"

230

"Are you in love with this woman?"

"I don't know. Yes. No. I have no right to be. But let me tell you the rest. There's more. I'm in trouble, the deepest trouble."

"Trouble? What is it? Something else? Something more?"

"Father . . ."

"Connected with this woman, is it?" Father Ryan's face was stony.

"Yes. But there's so much more, I'm afraid."

"Speak plainly."

231

Chapter 15

EVERY SIN IN THE PROGRAM

Father Din recounted the events of his day, speaking slowly, in measured tones, trying, with great effort, to be perfectly truthful and factual.

Father Ryan listened, puffing a cigar, sipping whiskey, as the story was told. "You mean then," he said, waving smoke from his face, "that this boy may still be lying in that alley?"

"I'm afraid that it's possible, Father."

"Oh, Michael," Father Ryan said, shaking his head sadly. "Charity requires that I think of you as being in the grip of madness. I'd have to sit down at my computer and reckon them up, but I do believe that you have committed every sin the program."

"I committed a mortal sin, Father, yes. Toddy is married. But my sin doesn't nullify my ministrations to Dedi Pavon. The grace of Christ flows through my office as a priest and not through me."

"That is indeed correct; but the boy—"

"Father, under the circumstances, I did what I could. Please try to see that my actions would influence the safety of others. This man is possessed, Father, a killer."

"What you say, Michael, may be reasonable; it's the logic of a soldier or a policeman, however, and not that of a priest."

"It's the way I think, Father. I'm *not* a priest. That's what I'm trying to tell you!"

"But I *am* a priest. I am no longer a man. 'I live now, not I, but Christ lives in me.' That is St. Paul speaking. *Tu es Sacerdos*. You're a priest!"

"Well, St. Paul was wrong! Christ can live in a man, and in a husband as well. This is a new age, Father."

"The Church thinks not. *Roma locuta est. Causa Finita est.* What is a new age in eternity? You've caught the contagion of the Father Corrigans, the worldly men. You *blaspheme*!"

"And what of using our own God-given minds?"

"*Pride!*"

"But Father, shouldn't we take pride in what God has given?"

"Michael, I need not instruct you in the knowledge of our Church; I know that you understand these things as well, and perhaps better, than I do. If you choose to be perverse in your polemic, what can I say to you? Again, you're using the argument of the public man, not of the priest, who reasons out of faith. You must give one thing up to receive the other. You, like a willful child, would have all that your eyes rest upon. I am tired, Michael. You're too clever for me; but, even now, you are not being honest with yourself, and you know it."

"Please, Father, be calm, for the sake of your health."

233

"I'm perfectly calm, Michael. Now then, let's start by asking ourselves what has to be done. What do you say?"

"I must leave the priesthood."

Father Ryan shook his head. "No, Michael, it isn't over yet. That would be the easy way, and later you'd never forgive yourself for having taken it. You are engaged in a battle, and it has to be won or lost. You can't simply back off from it. You must win your way through to what you are going to become, whether it be a priest or something else. But faith will come. However, that wasn't what I was referring to. I meant what do you think should be done now. I want you to act."

"Call the police."

"Exactly. We must have this man Monk arrested, and you must help to build the case against him."

"I've been told that he walks in and out of police headquarters as if it were a hotel. And think, Father, if he were to get away with this, he would take reprisals against everyone involved."

"Are you afraid?"

"Not for myself, Father. I'm thinking of Toddy Muir and of her husband and others. I can't witness against this man without naming Toddy. And if I name her, she'll have to testify. I have no doubt at all that this man would be quite capable of killing both her and her husband."

"Then what we must do is see to it that this information gets into the right hands. I know just the man to contact. He's a narcotics detective, an able and honest man. I'll make a few

234

phone calls and find him. I think I have his home number. I'll call there first. I don't think he'll mind if I wake him. Not for something like this. In fact, I think he'll be grateful."

"Why do you think that, Father?"

"Because his daughter died of drugs and he hates those who deal in it."

"You're referring to Lieutenant Figlia, aren't you?"

"That's right. I forgot, you helped with Rose Figlia's funeral."

"Yes. And now I understand so much more about the whole situation. I understand life so much better, and I've seen everything in a new light. Father, I would rejoin myself, deserted long ago . . ."

"Faith, Michael. Faith. It will come. In the meantime, go and clean yourself up. Shower, shave, and put on the garb of the priest that you are—now and forever. It is my intention to have the Diocese send you away for rehabilitation. There is a place that takes care of sick priests—drug addicts, alcoholics, priests who have fallen ill of soul. Priests like you, Michael. I only wish I could send Father Thom Corrigan there, too, but—"

"He's a celebrity, and I'm nobody."

"Go and clean yourself up—your outer self, at least!"

PART FIVE

CYCLE OF FEAR

Chapter 1

CALLING IN A FAVOR

Lieutenant Figlia sat at a desk in the middle of the squad-room. He had chosen a place here amidst computers and telephones, rather than in Hubbard's office, for a reason: he was having a great deal of difficulty staying awake—the noise out here helped. Figlia put a stubbly chin in the elbow-braced palm of his left hand and looked out on the scene around him. He saw Monk Stolz wherever he looked.

The bluecoat at the desk in front of his was checking in an odd couple: a tall, skinny black man, and a short, muscular white woman. The man had several bandages about the head and face, the woman had a bandage over her right eye. They were both drunk or drugged; and yet, Figlia thought, they had probably sat in the emergency ward of a hospital for hours. They must have been in dandy condition when they were picked up. He listened as they were checked in . . .

"O.K.," the bluecoat said, "I'm in a hurry. You. What's your name?"

"Torrance Amsterdam."

"Age?"

"Twenty-six."

"Address?"

He gave it.

238

"What's in that case?"

"A sax. I'm a musician."

"He only thinks he is," said the woman.

"An' you only *think* you're a man."

"All right, cut it," snapped the bluecoat. "Haven't you two had enough for one night? You. What's your name, lady?"

"Elga Hargo."

"Lady?" said Tory. "Ha!"

"I said cut it," the bluecoat warned. "You, Hargo, what's your age?"

"Forty-two."

"Address?"

She gave it.

"Occupation?"

"She's a dyke," said Tory.

Elga leaped, grabbed Tory by the collar, and pushed him down over the officer's desk. Figlia jumped up and helped the bluecoat separate the battlers. Elga was taken across the room and handcuffed to a bench. Tory found that very funny, until he was warned that if he didn't behave he'd be

239

handcuffed to her free arm. He sat on the floor in front of the bluecoat's desk on his saxophone case and fell asleep.

"What's the story?" Figlia asked, mildly amused.

"Fight over a pool game."

"A pool game?"

"Well, that's what I get from them two. But there was a bimbo involved."

"Over a woman?"

"More likely. He took a poke at her, then she preceded to shove a billiard ball down his throat and try to wrap a cue-stick around his head. One tough broad!"

"He's on junk, isn't he?"

"You should see his arms. He's got enough tracks to operate a trans-continental railroad."

"Did he have anything on him?"

"A few bags—not much. He's no dealer."

"A few bags. That's enough for a nice long vacation up-state. How about her?"

"No, she was clean." The bluecoat glanced at Elga, then looked at Figlia, smiling, "Well, you know what I mean."

"Yeah. Well, she's got a nice assault charge. She won't be seeing her bimbo for a while either. You better check with the medical people about the guy; he's going to need something before the night is over. We don't want him keeping everybody awake. And I want to speak to him later. Both of them. I think they might have starred in a porno-flick I saw recently. Tell me when they've sobered up."

"Yes, sir."

From across the room another officer called: "Lieutenant Figlia, there's a call for you. You want to take it at your desk?"

"Switch it here," Figlia called back. He put the receiver to his ear. "Yes? Figlia here."

"Lieutenant Figlia?"

"Yes?"

"This is Father Ryan."

"Well, Father! Good to hear from you."

"It's good to speak with you again, Albert. The Parish misses you."

"I know you're joking, Father."

"I have faith that you'll return to the fold, Albert."

"Perhaps so, Father. But what prompts this call? It's after four in the morning. It's hard to believe you'd wake in the middle of the night with a sudden urge to save me. How did you know where I was, anyhow? I'm only here on temporary assignment."

"I took the liberty of calling your home. I'm afraid I woke your lovely wife. But I simply had to talk with you. It's something of the utmost seriousness. Both a police matter and a matter involving the Church. In fact, it involves a priest, my assistant and curate, Father Michael Din."

"Well, what is it, Father?"

"Have you received a report on the body of a young boy—about sixteen years of age—being found? The body would have been found in an alley. The boy was small and dark-complected, a Puerto Rican."

"I haven't heard of anything tonight. Is this a certainty?"

"Yes."

"I'll check it out. But how does your priest fit in?"

Father Ryan told him. Now Figlia was wide awake. "The man called himself Monk?"

"Yes," said Father Ryan, "Monk. I suppose you'd like to speak with Father Din?"

"Absolutely. I'll have a patrol car pick him up. Have him wait there."

"He'll be ready and waiting. Albert, is Father Din in any trouble?"

"Not with us, Father—not if his story checks out. Sounds like he might be in a lot of trouble with you, though. And maybe with Monk Stolz."

"He's a good young man, Albert. You'll see to his interests, won't you? He's only confused."

"I'll look after him, Father. And, Father . . . Thanks. I mean for calling me personally. This is a big one. I think when I explain what's happened to Gena, she'll even forgive you for waking her up."

"Give her my blessings, Albert. And thank you."

Chapter 2

DEAD BIRD, LIVE FOX

Figlia issued the order for one of his patrol cars to cross precinct boundaries and go into Chelsea to pick up Father Din. It was made clear that he was only a witness and was to be treated with the respect due a priest. Figlia had in mind the fact that Father Din might not be dressed as a priest. He also ordered that Father Din be kept in the patrol car, and not allowed to enter the station. Figlia would go out to the car. If there were spies in the station, Figlia had no intention of allowing them to discover anything. He checked his pistol. If Stolz so much as blinked an eye, Figlia would put a bullet through it.

He put on his overcoat, hat, scarf, and gloves. Then he went and stood inside the front door, waiting for the patrol car to pull up. Outside was a kaleidoscopic lace of snow on night, broken only by the faint red glow of the turning beacons of a few parked prowl cars.

Figlia felt positively gleeful. According to Father Ryan, Monk was drugged, and sitting up in an apartment with the door wide open, in a drug-induced sleep.

Figlia smoked, and eventually a patrol car came crunching up, hubcap-deep in snow, to the front of the station. There was a big, dark fellow in the back seat. Figlia pushed through the door and went, slipping, down the steps, and got into the car next to the back-seat passenger.

"You're Father Din?"

"Yes."

"I'm Al Figlia. What's the address?"

"I don't know. But if you drive straight ahead, I'll point out the house. It's a few blocks."

"All right, Father, we're not going to set any speed records in this snow, so you tell me all about it on the way. Officer . . ."

"Yes, sir?"

"No siren, no noise, everything very quiet—got it?"

"Yes, sir."

"Go ahead, Father."

"Well, it's just as Father Ryan told you . . ."

"I want it from you, Father."

Father Din told him, and Figlia listened. "That's all of it, then?" Figlia asked.

"Yes. Except for details. My father was a cop," Father Din put in. "A Jersey City detective."

"He was?

"Yes. He always wanted me to be a priest, but I wanted to be a cop like him. I was in attendance at your daughter's funeral, Lieutenant."

"You were? You know then why I want this S.O.B."

"I understand," said Father Din.

"Douse the beacon," Figlia said to the driver.

"I have already, sir."

"There it is," said Father Din, "on the right there."

"Pull in here," Figlia ordered. The driver pulled the car in to the curb, climbing crunchingly up on drifting snow. They got out.

"You," Figlia said to the driver— "Stay at the door. No one out. You," he said to the driver's partner, "and you," to Father Din, "you come with me." He led the way into the alley beside the building.

"I don't see anything," said the driver's partner.

"There was no report on it," said Figlia, "the body's got to be here." The driver's partner waved a flashlight up and down the narrow, snow-filled alley.

"It was near the rear of the house," Father Din said.

"There it is," said Figlia quietly. He pointed to a small mound in the snow, near the wall of the next building. The driver's partner aimed the beam of the flashlight at the place.

They went to it. Dedi's twisted, smashed, rigor-mortised little body lay under a two-inch blanket of snow. It reminded Father Din of the corpse of a frozen bird—but no peacock, a dead sparrow. He looked away.

"All right," Figlia said, "that's that. Come on." The driver, the driver's partner, and Father Din, in that order, followed the fast-moving Figlia into the house and up the stairs. The alarmed, angry superintendent stood watching them ascend, his eyes crusted with sleep, shivering in his tattered robe.

Figlia took the stairs two at a time, gun in hand. At the fifth floor landing, he stopped and turned to the bluecoats behind him. Seeing that Father Din had followed, Figlia gestured for him to go back down the stairs. Then, too involved to give further thought to the priest, he turned and went on to Toddy's door. It was shut.

Father Din said he'd left the door wide open, Monk asleep. The shut door was a bad sign. Figlia tried it. It was locked. He cursed under his breath.

Figlia indicated that the driver's partner should kick the door in. The driver's partner was a big man, well over two-hundred pounds. One lunging kick over the doorknob and the lock snapped. The door swung open. There was no one in the kitchen. If Monk was in one of the other rooms, he'd be awake; he'd know. There was no point in being quiet.

"Stolz!" Figlia called out.

Silence.

"This is the police, Stolz," Figlia called. "Come out in the open. Let's see you." But even as he called, Figlia knew his man was gone. He edged into the kitchen, the two bluecoats following. Father Din waited at the door. He saw Figlia go into the livingroom, kick open the bedroom door, look, then with a very audible curse re-holster his revolver, and come back into the kitchen.

"You," Figlia said to the driver's partner, "go down and call the wagon. And the B.C.I. I want pictures of the body. Hold on. Notify the M.E. and the D.A.'s office. I want everything involved here on all the records. I'm going to play this strictly kosher, just in case it adds up to something later. And you," he said to the driver, "start searching this place, top to bottom."

"Don't you need a warrant?" asked Father Din.

"No," said Figlia, sniffing at the mouth of a Scotch bottle. He took a long draft from it, then went over to the driver and handed him the bottle. "Have a drink. Warm you up," he said. "It's on the house." Figlia looked at Father Din. "You told me he'd been drugged. That Scotch is clean."

"He had been," said Father Din. "The other bottle. But that was about three hours ago. He must have come out of it. He's very strong."

Figlia nodded thoughtfully. "And realized that he'd better get out," he said. "You realize, do you, that he probably intended to kill you?"

"Yes, I see that now."

"Only he had to play games about it. That's his weakness, and that's what saved you. If that girl Opal hadn't drugged him, he probably would've shot you up and tossed you off the roof, too. I hope you realize that you've behaved very recklessly, Father."

"Yes. I see that now."

"Where is Toddy Muir now, Father?"

From outside could be heard the faint whine of sirens.

"She's checked in at the St. Christopher Hotel."

Figlia shook his head disgustedly. "That whorehouse! All right," he said. "Shall I have you driven back to the Rectory?"

"I'd appreciate it," said Father Din.

"I'll want to speak with you tomorrow. I'll want a statement."

"I'll come in," said Father Din.

"Make it at three," said Figlia.

There was a clamor in the hall, and four officious policemen entered the apartment. Figlia told one of them to drive Father Din back to the Rectory. But as he was being driven along the Strip, through a blizzard of snow, Father Din remembered Toddy's last words: "I'm warmer than a principle."

He told the driver to let him out, and trudged the rest of the way through the storm to The Busy Nook, knowing that Father Ryan, and perhaps Figlia, would be furious with him. "To hell," he said, trudging on.

Chapter 3

GETTING IT RIGHT

The transom was shut and a towel hung over the doorknob, blocking the keyhole from all eyes, yet Toddy could not feel at ease. It was silly of her, she felt, to be so shaken by a Peeping Tom, but shaken she was. Something like this might have been expected in such a place, and Peeping Toms, she had heard, were generally harmless and quite timid people. But the events of the day had left her emotionally vulnerable. She had lain across the bed and cried for nearly an hour, until the shock had subsided. She should have left the St. Christopher, had she known where to go at this hour of the night—or morning—but for the thought that Sam—Father Din, she corrected herself—might return. He would not be able to find her, and she did not know where to find him. No, she must get hold of herself; it was only that the spookiness of her nerves tormented her.

The grotesque, leering face in the transom had come into her vision like a negative reply to a prayer. As if God had said: "See what you are asking? Well, here's your answer." But she knew that this was not God's answer; it was her own; her guilt whispering in her ear. And meanwhile, outside, over and over again—

ST. CHRIST PHER (RED)

(———————-)

ST. CHRIST PHER (BLUE)

250

(————————-)

ST. CHRIST PHER (RED)

(————————-)

It was stupid, she knew: but somehow that sign seemed to drill at her a warning. It was Christ, Christ, Christ, Christ, over and over, and it was ominous, frightening, for she had long ago renounced that Christ.

And down the street, only a few doors away, stood the scissors factory, its terrifying pair of forty-foot high shears always poised to cut the sky in half. She was being superstitious, primitive. Like Father Din, she was seeing signs.

She did not, for the moment, remember her own fascination, and even belief in, astrology, and other occult pseudo-sciences. The sinner always hopes that the experience of sinning will be a more profound one than it is. The sin turns out to be merely unhealthy, and the sinner sickly. She had thought of these things. Now, she got up from the bed and went to the window. She hadn't noticed how hard it was snowing, nor how wild the wind was. She stood looking out into a night that was paling with the coming dawn. The street below was aflood with heaping, drifting flakes. A ghost of snow moved through it with a gentle, sweeping motion; then, caught in an upper wind, whirled away, dissolved, was gone, mingled in the thick white air.

She did not know her own heart. "Suppose," she thought, "that Sam—Father Din—comes along in the snow, coming to me? Should I let him in? Would it be wrong? Should I turn him away?" And what about Jack? "Where are you, Jack?"

251

ST. CHRIST PHER (RED)

(————————-)

ST. CHRIST PHER (BLUE)

(————————-)

ST. CHRIST PHER (RED)

(————————-)

And so she turned with an idea, and went to the bureau and opened the top drawer. It was there! She couldn't save herself from a little, nervous laugh. "It's a plot," `she said aloud, taking the Gideon Bible from the drawer. "Everyone's trying to save me." She went to the bed, lay down, and began to read at random in the book. It was Job—whose story she read through. Then she shut the Bible and went back to the window. There were fresh foot-tracks in the snow in front of the hotel. And just then a soft knock came at the door. "Who is it?" she called, frightened and at the same time hopeful. "Who's there?"

"It's me—Michael."

Toddy gave a small, wild cry of relief, and ran to the door. She pulled it open and there stood a tall snowman.

"You're covered with it," Toddy said, backing into the room.

"I've been to see Father Ryan—my boss—and the police have been notified," he said. "They've picked up Dedi's body. Monk was gone . . ."

"Aren't you coming in?"

"No, I don't think so. I've been thinking things over . . ."

"But you must—at least for a minute. Please." Then, with inspiration—"Monk was gone. That means he could be anywhere. He might come here and find me. Please, Sam, you can't leave me here in this awful place alone."

Father Din looked at her. His eyes were red-rimmed, and had a tense, troubled look in them. Then, with a slight heave of his chest, he began slapping the wet snow from his coat. "All right," he said, "I'll stay with you till morning." He stepped in and removed his coat. Toddy took it and hung it near the radiator to dry. Also, his shoes, his socks. Father Din dried his hair and face on a towel. He slumped into an overstuffed chair.

"This Father Ryan," Toddy asked, sitting on the bed, "you say he's your boss?"

"Something like that," said Father Din. "I'm very fond of him, and I argued with him tonight. I think I hurt him very deeply."

"I'm sorry. I suppose it had something to do with me?"

"No, only with me."

"But he convinced you, didn't he?"

"What makes you think that?"

"It's obvious. You're in uniform. You're not the same man you were a couple of hours ago. It's funny; I thought that if you came back at all, you'd have decided to quit. I didn't expect you to come back having decided the other way. But you have, haven't you?"

Father Din studied the thin rug that was like mouse-skin. His wet foot prints walked up to him from the door. After a few seconds, he said: "Father Ryan made it seem so simple; even I could see it. I wouldn't agree with him—still being a stubborn, stupidly clever fool—but I understood. Ever since the beginning, when I was selected for the priesthood, everyone has been telling me that faith would come. All I had to do was to wait." He looked at her.

"Candidates are supposed to be selected because it's seen by someone who knows that such a person has a vocation. But in fact no one knows who has a vocation. The truth is, an overzealous, if well-meaning, Bishop can rob the cradle. It can happen for all sorts of reasons—political, personal—and then an unsuited guy like me ends up in a position where no matter what he does, he can't be right. Paul said that there are diversities of graces."

"You mean that you would be good in another circumstance?"

"I would hope so. And then there's the other thing. 'There are eunuchs who have made themselves eunuchs for the kingdom of heaven,' Christ said. I can't make myself a eunuch, though, God knows, I've tried."

"If you feel that way, why are you wearing your backwards collar?"

"I'm not sure. Some last concession to Father Ryan, a man for whom I hold a deep affection. And I also feel I've got to end this thing in the right way. I started it with a lie, maybe I can end it closer to the truth. I'm still a priest and I'm going to dress like one until I'm not one. No more false flags."

"But you only came to give me my key back."

"And to tell you what happened. I had to see you again, to say—"

"I know. You don't have to say it. In a way, I feel relieved. I was more than a little afraid of the idea, though I might have gone through with it. Do you understand?"

Father Din looked up at her and nodded. She was beautiful.

"You love Jack."

"I suppose I do; but it's hopeless."

"Don't let yourself believe that."

"Do you know," Toddy said, half serious, half amused, "I prayed for you to come back to me tonight. But I didn't expect that you'd come back to me as a priest. Maybe the Lord knows what I really need."

"I think so," Father Din said, his eyes dropping. She kissed him lightly on the forehead, then went to bed and fell into a troubled sleep.

Chapter 4

MAHMOUD SAVES CAMILLA FROM THE MADMAN

At three o'clock that morning, Ansar, Mahmoud and Camilla were not so much released as expelled from the station. There were no charges against them. But where could they go? Ansar insisted that they go back to the Saints and Sinners Club, which stayed open till four. He wanted to retrieve his paper bag full of paraphernalia from the garbage can outside Tiger's where he had stashed it during the excitement.

It wasn't a long walk from the precinct house to the Saints and Sinners Club, but it was a cold one. The three exchanged very little conversation. Ansar went immediately to the garbage can and retrieved his Saks shopping bag. Mahmoud and Camilla went inside.

Opal, whom Mahmoud knew as Tory's girl friend, sat at the bar. Mahmoud saw an opportunity to get Camilla clear of the crazy Ansar, at least for the night. He introduced Opal and Camilla and asked if Opal would let Camilla spend the night with her. She agreed, saying: "I'm not going back to my apartment tonight, but I'll find a place for us. I know lotsa people around here. I'm all by myself tonight anyhow. Tory and Elga are in jail."

"I know," said Mahmoud. "I just left Tory. You probably won't see him for a day or two. He's going to be charged, for sure. Drunk and disorderly, for Tory, assault and battery for Elga, from what I hear."

Just then Ansar walked up to them. "Now I must find a place to do my work," he said. He was carrying the paper bag. He pointed up the bar at Tiger. "Tell that Zionist he cannot win."

"Opal," said Mahmoud, ignoring Ansar, "Ansar and I need a place to stay. I don't know about him but I've got to get some sleep. Where can we go at this hour?"

"Only one place close—The Busy Nook—I mean, the St. Christopher Hotel—right on down the avenue."

Mahmoud explained to Ansar that Camilla would stay with Opal, "because that's no place for a nice young girl."

"Then she will meet us here tomorrow," said Ansar, "at five o'clock. You will bring her. I have very important business in the meantime. *You* may need to sleep," he said, looking at Mahmoud, "but Ansar must work."

"What are you doing, anyway? What is this work?" asked Mahmoud. "Look, Ansar, I don't know you, and I try to mind my own business, so I haven't asked what you're up to, but if I'm going to spend the night with you—"

"I am preparing to make a statement. Where and when is not important—only the statement is important."

"But not tonight. Not with me. Right?"

"It is impossible tonight. But if it were, then I would do it tonight."

Chapter 5

THE DREAM IN ROOM 28

Ansar dreamed back from room 28 at The Busy Nook to a lost childhood in Hebron, the poorest and least developed of the West Bank's major towns. His hometown was largely agricultural, low in applied technology, a town that young people left, looking for work. They might try the Persian Gulf, they might try Jordan, and yet, being children of the country, hicks of a sort, they could hope for perhaps no more than a hillbilly finds in the Marine Corps—at best a clean barracks life.

The possibility was great for much less. And Ansar had never been particularly clever. Indeed, his associates had often thought him a fool, a man capable of stepping backwards off a balcony. Without quite understanding what others saw in him, but understanding that it was difficult for him to earn the lasting respect of others, Ansar had developed, as a sort of performance that had become second nature, his gruff, pseudo-decisive manner, which earned him a short-term, grudging respect, that fell away when he was better known.

But always, Ansar said, things would be different this time, and he had been constantly driven to more and more extreme behavior. He was not really an ideologue, a word too complicated to represent him, nor did he hold the tenets of the Muslim faith with a very strong grip; but these were what Ansar had to use.

ST. CHRIST PHER (RED)

(—————)

ST. CHRIST PHER (BLUE)

(—————)

Now he puzzled into the night over his bomb book. He tried
to follow the diagrams, but things kept getting lost between
his eye-on-the-book and his eye-on-the-materiel. The dia-
gram of the bomb did not look like the stuff on the table
beside it. Ansar shook his head and began to rearrange
things. He had to get this right. It was the supreme test of his
life. But he had still made no decision as to what he would
blow up. Perhaps the Police Station. That would certainly
earn him respect.

Chapter 6

THE DREAM IN ROOM 29

ST. CHRIST PHER (RED)

(————————-)

ST. CHRIST PHER (BLUE)

(—————-)

In room 29, Mahmoud had undressed and carefully folded and hung up his clothing and now lay back on the bed in his clean white underwear, his arms up behind his head, waiting for sleep. But he was overtired and must wait for his nervous system to relax and prepare the ease of his dreams.

He was comparing this Ansar and himself and some others of his acquaintance to his brother, Tory, who did not seem to have faith in any human enterprise but music. Tory would not join in any effort or cause. Even when it came to his beloved jazz, Tory was without discipline. He had never been at his best in the cooperative effort of modern jazz but always preferred the long, almost lonely riffs of Dixieland. The more on-his-own he was the more brilliant he was, the more in unison, the flatter he became.

Mahmoud, who used to be Morris and sometimes Maurice, had been the leader of their early groups—there had been a dozen or more—but he could never contain Tory and they had fallen out many times.

Then Mahmoud had found the most important group of his life, the Muslims. Hope in a New Order. But Tory did not desire hope any more than he desired order. Tory was his own lonely song. And now he sat in the local tank awaiting charges. But what could ever happen to Tory, Mahmoud asked himself. He would be the same in jail or out. He would always be the same. Why, Mahmoud wondered, did he envy his brother?

Chapter 7

TATTOOS

"That little dog!" Pilar exclaimed, between spoonfuls of soup. "He promise me to come home at night. I twist his ears off when I get him!"

"Oh, Pilar," Jack Muir said wearily, "he stays out all the time."

"No he don't!" Pilar almost shouted. "I tell him and he do what I say."

Muir shrugged indifferently and lighted a cigarette.

"I should have let him go into the shit-bowl," Pilar said.

"He'll be all right," Jack said, his thoughts elsewhere.

"You love him, too, don't you, Jack?" Pilar said, her almond eyes warming a bit. Muir looked at her. He smiled. "Sure I do," he said, reaching across the table to pat her hand. "Don't worry about him; he's tough, like Humphrey Bogart."

"Oh, he love Bogie," Pilar said, enthusiastic. "He watch him all the time. He love video classics."

"I know," said Muir, slipping back into his thoughts.

Pilar finished her soup. She put the cup in the sink. A roach ran out of the sink and up her arm. She jumped back, squealing, and slapped the bug off. "I need a fix," she said.

262

"I've got meth . . ." Muir offered.

"No, I need a fix," said Pilar. She went to the sideboard and got her pocketbook.

"Do it in the bathroom," said Muir.

"O.K.," Pilar said, unoffended. She went into the tiny bathroom and shut the door. In a minute, Muir heard water running. In a few more minutes Pilar came out, her eyes already turned into opaque, well-oiled glass. "Come to bed, Jack: I got a surprise for you."

Indifferently, Muir followed her into the small bedroom the windows of which looked out on a narrow, ugly street. With her back to him, as he sat on the bed removing his shoes, Pilar took off all her clothes but her bra. She had a slim, muscular body. Her calves were wiry and thin, her thighs of hard, medium thickness, her buttocks were a gleaming gold, and deeply, darkly etched in the middle. Her waist was narrow, her torso, from the back, very V'd, and her shoulders broad. Out of her shoes, she looked much shorter, but at the same time much stronger, than with them on. For the first time in weeks, Muir felt the stirrings of sex. Pilar turned to him then, her eyes gleaming. Her small breasts, where they swelled up out of her bra, had the same dusky golden hue as her buttocks, and the same dark etching in the middle, between them. "Take off your bra," Muir said. He was undressed now, and under the covers.

"Wait," said Pilar. She turned on the bedside lamp, then turned off the overhead light. Then she got into bed.

She sat next to Muir, turning her breasts toward him. She reached behind her and undid her bra. "Look," she said. The bra fell away. At first, Muir saw nothing but the two round, golden, bouncing little breasts. Then he saw that his name had been tattooed over the brown, full nipples—JACK over the right nipple, and MUIR over the left.

"My God," he said, "what have you done?"

Pilar's face, which had been for a moment like that of a child's who had a surprise gift to give, showed sudden panic.

"You no like, Jack?"

Muir grabbed her into his arms. He pushed her dark head down on his shoulder, and sat rocking her.

"Don't you like what I did, Jack?" she asked again, in a few moments, her voice muffled against Muir's shoulder. "You see how I love you," she said. "You see how I love you? It hurt, Jack. See how I love you?"

"Yes, yes," Muir said softly, rocking her the while. He was appalled; but his feeling of pity for Pilar was even stronger than his revulsion. "Yes, I see how you love me," he said, but he said it so softly that Pilar couldn't hear.

"What?" she said, lifting her head from his shoulder. "You no like, Jack?"

"No," said Muir, "it's fine, it's fine."

"You like them?" Pilar brightened visibly.

"Yes," Muir lied.

Pilar put her head back down on his shoulder. She reached down and put her hand between his legs, edged it up to his crotch. Muir kept rocking her gently. "Oh," he moaned, not with sex but with a vague yet terrible guilt. Then Pilar's hand fell away from him. Her head became heavy on his shoulder. Gently, he stretched her out on the bed, covered them, and lay looking into her drugged, sleeping, Aztec face. He lay like that for half an hour, during which his pity left him, as his attention gradually shifted from thoughts of her soul to thoughts of her tawny, animal body. The girl had a beauty of her own, and his artist's eye began to discover it. One of Pilar's hands rested on the pillow, next to the black stream of her hair, and the fingernails of it were large and long and blood-red. The hand was like an exotic talon. Muir kissed its palm. He rocked her in his arms till they both fell asleep.

Muir woke with a start. He got out of bed, slipping his feet into his shoes, threw his army overcoat over his shoulders, and went to the window. Outside, a heavy layer of snow lay on the street, with still more of the intrepid stuff dancing down out of the faint dawn sky. He sat by the window for half an hour, watching and smoking. Then Pilar stirred in bed and called him to her. He went back and got in bed with the warm, naked girl.

"Jack?" she whispered, out of her sleep.

"Yes . . ."

Pilar took his shoulders in her hands, her long nails cutting into his flesh, and pulled him down upon her.

"Love me, Jack," she whispered.

265

Chapter 8

CHECKING OUT

A sleep-refreshed Felix Potter knocked on the door of room 22, waking Toddy and Father Din. Father Din pulled himself out of the overstuffed chair in which he'd slept, and went to the door. He opened it. "Yes?" he said.

"Oh, it's you," said Potter, surprised; indeed, shocked to see Father Din's priestly collar. He cleared his throat and became official. "It's noon," he said. "It's check-out time. You'll have to vacate."

"Noon?" said Father Din. "Yes, all right, we'll be out in a few minutes."

"Well, hurry, please; the maid will be here soon to change the sheets," said Potter, with concealed mischievous pleasure. Actually, the maid would only put the top sheet on the bottom and a clean sheet on top.

"All right," said Father Din, closing the door, "we'll hurry." But before he could shut it, the door was pushed open again by a uniformed policeman. "Who are you?" asked the bluecoat. He looked past Father Din and saw Toddy, who was sitting up in bed. "Mrs. Muir?" he called to her.

"Yes."

"Excuse me," said the bluecoat, "I thought you were alone in there."

"Is there something wrong, officer?" asked Potter, who stood to the side.

"No, I guess not," the bluecoat said. "You go along."

Potter gave him an imperious look, and went down the hall. The cop looked in. "I was detailed down here last night—or I should say this morning—to keep an eye on your door. I was told that when you woke I was to bring you to the station for questioning. Nobody said you'd be . . . I thought you were alone." Father Din explained his presence. "Well, looks like you didn't need me," said the cop. "I'll go down and see that there's a car waiting."

"I must be important," said Toddy, when Father Din closed the door.

"You are," he said. "And good morning." He ran fingers over his chin.

Toddy sat in the bed, smoking.

"I have to be at police headquarters at three," he said. "That's in three hours. Right now, I'm going to see Pilar Pavon—to see if I can help her in any way."

"Do you know where she lives?"

"She and Dedi lived together, didn't they? That was the impression you gave me."

"Yes, they do; but I don't know where she lives."

"Well, I know. I took a clinic card out of his wallet last night, when Monk wasn't looking. Pilar will be at that address, I hope."

"I guess so," said Toddy, rubbing her eyes. "It's too early for me to think. I don't wake up until dark. If I wait for you at the police station, will you eat with me?"

"I'll be there at three," said Father Din, "but you'll have to wait for me while I make my statement. Better have a little breakfast as soon as you can. I'll see you then."

Father Din shut the door behind him. The bluecoat, sitting tipped back on a chair in the hall, nodded, "I've got a car waiting outside," he said. "She won't be long, will she?" Father Din smiled, shrugged, and went on down to the lobby.

He paid the hotel bill, and then went into the snowy street. He had walked a block, when a fareless taxi came grinding along on chains. The snow was like a thick white fog through which one could barely see. The driver made no attempt to pull his cab over to the curb, but stopped it in the middle of the street. Father Din negotiated a mountainous snow-drift and slipped-slid to the door of the cab, and got in.

"Where to?" asked the cabbie.

Father Din gave him the address.

"Some storm, eh?"

"Yes, quite a storm," said Father Din.

"Supposed to turn to sleet later."

"Is it?"

"Yeah. Then it'll freeze."

"Probably," said Father Din. "Like hell freezing over, isn't it?"

Chapter 9

CHECKING IN

Curious and annoyed, Felix Potter slid on down the hall, knocking on doors and calling, "It's noon. Check out Time. Anyone wants to stay, they've got to pay." Mahmoud opened the door to room 29. He was dressed. Potter pounded Ansar's door, but no answer came.

Mahmoud said, "Use your key. He's probably asleep."

Potter shrugged, lifted his key-chained keys and unlocked the door, pushing it open.

Mahmoud stepped in front of him, blocking his view, and in. He saw at a glance the situation was as he'd feared. Ansar had fallen asleep at the room's one small table, paraphernalia scattered about it.

Mahmoud did not want Felix Potter to see inside. He turned back to Potter, who stood trying to peer past him, and said, taking a roll of bills from his pocket, "Look, my friend and I will keep this room for the rest of the day. He's exhausted. Needs some sleep. What do we owe you?"

Felix Potter felt that the world owed him an explanation, but he could see that he was not going to get one. He looked at the roll of bills and said, "Fifty dollars for two." Why not? It was incredibly high for the Busy Nook. Potter could pocket at least half of it. The several bills warmed his palm, and the warmth scurried up his arm and into his heart.

Chapter 10

THE VISITORS

Two hours earlier, at ten, Pilar Pavon woke to find herself alone. Jack Muir was gone; apparently Dedi had never come home. At first Pilar thought Jack must have gone to get something at the store, but when he did not return by noon she knew he wouldn't be back. Men!

She got up, put on a pot of coffee (the weak percolated gringo coffee that Dedi liked), washed, brushed her teeth, poured herself (when the last perk sounded) a cup of coffee, and sat down (still wearing her warm winter housecoat) at the kitchen table to drink it. "And a good-looking *muchacha*," she said, extending a draped, curving calf, which was perhaps a little too thin, and studying it. "*Stupidos!*" she spit, tossing her tousled raveny hair out of her face, and taking a sip of hot coffee.

Suddenly she frowned, the cup poised at her lips, as if remembering something. "No, he would never do a thing like that," Pilar said aloud, and, surprised at the sound of her own voice, looked about the empty room.

Early that morning, before falling asleep for the second time, she had gone on a match hunt and found the revolver in Muir's army-coat pocket. She'd asked him what he was doing with it. He'd told her it had been given him and that he intended to sell it. At that point, her mind had been too hazed-over for her to put things together. Now it occurred to her that when she'd picked Muir up in front of Toddy's building, he'd had a gun, and she saw what that might mean. "Maybe

271

he gonna kill Monk, or maybe Monk gonna kill him," she thought. "What I should do?" But she could think of nothing to do but wait for Dedi and Jack Muir to find her. She could not find them, especially in a blizzard. While she waited to hear something from them, she busied herself with house-keeping chores, stopping occasionally for more coffee, cigarettes, and pills. It was a little after noon when the door-bell rang. She breathed a deep sigh of relief, thinking it was Jack returning, or maybe Dedi, who always lost his keys. The buzzer to let people in no longer worked. She would have to go down three flights of musty, littered stairs to open the door.

But it was not Jack at the door. It was Opal and a strange girl. "What you want?" demanded Pilar, holding the collar of her housecoat against the swift, cold breeze that swept in through the open door.

"I thought somebody ought to come see you," said Opal. She stood, booted and bundled for winter, her back to the whirl-ing, wind-driven snow.

"What you mean?" asked Pilar sharply. "What you want?"

"You mean nobody's told you yet?"

"I don't know what you are talking about. You tell me, or go away."

"I got to talk to you," said Opal. "I got to tell you some-thin'. Can we come in?"

"Who is your friend?"

"Her name's Camilla."

"Hi," said Camilla.

She nodded at the girl. "Is it important?"

"Yes."

"O.K.," said Pilar, "but it better be important. Come on. I live upstairs."

As Father Din's cab pulled on to Pilar's street, Opal's cab could still be seen grinding in the snow a block ahead.

"This is it, Father."

"Will you wait for me?"

"How long will you be? It ain't so good to sit still in this weather. I'm thinkin' of the car."

"Maybe a half hour at most."

"O.K., Father, I'll tell you what"—he looked at his watch—"I'll be back in a half hour. You know you owe me a lot of money already, Father, but let's forget it. I don't like for a priest to pay. And you can depend on me—I'll be back."

"Here," said Father Din, handing the cabbie a bill, "get yourself some coffee."

The building was a sad and dreary replica of the ones to each side of it, only featured with uniqueness insofar as its scars were differently placed. There was a broken window on the first floor, backed against the cold with a jagged piece of cardboard. There was a crudely drawn swastika, done in red paint with a two-inch brush, near the entrance. There were hearts, names, and curses carved into the chipped, slimy-green-painted wood of the rickety outer doors, through which wind had driven snow, so that it was nearly as deep between that outer and the inner doors as it was in the street. None of the mailboxes had locks. Only a few had names on them. Pilar & Dedi Pavon. Father Din rang the bell under the mailbox and hoped it would work. After a moment, he rang again, and then heard someone descending the stairs.

Opal opened the door. She did not recognize Father Din as Sam Hopkins. Clean-shaven, his collar sticking stiffly up under his chin, he was a stranger, a priest. "What is it?" she asked.

"It's me, Opal—Sam."

Now she saw. "Sam! Why, you a priest. Why you dressed like that?"

"I *am* a priest, Opal."

She stood for a moment, blinking.

"Why if that don't beat all! Toddy know that?" She raised her eyebrows.

"Yes, she knows."

"Well, if that don't beat all! I just don't know what to think. What do I call you then?"

"My name is Michael Din. You can call me Father Din if you want to—or Michael, or Sam, Opal, I don't care."

"But what was you doing—?"

"That's a long story. Perhaps I'll be able to tell you about it some time. But I've come to see Pilar—about Dedi."

"Me too," said Opal. "But when I come, I didn't think I'd have to *tell* her about it. I only come to help. 'Sides, I'm afraid to go back to that house, and last night Elga—you remember her—and Tory, they got into a fight and both of 'em is in jail, so I didn't know what else to do. Two places I know I'm not going near, that house or that jail."

"You mean to say nobody has notified her yet—I mean, before you?"

"Ah-ah! Nobody. I just told her." They were standing in the hallway now, on the first floor. Opal closed the door.

"My God!" Father Din exclaimed, slapping his forehead, "they probably can't locate her, and it's my fault."

"Why is it your fault?"

"I took the only I.D. card Dedi had on him from his wallet last night. That's how I knew the address here. I never even thought of it until this morning. I should have given it to the police last night."

"That could get you into some kind of trouble, couldn't it?"

"I suppose it could," said Father Din. "When I saw that Dedi was dead, I stuffed the card in my pocket, I forgot about it until this morning. And no one asked me about—"

275

"Well, you're a priest," interjected Opal. "They won't do anything to you. Will they?"

Father Din snorted without humor. "How is Pilar taking it?" he asked, shifting from thoughts of Figlia's wrath.

She rolled her big, cherub-like eyes up toward the apartment. "Oh, not so good. She just keeps cryin' and cryin'. Can't stop her. Maybe shouldn't. I'm doing what I know how, but what can I do? What can any old body do? She some musta loved that poor little boy. Maybe you can help her."

Father Din followed Opal up the three flights of creaking, littered stairs and into the apartment. Camilla sat across the table from Pilar, like a dark little lady-in-waiting.

"What do you want?" Pilar snapped, as Father Din entered. "I no call for a priest. I got a spiritist."

"Do you remember me, Pilar? My name is Michael Din. We met for a moment last evening. But perhaps you don't recognize me, dressed as I am?"

Pilar studied him for a moment with angry, tear-stained eyes. Then she said: "I remember you. You are the one who stop me from cutting Miss High-Class nose off, when I lose my temper. You were nice to me. How come you no dressed like a priest last night?"

"That's just what I asked him," said Opal.

"That's a long story, Pilar. I've come to—"

"I know. Don't tell me no more."

276

Father Din nodded and smiled strainedly. "I have your brother's card here," he said after a pause. "I've brought it to give you." He placed the card on the table in front of Pilar.

She looked at it, reached out and touched it with her fingers, but didn't pick it up. "Clinic card," she said. "He always sick. If he had took the medicines I fixed for him, he would be strong like a bull. But he would lie and not take them, and that is why he always sick. The clinic don't help. He had sores all over on him when he was born. Our father, he was drunk and he wanted to kill Dedi—maybe me too. Our mother was sick . . . they left us, then we only had each other . . ." Her face twisted grotesquely with mingled hatred and heartbreak, and she put it in her hand on the table. She let out a long groan that rose in timbre into a high, shrill wail. Opal went over to her and put a hand on her back.

Father Din stood in the middle of the small kitchen, again feeling as helpless as he had last night when her brother died. He tried to make himself say consoling words, but it was no use: it wasn't in him. He felt that such words would burn, rather than soothe, like salt in a wound. He was speech-less now listening to Pilar's moans of mourning and anguish.

"*Stupido!*" she said in a weak voice, banging the table top with a small fist. "*Stupido!*"

Father Din had seen Dedi Pavon alive and dead, now he saw Dedi's sister in her grief. He stood in silence before this poverty-stricken, morally-stricken, grief-stricken woman whose every sound of grieving cut him to the quick, and waited.

277

"There, baby," Opal cooed over Pilar's shaking shoulders—"there, now, there—"

Finally, Pilar raised her head, wiped her eyes on the sleeve of her housecoat, and asked Father Din: "You know what happened?"

"He was there," said Opal.

"I forget," said Pilar. She looked hard at Father Din. "Why you not *do* something, eh? You a priest? Why you not save him?"

Humbly, softly, Father Din answered that he didn't know how to.

"So," said Pilar, nodding. "Big good you are! I am *Catalicos Romanos*, too, see: but what good can it do for me? I cannot tell priests like you that I must sleep with men to make money to feed my little brother. What would you say, if I said that? You would put a curse on me."

Father Din did not speak.

"*He* knows," Pilar went on. "But *I* know who will help me. Jack will help me. He will go and kill Monk with that *pistola* that he has. He always say he will, but he don't. But now he is. He will do it for Dedi—for me. He will do for me and for my brother what he don't do for his wife. You will see."

"Jack Muir has a gun?" asked Father Din.

"*Si*. And I already put a spell on Monk yesterday that he would die before midnight tonight. And it is Jack who will kill him."

"Then you must help us stop him."

"Why? What you mean?"

"Because, if you care for him, you don't want to see him get into serious trouble, do you? He could be killed—or go to prison . . . ."

"Sam—I mean the Father is right," said Opal. "You don't want to see Jack get into no bad trouble, Pilar."

"Yes," said Pilar, "you are right."

"But," said Father Din, "you say he has a gun."

"Yes, *si*." Pilar looked thoughtful. "He has kicked," she said, after a moment.

"Kicked?"

"*Si*, he has kicked. He no use anymore heroin. Only meth."

"Wow!" exclaimed Opal. "That's why he didn't show up last night. When he kick it, baby?"

"A week. Maybe more. He has done this by himself. He has done this thing for his wife. He will go for her soon. I knew it this morning."

"I see," said Father Din. "Where is Muir now? Do you know?"

"He left before I woke up," said Pilar. "I do not know where he is. I would tell you. I speak the truth."

"I believe you," said Father Din. "Now won't you let me drive you down to police headquarters? I have a cab coming to pick me up in a few minutes and the police will want to talk with you."

"You should go with the Father, baby," said Opal. "You want to see Dedi once more, don't you?"

"You'll have to identify him," Father Din said softly, "and through my mistake the police don't know where to find you."

"Yes," said Pilar, "I go with you."

Chapter 11

THE MORGUE

When they got out at the police station, Opal said: "This is close enough for us." She waved her hand and walked away, pulling Camilla Azziz in the direction of the Saints and Sinners Club. Father Din took Pilar inside.

In the station, Father Din saw Toddy sitting alone in a far corner of the squad room. She started to rise and come over to him, but he signaled, not letting Pilar see, for Toddy to stay where she was. He led Pilar up to a bluecoat and asked to see Lieutenant Figlia.

In a moment, another bluecoat came and led the way to Captain Hubbard's office (Hubbard had called in sick that morning), inside of which, behind Hubbard's desk, sat Figlia eating chicken from a cardboard barrel. When he saw Pilar with Father Din, he got to his feet and came out from behind the desk. His clean-shaven face was gray. "Hello," he said to Father Din, and glanced at Pilar with a question in his eyes for which he also seemed to have the answer. "Relative of the boy?"

"Lieutenant," Father Din said, taking Pilar's elbow, "this is Pilar Pavon. She's Dedi Pavon's sister."

"Yes, yes," said Figlia, looking thoughtfully at Pilar. His eyes threw a question at Father Din. Father Din answered it: "She wants to see her brother's remains, Lieutenant."

"Can I see him?" Pilar asked.

"Yes," said Figlia. He went to his desk and pressed a button. With a reply, he said: "Send in a policewoman." He pulled a chair out for Pilar. "Please sit down, Miss Pavon," he said. Pilar sat down. Figlia looked at her, kindly. "You have my condolences, Miss Pavon."

"Thank you . . ."

"Are you Dedi's closest relative? I mean, don't you have parents?"

"No, sir. We got nobody, just us."

Figlia glanced at Father Din. "I had a hunch that you'd know where to find whoever the body belonged to, but we haven't been able to find you. I should have asked you last night, but I'm afraid I wasn't in top form. That's what happens when you get too involved; you're inclined to forget routine procedures."

"It was my fault, Lieutenant," said Father Din. "If you'll wait a moment, I'll tell you about it." He indicated a reluctance to speak before Pilar, who, in any case, showed no interest in what was being said.

"Your fault?" said Figlia.

A knock came at the opaque, beveled glass window in the door. A bulky shadow fidgeting. Figlia called for the shadow to enter, and a policewoman came in. "Sir?" she asked.

"Please take Miss Pavon here to identify a relative's remains. There's a tentative I.D. on it. She'll tell you who. Miss Pavon?" Pilar looked up, dreamily. She looked quite ugly now. "Will you go with this officer, please."

"*Si*," said Pilar listlessly. She got up, nodded at Father Din, and followed the policewoman out.

"Now what's this business about it being your fault?" asked Figlia with low heat. He sat down behind the desk, reached into the cardboard barrel, and drew out a drumstick. "I'm sorry, but I have to eat sometime. You don't mind, do you? Would you like a piece? It's very good. Colonel Drummond's Deep Down Done. I've become very fond of it."

"No, thank you," said Father Din. He hadn't eaten in so long that he'd lost his appetite, and the odor of chicken was nauseating. "I'm terribly sorry about this," he went on, "but I'm afraid I'm responsible for your not being able to locate Miss Pavon."

"So you said, but how comes it?"

Father Din told him about taking the card from Dedi's wallet.

"Well," Figlia said, "your intentions were good, Father. I don't suppose I have a right to be too angry about it; it's partly my fault for not asking. Neither of us were quite ourselves last night."

"Then they'll be no charges? I mean, for tampering with evidence or something?"

"No, Father; but if you keep trying . . ."

"I won't, I promise you," said Father Din.

"Here's another question I should have asked you last night—in a few minutes I'm going to have you make a detailed statement—but tell me, did the Pavon boy have any money on him, and, if so, how much? I'm assuming that Stolz took it."

"Yes, perhaps two-hundred dollars that Monk took from his wallet."

Figlia flipped the clean bone of the drumstick back in the barrel.

"He also had a tape-wrapped iron bar about ten inches long."

"Yes, I saw that."

"You see," Figlia said, "he fits the description of a robbery perp, kid who knocked over the St. Christopher Hotel early yesterday evening. Same type, the bar, a junkie—it all fits. Plus the money—just about the right amount. Well, that's not very important now, is it?"

"I suppose not," said Father Din, remembering Dedi and the "hot watches." "There's something else that you should know, Lieutenant. I think it is very important."

"What's that?"

"You've talked to Mrs. Muir?"

"Yes, and we have her statement."

"Well, this boy's sister, Miss Pavon, has been seeing Mrs. Muir's husband."

"Jack Muir, also on junk, according to his wife."

"Yes—that is, he was; but he isn't now. Miss Pavon told me that he said he'd kicked his habit."

"Yeah?"

"Well, he's got a gun."

"I see," said Figlia. "And you think that Muir is looking for Stolz?"

"It's possible."

"Yes, it is, isn't it?" said Figlia, his worried eyes darting with thought. "This is a very bad situation. I could almost wish that Stolz were gone—I don't want bodies all over the streets down here. But I want that man myself. I only hope he's crazy enough to have stayed. And he might be. I've been studying psych reports on him. He's a periodic alcoholic. He stays cool and sober for months at a time, but when he goes, he goes for two or three weeks. He usually tucks away in a hotel room or an apartment—some casual place he decides on—gets himself a lady, and maybe a gofor, and sits around making a dangerous nuisance of himself until he's ready to rejoin the world. It looks like he's on one now. At such times he can be especially dangerous. Booze doesn't square well with his kind of mind. He gets delusive. He's hurt people before during these toots. It's on the record. My feeling is, from what you and Mrs. Muir told me about the state of things last night, that he won't be able to let the situation drop. I have good reason to know that he believes in revenge."

"You mean, he'll look for her."

285

"I think he'll be looking for anyone who was there. But I doubt if he'll be on the street. He's too easy to spot, and he knows it, and he knows that we're looking. No, he won't show up on the street, and that'll severely limit his search. But I'm almost certain he'll sneak back up to Mrs. Muir's apartment to have a look—I'd bet on it—and that's why I've got it under twenty-four hour a day surveillance. And I've told Mrs. Muir that—although I'm not instructing her, or using any coercion whatsoever about it—I don't think she should go back there. Unless it's to get some clothes or something, and only for a few minutes—in and out quickly. You understand—that's only advice, not an order. As I say, the apartment is under surveillance. She'd be safe enough. But . . . ."

Father Din saw what Figlia was getting at.

"You really want to get that man, don't you?"

Figlia nodded slowly, seriously.

"Now you're on record advising her not to return to the apartment, but I can see that you half hope she does so that she can act as bait for Stolz."

"I've advised her not to. But, as I say, the apartment is being closely watched. She'd be safe if she did—but only for a short time. We've got an A.P.B. out on Stolz. If we can pick him up we might save ourselves some confusion."

Father Din felt a sudden dislike for Figlia. "You want my statement?"

286

But just then a bluecoat stepped in. "We got him, Lieutenant!" The officer was flushed with excitement. "We got Stolz outside in the squad room!"

"How?" said Figlia, standing. "What happened? Tell me!"

"We just picked him up off the street. He was stumbling along the Strip, drugged to the gills. Drunk and drugged. A patrol car spotted him—they weren't sure it was Stolz—they pulled over, went up to him, and took him. According to the boys, he just stood there swaying. But he was clean—no drugs, no weapon. If he had any, he must have stashed them somewhere. But he looked sick, he was having trouble breathing, so they took him over to St. Vincent's emergency before bringing him here. Docs over there said he was O.D.ed on some kind of barbiturate. They shot him with uppers of some kind. Then the boys brought him over here. We're feeding him coffee. He's in pretty good shape now. We got him cuffed to a bench out in the squad room. A mean looking S.O.B.!"

Figlia seemed to sway behind the desk. "At last!" he sighed.

At that moment, in the hollow coolness of the morgue, Pilar Pavon's knees gave out from under her, and she was only saved from falling to the floor by the buxom policewoman who caught her about the waist and shoulders in almost the way a man takes a woman into his arms to kiss her. In a moment, she was standing straight again, but leaning a little against the big policewoman's shoulder. The policewoman held her elbow. When the sheet was pulled aside, she looked into her dead brother's face, and then looked quickly away. She tried to scream but gagged on it. Choking, her eyes alone went back to Dedi's face. She did not see his body, and so could not know how his joints had had to be cut,

287

twisted and snapped back into place so that he could fit on his bier, nor did she observe that the back of his head was missing.

PART SIX

THE BIG BANG

Chapter 1

FREEDOM HOUSE

FREEDOM HOUSE shone on a brass plate affixed to the red brick facade of the four story house on Washington Square North. It was an historical site. But unlike many of the other buildings on Washington Square, it was not owned by New York University. It was owned by Father Thom Corrigan, the best-selling author. It had been in his family since the days when it was used as a staging area for the fugitive slaves of the Underground Railroad. Corrigan's ancestors had come to the New World as radical followers of the Unitarian Universalist, John Murray, but by the time of the great Irish immigration in the 1840s, one of them, possibly for political reasons, had made his conversion to Catholicism and the family had been Catholic, if of an exceedingly radical stripe, ever since. The Corrigans had prospered and by the time of the Civil War, possessed much valuable real estate. It was Thom Corrigan's great-great-grandparents, dedicated abolitionists, who set up Freedom House to aid fugitive slaves on their way to Canada.

Over the past few years Father Din had been a more and more frequent visitor here. He had sat with Father Corrigan and his mistress and listened as Corrigan expounded a doctrine comprised of a mixture, in almost equal parts, of Marxist philosophy, Zen Buddhism, Unitarianism, and an almost unrecognizable form of Catholicism, anti-papal and pro-Communist, wherein Christ was shown to be the first true Marxist.

290

Corrigan was a Jesuit, of the teaching order, and to Father Din, almost magically free of the constraints of an ordinary parish priest. He seemed to do and say as he pleased and come and go as he willed. It was understood that he had been "corrected" many times, but he was very rich and famous and clearly more in agreement with the times than with the Pope. No man could be less like Father Ryan.

Father Corrigan had just returned from Central America and a group of his friends were throwing him a welcome home party. In attendance was a Hollywood star, a Harlem pimp, a famous radical lawyer, and a number of people from city, state, and national government. Corrigan had just finished singing a loose medley of Pete Seeger songs with his mistress when he was called to the telephone. He picked up the receiver in a high mood. "Corrigan, here," he said.

"Hello, Father Corrigan. This is Father Ryan over at Saint Saviour's."

"Well . . . good to hear from you, Father."

"Father Michael Din is my curate."

"Yes, I know that, Father. I know who you are. Good to hear from you. Can I assist you in any way?"

"I was wondering," the voice hesitated. "I was wondering if you had heard from Father Michael. I understand that you see him occasionally."

"No, I haven't, Father. I've been out of the country—Central America. As a matter of fact, some of my friends are throwing me a homecoming party right now."

"Oh, my compliments on the publication of your new book."

"Thank you, Father. Have you read it?"

"Yes. Just last evening."

"What did you think?"

"I think we disagree on many things."

"Oh, I'm sorry to hear that, Father. Perhaps we could get together and talk them over. Your parish isn't far from my house."

"Yes. We're very close, aren't we?"

"About Father Michael . . .?"

"I'm afraid that he is in very serious trouble."

"Of what sort, Father?

"Of all sorts. I think he may be in trouble with the police. I think he may be in danger. He is certainly in trouble with our Church. He may have to be sent away for rehabilitation."

"In order for him to remain a priest, you mean? But Father, Father Michael and I have grown to be friends. I think I know him quite well now. All men are not suited to this calling, and shouldn't we set them free if they aren't? Father Michael is a good person, but I think one not made for the priesthood."

"His deepest problem, Father, is one of faith. And as you know, faith will come."

292

"Faith will come has been repeated ad nauseam to people like Michael. It is not always true."

"We disagree on that, too" said Father Ryan. "I have lived with the problem myself and I say that it finally comes. He has made so many mistakes. I am afraid for what he might do next. But you haven't heard from him, then?"

"No. Is there somewhere else he could be?"

"The only other place I can think of—the only other possible contact I may have with him—is through a police Lieutenant named Figlia, a former parishioner here. I just now hung on the phone until it went dead. But I'll try again. I want to help Father Michael. I'm terribly worried about him. Will you contact me if you hear from him?"

"Absolutely, Father."

"Christ is in Father Michael."

"Absolutely, Father."

"Goodbye, Father."

"Goodbye, Father."

Chapter 2

FALSE WITNESS

Toddy Muir cowered in a corner of the squad room. She had seen Monk brought in and now sat many desks away from him, across computers with rattling printers, beeping Fax machines, and ringing telephones. Fear and relief fought inside her as she watched Lieutenant Figlia and Father Din approach Monk. Suddenly Monk bayed like a wolf that has spotted the moon, and the eerie sound ricocheted about the squad room. Cops and suspects and witnesses alike seemed to duck and dodge. Now he roared for all to hear, "You're a priest! I knew there was something strange about you, you filthy hypocrite!"

"Is this the man?" Figlia said.

"This is the animal," Father Din said.

"And you, Figlia, you haven't got a damned thing," said Monk. "Your daughter was a junkie who O.D.ed. What's new? Just because I was there—that's no evidence of any-thing. If the Sawyer kid wants to say I was there, so what? So was he, and he's a junkie, I'm not."

"*You . . . killed . . . Dedi . . . Pavon*," said Father Din, leaning forward, emphasizing each word, for he believed that, in a sense, Monk *had* killed the boy.

"You lie, you filthy priest! He was dead and you know it. I just gave him the toss. You want to charge me with messing with dead bodies, go ahead. It's laughable. You people haven't got a thing worth wasting my lawyer's time on and you know it. You might as well let me walk now."

Lieutenant Figlia and Father Din looked at each other grimly. They both knew that Monk was right. It was all a couple of handfuls of air. Monk was grinning at them as if at a pair of fools. He knew he would walk, now or later. One phone call and he would be free to destroy the lives of Jack and Toddy Muir. He would even the score with Opal. He would search out Tory. He lived for vengeance.

Father Din decided that, at whatever cost, this man, this monster could not be allowed to walk free. He remembered what his own father had done in a similar situation. No. He had decided. A black tension twisted his face. He said, "But Dedi Pavon was *alive* when you threw him off the roof. He begged you not to do it. I saw it. I heard him beg and I saw him struggle. It was deliberate murder!"

It seemed for a moment that Monk could not understand what Father Din was saying. He looked blank. Then he appeared to go into what looked like anaphylactic shock. "You *lie!*" he shouted. He glared at Figlia. "He's lying, I tell you!" He looked back at Father Din, furiously trying to free his cuffed wrist. "You can't do this—it's a *sin!* He's lying, I tell you!"

"A priest wouldn't lie," said Figlia. "And who do you think a jury will believe, you or a priest?" He turned to Father Din. "You will swear to this in court, on the Bible?"

Father Din nodded, staring straight at Monk with an almost supernatural look of loathing on his face. He did not blink, whatever was going on in his mind. "I will swear in court on the Holy Bible that I saw this man deliberately murder Dedi Pavon. I will swear that the boy begged for his life."

"You'll roast in hell for this, priest!" said Monk, his voice thick.

"You *are* hell," said Father Din. "You yourself are hell. Where you go is hell," he paraphrased Satan in Paradise Lost.

Figlia looked gleeful. "Put him in a holding cell," he told Verdi. "Would you please come with me, Father. We have some work to do."

Chapter 3

VANISHED!

Furiously, Monk calculated with the abacus of his mind. He would not get bail on a capital crime. He had too much money and a long record. No judge would set him loose this time, not with a priest as prime witness to a murder. Monk believed himself to be innocent of Dedi's death, but he knew that nobody else would. He would never see the outside again if he remained in custody. There was only one thing to do. He had to get out now—right now, through the front door. Once out, it would be no trouble to find his way to South America, where he had friends and could live like a king. Extradition was improbable from Colombia. But this was his last chance at freedom. It was now or never.

Monk took a sip of coffee. He seemed to be stalling. Verdi didn't like that. "Come on," he said, "let's go," unlocking the cuff from the bench. The cuff fell loose. Verdi jiggled the key free. The cuff came up across his face, cutting open his cheek. Verdi reared back, blood flying.

Monk cannonballed toward the door, knocking two bluecoats aside like bowling pins. Verdi pulled his gun and charged out the door, holding his bleeding cheek with his free hand. Monk was halfway up the block, shooting steam in the cold. The cold hit Verdi hard. He wore no coat. He felt the presence of several patrolmen panting behind him. But he couldn't look back, afraid of losing sight of Monk. He would catch merry hell if he couldn't catch this bastard.

Verdi saw Monk swerve and slide at the corner of Third Street like an out-of-control van. He was actually kicking up a spray of snow and ice behind him. At the corner, Verdi cursed, seeing what was in store. Monk was heading toward the Bravos' club house. "Shit," he cried, "the sonofabitch!" And up the steps and through the door that was never locked. And then Verdi was inside the door himself, and Monk was ahead of him on the stairs, banging at every door with the flying handcuffs, shouting, "RAID! RAID!"

In a New York minute, the hall was filled with Bravos. None of them laid a finger on Verdi, they just filled the halls and stairs and blocked him and began to chant—

> *If you can, then kill a cop,*
> *Cut his belly, make him pop!*

By the time Verdi got to the roof door, Monk was half a block down, making his way along the connected roofs, a moving silhouette against the tragic winter sky. Verdi hit the roof and his feet went out from under him in the snow. He slid and slipped to his feet and saw nothing, no one. Monk had vanished.

The late winter afternoon was darkening before Verdi's eyes, as was his hope of promotion. The wind knifed his coatless torso. It seemed to take a special aim at his heart. He felt his cheek. It was deeply gashed, but the blood had caked with the cold. "Damn! Damn! Damn!" he cursed. He walked in a circle, kicking out at air.

Back down on the street, two patrol cars had joined the chase. Verdi ran up the street to the vague point where Monk seemed to disappear. Bluecoats ran up and down the street in a disordered search.

At the station house, an officer burst in on Figlia and Father Din. He looked scared. He said, "Something's happened, Sir." He shook his head. "Stolz got out of the station. But don't worry. We think we know where he is. We got everybody out there. We'll get him."

"Dammit to Hell!" Figlia yelled. "Let's go!"

Father Din followed Figlia out of Hubbard's office, but not out the front door. Instead, he went to Toddy. "Did you see what happened?" he asked her.

"I saw it all, everything," she said. "Oh, my God, he's loose again! What are we going to do?"

"I'm going to take you somewhere where you'll be safe." He picked up a telephone from an empty desk and punched in a number. "Hello," he said, "I want to speak with Father Corrigan." He stood waiting for a minute, then said, "Father Corrigan? I must see you." Father Din followed Figlia back to Hubbard's office. Just inside, Figlia said, "When you told me about the Pavon boy, earlier, you said he was dead from an O.D. Now you say he was alive when he was thrown off the roof. Which is it?"

"That boy begged for his life."

A look of deep doubt crossed Figlia's face. Then he gave Father Din a sad little smile. "But you won't change your story again, will you?"

"No. Never!" Figlia reached out and put his hand on Father Din's shoulder. "Good," he said. "Then we've got the son-of-a-bitch!"

Chapter 4

CRAZIER THAN SATAN

While Ansar slept, Mahmoud went out and bought several containers of black coffee. Back in the hotel room, he drank coffee and read Ansar's "bomb book" through from cover to cover. He was sitting up on the bed reading when Ansar stirred. Ansar looked up at him, a dazed expression on his bearded face.

"There's a container of coffee there," said Mahmoud, "sitting on the heat vent. Probably still warm."

"I think I have made it so that it will work," said Ansar.

"I doubt it," said Mahmoud. "I've been reading your instructions. You haven't got the trigger mechanism hooked up right. If I thought that thing would go off, I wouldn't be sitting here."

Ansar had retrieved the coffee and was sipping it.

"Now what in the name of the Unspeakable do you intend to do with that thing?"

"I told you, Ansar is going to make a statement."

"What kind of statement, you idiot? What do you intend to blow up?"

"Do not call Ansar an idiot. What does it matter what I blow up? It is the statement that matters. I can blow up the police station. I can blow up the United Nations. I wish I could blow up the whole world. Send us all to Allah to be judged for the wicked creatures we are.

"Now you listen to me, Mahmoud. I am no fool. I did not hook up the trigger mechanism properly yet, so the bomb would be safe. But now, look."

Before Mahmoud could rise, Ansar had turned a few wires. "Stay back! The bomb will go off now. Now you listen to Ansar. You think you are a Muslim? Then you should not be afraid to die in the Jihad. You will travel with Ansar over Al Sirat, the bridge over the infernal fire to paradise. You will become a hero in paradise. You will have died at the right hand of Ansar!"

"The Great?" said Mahmoud. "This is just plain vanity and stupidity. Islam is a faith of peace. You're even crazier than Satan!"

Chapter 5

PENANCE

"It was almost physical. I felt struck across my . . . soul," Father Din confessed to Father Corrigan, "as if by a giant mailed fist right out of a cloud.

"Not five minutes before, I had borne false witness against this man, believing myself justified because he was a monster.

"But it was like a sign from God, when he was able to escape from that crowded police station. It was a sign and I knew it immediately. It was *I* who had been the monster. I had committed a mortal sin in a moment of anger and passion and God had let Monk escape.

"I'd broken two of the ten commandments; adultery and bearing false witness. God was angry, repulsed by me, and showed me how He felt by letting Monk go. I knew I had to confess as soon as possible. Somehow—I don't quite know how—I've become a Judas priest. I will *not* remain one, even if I leave the priesthood, which I think now is inevitable."

Father Corrigan said: "The essential condition for receiving the sacrament of penance is having the right disposition. "You know that. If you are genuinely sorry for your sins and do not intend to repeat them, do not intend to repeat the offence against One Who is All Good, then God may return to dwell in your soul, from which, by your sins, you have expelled Him.

"And if you have a firm resolve to amend your life, you're not required to guarantee your future sinlessness. Michael, we all fail, and ask forgiveness, and try again.

"I know the priestly life has been difficult for you. It may even have contributed to your moral problems. I mean, perhaps a more normal life would have found you a better man. Your confessions of the past have made me aware of your difficulties. Michael, I know how long you have struggled with these matters. What has happened to you in the last couple of days is the direct result of an imperfect vocation. You have horrified yourself. Shall we call that your penance?

"You know, Michael, I have a vision of the future. I see you married, a husband and father. I see you living the life you were meant to live. I want you to refuse rehabilitation. I want you to leave the priesthood. I think that is what you want to do and I think that is what should be done. I can put you in touch with a halfway house for former priests, run by a friend of mine. A former bishop, believe it or not. Now say me the Act of Contrition."

Michael put his hands up in prayer. "O my God, I am heartily sorry for having offended Thee and I detest all my sins because I dread the loss of heaven and the pains of hell, but most of all because they offend Thee Who art all good and deserving of all my love. I firmly resolve, with the help of Thy grace to confess my sins, to do penance and to amend my life."

"To the degree that you and God share an understanding of your heart, you are free of sin. Go, and sin no more." Father Corrigan patted Father Din's shoulder. "You and your friend are welcome to stay here as long as you wish. I have a few

303

empty bedrooms. The young lady will be safe here, and you'll have time to think. You talk it over with her while I see to my guests. And—call Father Ryan. He's worried sick about you. I'll send the young lady in here so you can talk."

In a moment Toddy entered Father Corrigan's study. "Do you know who's out there?" she said. "There are celebrities of all sorts."

"Toddy, Father Corrigan has offered to put you up here for a few days. You'll be safe here. What do you think?"

"It would be wonderful to be somewhere where I didn't have to be afraid. But I don't have anything with me. Nothing. I need my bank book. I need some clothes. I need—all kinds of things."

"I'm going to call the station and talk to Figlia, if he's there. It's possible that they've got Monk by now."

"Oh, God, that would be wonderful."

Father Din called the station and got an answer. In a moment he had Figlia on the phone. "Did you get him?" he asked.

"No," said Figlia. "The bastard eluded us somehow. He probably knows every rat hole in Needleneck. But we'll get him."

Father Din told Lieutenant Figlia that they would be staying with Father Corrigan, gave him the address and phone number. "Would it be safe for Mrs. Muir to get some things from her place?"

"The apartment's covered. Just get in and get out."

Chapter 6

GOOD NEWS AND BAD

As they headed cross town in a cab, Father Din said: "Toddy, I have some good and some bad news for you. Which do you want first?"

"The good news, I guess. I really need it."

"Pilar told me earlier today, before we went to the police station, that Jack has kicked, or is kicking the drugs."

"Oh," said Toddy, staring ahead. She seemed to be absorbing the information. Turning to him, she said, "Is it true? If it's true, it changes everything. Why didn't you tell me this earlier?"

"Because of the bad news that goes with it. I thought about telling you, but I really didn't want you to have any more to worry about than you already had."

"Oh, God, now I'm afraid to hear. What is it?"

"Well, he has a revolver on him and Pilar thinks he just might be out looking for Monk, to settle the score."

"Oh, my God," she said. "The fool! Monk'll kill him!"

"Now you see why I didn't tell you sooner," Father Din said.

"But Jack . . . he's really off the stuff?"

"Pilar says so."

"She wouldn't lie about that . . . I know. Oh, Lord! Just when he's off—finally! And then he goes looking for even worse trouble. And what if he's heard about Dedi, if he heard about how it happened? He loved that poor kid."

"Try to take the better view, Toddy. Tell me this, though, would you try again now—knowing that Jack's quit the drugs—if you had the chance?"

"You're a priest. Isn't it your duty to order me to try?"

"Don't be difficult, Toddy. I asked you as a friend."

"I'm sorry." She paused. "Yes. Yes, I would try. If it were true."

The cab drew up to the curb in front of Toddy's building. Father Din told the driver to wait, that they would only be a few minutes. He took Toddy by the hand and stepped up to the two bluecoats sitting in the patrol car. "This is Mrs. Muir. She's going up to the apartment to get a few things."

"Yes, Father. We got a call from Lieutenant Figlia. I'll go up with you and check out the halls and the apartment. There's no ground floor back door. We checked. It's in the super's apartment." He told the other officer to keep an eye on the door and led the way up to Toddy's apartment. After checking the rooms and the hall, he returned to his partner in the patrol car. Toddy hurried about the apartment, gathering her things while Father Din waited.

Chapter 7

SHOCK WAVES

Opal and Camilla waited for Ansar and Mahmoud at the Saints and Sinners Club, Opal lubricating herself with a gin and tonic, and Camilla sipping some of Tiger's ever-brewed coffee.

Tiger held a cup of coffee too. He listened as Opal told the pretty young Camilla all the reasons she should return to Chicago and her parents. He nodded in agreement at each and every one.

"But I haven't got any money," Camilla objected. "I'll have to find a job and make enough to pay my fare back, and, if I do that, why should I go? If I have a job, I might as well stay here."

"You should go because that fellow you're with is going to get you into a lot of trouble," Tiger said. "You should listen to Opal. Young people can't see very far ahead, and that's how they get into trouble. That boy is dangerous."

"I know he's a little weird, but—"

"Look," said Opal, "you're a very pretty little girl, and nobody can get themselves into more trouble than a very pretty little girl. I should know. I was a very pretty little girl once, wasn't I, Tiger?"

"Still are. Look," said Tiger, "I've got an idea. Why don't you let me lend you the money to get back to Chicago? You can pay me back some day, no hurry."

"Tiger, that is the sweetest thing!" said Opal.

"Oh," said Camilla, "I couldn't do that."

"You can and you will, girl!" said Opal, slapping the bar.

Tiger left them for a few minutes and returned with an envelope. "Opal, there's five hundred dollars in this. I want you to take this young lady out to J.F.K. and stay with her until she's on a flight for the Toddling Town. Buy her ticket, give her some spending money, and what's left is yours. Bring it back here and spend it."

"I don't know how to thank you," said Camilla, her eyes moist. She reached across the bar to pull her walleyed hero close for a kiss when the remaining plateglass window of the Saints and Sinners Club was blown out. Shards of glass sprayed the room like hail. Suddenly everyone was wearing little cuts. The room had actually rocked, as if in an earthquake. The boom engulfed them. Then there was a series of smaller explosions that seemed to go on and on, with short pauses here and there.

When it seemed that the worst was over, Tiger looked about. Nobody seemed to be seriously hurt. What was it? Had Monk kept his promise to lob a Molotov Cocktail in on him, to burn him out? But there was no fire. He climbed over the top of the bar and went to the door amid screams of fear. And now, outside, he saw that the Busy Nook was burning. Fire trucks were already gathering in front of the hotel. It looked as if several floors were gone. The fire raged up through the place where the roof should be, brightening the night sky like a giant torch. There was a bittersweet smell in the air.

Chapter 8

ARMAGEDDON

There was a pervading sense of unreality about Toddy's apartment, like an evil place remembered in a bad dream. But the bad dream was still alive. Had it only been the day before, since Dedi's death? Father Din would be glad if he never had to look at this place again.

He was startled out of his reverie by half a dozen rapidly fired shots. Or were they backfires? He raced to the front windows and pulled one up. For a moment, he saw nothing unusual. The police car. The building across the street. Jack Muir's loft. Snowbanks. The cab. Where was the cab? It was halfway up the block. Then the police car again. Then the bodies of two bluecoats, one hanging out of the car, one lying spreadeagled in the snow.

He stared down in horror. Monk! He must be here, in this building.

Out of the corner of his eye, somewhere up the Strip, near the Saints and Sinners Club, he saw a flame that looked like a red whale shoot across the sky. Toddy's building seemed to tremble. He whirled about and grabbed Toddy. For a moment they appeared to dance.

Then the door burst open. Monk, his face razor slashed and bleeding, pushed Jack Muir into the apartment in front of him. "I've been waiting for you two to show up. I've been watching the cops watching for me. But I picked up a secret weapon at Pilar's, this bullet-proof shield," he said, jerking

310

Muir's arms tighter. "The bitch tried to slice me up with a razor blade and now she's with her brother in hell. But the one I want most is you, you filthy, lying priest! I'm going to blow you into eternity where you can roast in hell forever. Then I'm going to take care of these two . . . lovers."

As Monk raved, Toddy screamed a scream that sounded endless until Father Din realized that the last part of it was the sound of a siren outside on the street.

"Hear that explosion?" cried Monk. "*I* did that. That was Tory doing my bidding. Tiger will never threaten a man like me again. I always even my scores." He stared wildly: unkempt, disheveled, confused, but plainly sober. He kicked the door shut behind him.

As he did so, Jack Muir lifted his arms and slid between Monk's to the floor. Father Din saw that Monk had a new weapon, perhaps a hastily acquired Saturday Night Special. Or was it Jack Muir's own pistol?

Monk kicked Jack Muir in the ribs, hard. There was a cracking sound and Jack screamed in pain. Toddy cried out and ran to Jack. She tried to pull him away from Monk, across the room. Father Din dove at Monk, gathering the arm that held the gun in both of his. He tried to drag Monk to the floor with his weight.

"Stolz!" Figlia called from beyond the door. "Let 'em go!" he shouted, plunging into the room.

Jack Muir kicked backward along the floor, Toddy dragging him by the shoulders. A bullet that was meant for Father Din broke a floorboard in half. Monk began beating at the back of Father Din's neck with his free hand, but Father Din

311

twisted around, taking the blows on his shoulder, and then faced Monk, holding the revolver-wielding arm in both of his, as Monk tripped backwards.

Father Din landed on Monk's stomach, the gun arm between himself and Monk, and the explosion came muffled and smoky between them. For a moment, Father Din thought he'd been shot. Then Monk's head fell back, like a man putting his head down on a pillow after a hard day.

Two bluecoats helped Father Din to his feet. He looked about. Toddy and Jack Muir lay huddled, halfway into the livingroom.

Father Din looked at Monk. "Is he dead?"

"No," said a cop, bending over Monk, removing the revolver.

Father Din knelt down beside Monk. He took the hand that had held the revolver in his own.

"Help me," came the sound from Monk's twisted mouth. He gathered strength and said, "I've been . . . crucified . . ." He was hit with a seizure of coughing. ". . . by my own . . congregation . . ." Then something incoherent. Figlia bent down close to his mouth to hear.

Father Din said, "What's he saying? What is it?" Figlia looked at Father Din. "The scum wants you to give him Last Rites."

"Yes," said Father Din, dazed. "Yes." He fumbled through his pockets, found his small vial of Holy oil, and anointed Monk's forehead with trembling fingers. "Through this Holy unction," he said mechanically, "may the Lord pardon thee whatever sins thou hast committed . . ."

He looked over at Toddy. From across the room Toddy looked back at him, then buried her face in Jack Muir's hair.

CPSIA information can be obtained
at www.ICGtesting.com
Printed in the USA
BVHW03*1010200718
522187BV00005B/28/P